ANOTHER MAN'S FREEDOM FIGHTER

LINDA NAUGHTON

ISBN 979-8-9868525-7-7 (E-Book)
ISBN 979-8-9868525-2-2 (Paperback)
Library of Congress Control Number 2022922360

Published 2022 by Wordsmyth Creations, LLC, Pittsburgh, Pennsylvania, USA.

Visit the author's website: www.lindanaughton.com

Cover design by Deranged Doctor Design:
www.derangeddoctordesign.com

CHAPTER 1

THE EXPLOSION CAME WITHOUT WARNING, shattering the quiet night in the domed city. It turned the southwest corner of the guardhouse into a million shards of brick, mortar, and glass. A fireball stretched out in every direction before collapsing back in upon itself.

Caitlin Farland let out a shocked cry and slammed on the brakes, bringing her ambulance to a screeching halt in the middle of the street. The vehicle was out of immediate danger, but Caitlin still heard the metallic patter of debris raining down on the roof and hood.

"Holy…" The stunned outburst came from Caitlin's partner, Vince Castellano. Just shy of thirty, Vince had a few years on Caitlin, but his youthful good looks belied his age. His short, black hair had a case of bed-head after waking in the middle of the night for their previous emergency call.

The guardhouse roof sagged, half its support gone. Smoke billowed through the remnants of the ceiling, up into the rafters of the dome. Waycross, like all Martian cities, was encased in a dome to protect the inhabitants from the inhospitable conditions outside. Fire was an ever-present danger in the enclosed environment. Air scrubbers struggled to keep the ash and fumes from being recycled into the city's breathing supply.

Caitlin reached for the radio microphone mounted on the dashboard, unable to tear her eyes off the burning structure. "Medic Five-One to Dispatch: There's just been an explosion at the fort's guardhouse. Fully involved structure fire; unknown injuries." Her heart pounded in her ears. Bombings weren't unheard of in the Martian cities, the rebels fond of striking against Peacekeeper bases and supply convoys, but Caitlin had only witnessed one other as it happened. Usually, the firefighters arrived after the fact.

She heard the dispatcher acknowledge the message and activate the alert tone for the rest of the department. It would take them at least ten minutes to arrive. Until then, Caitlin and Vince would be on their own. She started the ambulance moving again, steering towards a safe spot across the street and well away from the burning structure.

"So much for getting some rest tonight," Vince griped, rubbing his eyes. His new baby had been keeping him up at home. Now they'd be up all night handling the fire. "Wasn't there a ceasefire?"

Caitlin shook her head. "No. They've been talking about it, but the Federation never met the terms."

The political wing of the independence movement had been making peace overtures for months, but the Federation refused to budge. Amnesty for political prisoners? No. Investigations into charges of brutality? As if. They expected the rebels to lay down their arms for nothing but empty promises. It had surprised nobody when the deal fell through.

Flames poured from every opening of the guardhouse. The blast had hurled broken glass and charred chunks of brick for a hundred yards. The street looked like a war zone. Beyond the wall, Peacekeeper soldiers charged out of their barracks as if they feared the bombing was the prelude to an invasion. Many donned full battle gear over their black uniforms. One tried to get close enough to help the men inside, but the oppressive heat turned him back.

"There's no way anyone's alive in there," Caitlin murmured. Even the optimistic Vince didn't contradict her.

Caitlin hopped out of the ambulance cab. She grabbed a helmet and flame-resistant bunker jacket for each of them from the driver's side compartment. She had just come around the front of the truck when she noticed a Peacekeeper across the street pointing at the ambulance. He shouted orders like he was in charge, but he wore civilian clothes. His black hair was longer than the standard Peacekeeper buzz cut. The only thing identifying him as a soldier was the pistol in his hand.

The officer gathered up two other soldiers and began marching toward the ambulance. Frowning, Caitlin wondered what they wanted. Probably just to hassle us for not rushing into the burning guardhouse to "save" their friends, she thought. She braced herself for an argument. It's too dangerous, she would tell him. We need to wait for the fire engines to arrive. She wouldn't tell them there was little hope of anyone surviving that inferno; if his friends were lucky, the explosion got them before the fire did.

"Step away from the vehicle! Drop the bags and raise your hands!" The officer's shout froze a stunned Caitlin. He quickened his pace, leveling his pistol at Vince.

Vince glanced at her, his face mirroring her own confusion. Caitlin just shook her head. Vince set down his medical kit and took a step forward. He held his hands out to the sides in a non-threatening gesture. "What's the problem?"

The officer didn't answer. He closed on Vince, weapon still trained on him. "On the ground! Now!" Caitlin flinched as he shouted at her, "You, too!"

One of the soldiers wore a muscle shirt with his standard-issue black uniform trousers. Bald and taller even than Vince, he had a broad chest and arms that would make any weightlifter proud. "He said on the ground, asshole!" he snarled.

Without slowing down, the big soldier swung his rifle and clubbed Vince in the midsection. Vince dropped to his knees, doubled-over and gasping for air. The soldier pushed him facedown onto the ground, shouting in a thick British accent, "You deaf? Or just stupid?" He kicked Vince in the side and then slipped zip-ties around his hands.

"Stop it!" Caitlin dropped the bunker gear and charged forward without thinking. She skidded to a halt when the officer turned his pistol on her, fear overcoming her anger. She raised her hands, fists clenched. "What the hell is the matter with you? We're paramedics, for God's sake!"

The officer sized her up with a piercing, dark-eyed stare. For the first time, Caitlin noticed the military police badge dangling from a chain around his neck. "We'll see about that. Sykes, detain them. Edwards, check the truck."

Caitlin gaped as the British soldier, Sykes, zip-tied Vince's hands behind him. As the other trooper approached the back door of the ambulance like he was preparing to breach a hostile building, the sinking realization hit her.

"You think we had something to do with this?" Grabbing her arm hard enough to leave a bruise, Sykes jerked her around and shoved her face-first against the side of the ambulance. "This is insane!"

Sykes' voice rumbled in her ear, "Right, because the insurgents have never laid a trap before." Caitlin felt the pressure of zip-ties pinch her wrists.

Vince said through gritted teeth, "We were on our way back from a call. Check with the dispatcher, for God's sake."

Sykes didn't answer. He tugged her arm once more, shoving her down next to Vince. Caitlin winced as her knees bruised against the pavement.

"You all right?" she asked Vince.

"Quiet," Sykes warned, punctuating the word with a shove that had her struggling to keep her balance.

"PK bastards," Caitlin mumbled under her breath.

Sykes grabbed her chin in a vice-like grip and cranked her head back against his knee. Caitlin gasped and tried to pull free, but she had no leverage. The big man's voice rumbled by her ear. "What was that now?"

"That's enough, Sergeant," the officer said. Sykes squeezed her chin once more before releasing it.

A few minutes passed, neither of them daring to speak, until finally the other soldier climbed down from the ambulance. "Captain Decker? Truck is clear. The dispatcher confirms their story."

The officer—Decker—seemed almost disappointed. "Cut them loose, Sergeant."

Sykes hauled Caitlin to her feet first, making sure she saw the blade he used to cut her free from the zip ties. "You sure we can't find a reason to haul them in? This bint's got a mouth on her."

Caitlin just glared at him, clenching her jaw to keep herself from saying something that would land her in a Peacekeeper holding cell.

It was Vince who spoke up, still grimacing from the shot to the ribs. "Look, we don't want any trouble. We're just doing our jobs." He rubbed his wrists once the restraints were removed.

Decker's mouth twisted in a cold, mirthless smirk. The crack of a gunshot split the night air, cutting off any reply. It sounded close, like it had come from their side of the street.

Caitlin ducked, scanning the darkened buildings. Movement caught her eye in the shadows, followed by the staccato sound of automatic gunfire. The flash from the muzzle of a rifle illuminated a masked figure in an alley, firing on the soldiers near the ruined gate. More shooting erupted from further down the street.

Caitlin's stomach dropped through the floor as she realized they'd stumbled into a full-on rebel attack.

[[—＊—]]

"Take cover! Damn it, get into cover!" Captain Jack Decker shouted at the soldiers caught flat-footed in the street as the gunfire erupted around them. He saw fear etched into the faces of the young troopers scrambling behind concrete barricades lining the fort's short driveway. The guardhouse still blazed behind them, silhouetting them in an eerie light.

Sergeant Sykes knelt beside the ambulance's front bumper, firing a few quick rounds at the muzzle flashes. Jack stood behind him, scanning the buildings. The insurgents kept moving and popping up in different places, but Jack guessed there were maybe five total. Only a handful against the several hundred soldiers in the fort, but hit-and-run tactics were their specialty. The Peacekeepers had guards on the walls, patrols in the area, and cameras watching the surrounding buildings 24/7. Somehow, it still wasn't enough to defend against these damned guerrillas.

At the back of the ambulance, Corporal Edwards leaned out to fire. He crumpled without a sound, clutching at his neck.

"Edwards!" Jack shouted. The young corporal didn't answer.

Jack and Sykes returned fire at the muzzle flare, but couldn't see if they'd hit anything.

The two medics they'd detained earlier scrambled to Edwards's side. The woman clamped her hand against the neck wound. Even in the flickering glow of the fire, Jack could see the growing pool of blood beneath Edwards's head.

The other soldiers in front of the fort had started firing back. Sustained gunfire splintered bricks and shattered windows in the industrial buildings lining the street across from the fort. The insurgents' attack slacked off, and they soon slunk away into the darkness. Without the muzzle flashes to aim for, the soldiers had no targets. Calls to cease fire rose from the squad leaders.

Jack moved to where the medics were working on Edwards.

The female medic rocked back on her heels, removing her hand from the wounded soldier's neck. She lifted her eyes to

Jack's and shook her head. "I'm sorry; there was nothing we could do. The bullet severed his artery."

Jack's jaw clenched, the rage building. The last six months had seen a dramatic rise in insurgent activity: sabotage, attacks on Peacekeeper patrols, raids on outlying supply depots, and now this—a strike against Fort McChord itself. As head of the fort's counter-terrorism task-force, Jack led a team that had thwarted more attacks than any other group on Mars. Tonight, though, they'd failed. He looked down at Edwards, thinking of the young soldier's wife and the second baby they had on the way.

Tonight was personal.

Sykes appeared beside him. "What now, Captain?"

Jack activated the radio microphone clipped to his collar. "Citadel One to control. We need a perimeter west of the fort and all available patrols to start a search grid. We have approximately five armed insurgents moving westward." He heard the command center acknowledge his report, then a flurry of radio traffic as other squads received their assignments.

"Come on," Jack said to Sykes, "We're going after the assholes that did this."

CHAPTER 2

CAITLIN TAPED A BANDAGE IN place around the arm of the soldier she was treating. A bullet had creased his arm, leaving a deep groove. "You'll be all right," she assured the wide-eyed kid, who looked like he was barely out of high school. "Just need to get you over to the medical center to get this cleaned up. Go wait with the others in the truck there."

The soldier mumbled his thanks. He wandered over to the vehicle waiting to take the lightly injured ones who didn't require an ambulance. The Peacekeeper base had only a small clinic and barely any medical staff, so the military relied on the city's fire department and medical center for treatment and transport of anything significant.

Caitlin stripped off her medical gloves and rose, taking a moment to survey the scene. Even from a distance, the heat from the guardhouse warmed her face. Flames had engulfed the building. Thick black smoke poured from the roof and windows. They wouldn't be pulling anyone out of there, but a few soldiers in the vicinity had suffered minor shrapnel injuries. The firefight had also left a few injured and two dead, including the one she and Vince had tried to save. It could have been so much worse. Caitlin had been in many intense situations during her career with fire and EMS, but tonight ranked high among them.

The rest of her fire station's crew went to work, charging lines and hitting the blaze with fire-retardant foam. As they closed in on the structure, Caitlin heard a flurry of chatter over the radio.

"We found someone!"

Caitlin and Vince exchanged a stunned glance. How had anyone survived that inferno?

Stepping over a charged hose line, Caitlin met the firefighters carrying the victim out. The soldier lay still on the portable stretcher, much of his uniform burned or torn away. His face bled from several deep lacerations. Of greater concern were the charred, leathery third-degree burns covering much of his body. Caitlin bit back a disgusted sound as the sickening stench of burned flesh filled her nostrils. There was no forgetting that smell.

She tugged on a fresh set of exam gloves. "Where'd you find him?"

"Around back," replied Kim Zhang, one of the few other female firefighters in their crew. "Looks like he got blown through a window."

"Get him into Five-Two." Caitlin gestured toward their second ambulance. The second medic crew met the firefighters at the rear doors of their vehicle and got the patient strapped in and assessed.

"His airway's burned to hell. We'll have to crike him." Chris Tierney, just a year out of paramedic school, had an ego to match his inexperience.

His partner, Andrew Park, started an IV line through the soldier's peeling skin. Burn victims were always tough to get a line in, but at fifty-five, Park had been in the profession longer than Tierney had been alive. Tierney started digging out supplies from the airway kit for a surgical incision in the man's throat.

Park frowned. "Why don't you let Cait try first?"

"His throat's completely swollen. Nobody's going to get a tube down there," Tierney insisted.

"Just let me have a look." Caitlin climbed up into the truck and maneuvered around the stretcher to the captain's chair at the head. Tierney mumbled something under his breath about 'impossible', but vacated the chair in deference to the more experienced medics. Caitlin picked up the laryngoscope and opened the soldier's mouth.

As Tierney said, the throat had almost swollen shut. But she pushed the scope just a little further forward and the tiny dark circle of the trachea came into view. In a few more minutes, it would close off completely, but right now a tiny sliver remained open.

"Give me the tube." She heard a package being opened, then felt the soft plastic pressed into her gloved hand. She slid the tube through the narrow opening between the vocal cords. "Check it?"

Park began squeezing the bag to push oxygen into the soldier's lungs. A skeptical Tierney checked the monitor and listened with a stethoscope, making sure she had gotten the tube into his lungs and not his stomach. His brows shot up and he admitted grudgingly, "Good lung sounds. Monitor's reading CO_2. You're in."

Caitlin allowed herself a bittersweet moment of satisfaction. They may have gotten his airway secured, but the man had a slim chance of surviving burns of this magnitude. She wondered if they'd done anything more than prolong his misery.

She secured the tube in place with a plastic holder, and Park continued ventilations. "Want me to ride along?" she offered. It was customary to have two paramedics in the back for a critical patient. Vince and the Peacekeeper medics could manage the remaining minor patients at the fort for a while.

Park opened his mouth to respond, but an alert tone over the radio interrupted him. The dispatcher's voice echoed in the back of the ambulance. "Attention all units: report of shots fired in the vicinity of Frontier and Seventh. Stand by for further information." The address was just two blocks away. Was it another rebel attack?

Park frowned. "Sounds like you two are going to have your hands full. We'll be fine—it's not far. We'll try to do a quick turnaround at the hospital in case you need us." He said to Tierney, "Let's go." Tierney got out through the side door and went around to the driver's seat.

Caitlin hopped out and closed the back doors behind her. The truck pulled away from the scene, red lights flashing. She turned around and saw that the fire at the guardhouse still raged on. Her fellow firefighters were setting up more hose lines to douse it from all sides. She almost wished she was with them. Fire didn't take sides; it couldn't be categorized into the "good guys" and the "bad guys".

But most of all, it didn't make her feel like she was helping the enemy.

[[— ✳ —]]

Jack and Sykes pursued the terrorist through the alleys of the industrial district, moving at a pace that blended haste with caution. The last thing they wanted was to run headlong into another ambush. Jack had begun to worry they had lost their quarry when they heard gunshots, perhaps a block away.

A woman's voice came over the radio, calling for backup. "Echo Five taking fire. One man down. We're in an alley on the west side of the Cross plant, between Sixth and Seventh."

Jack radioed that they were approaching, and they closed in on the location. "Status?" he demanded of the frazzled young lieutenant giving orders at the mouth of the alley.

"Sir, we thought we spotted someone in the alley, but he opened fire before we could get into position. Looks like he went into a window behind that dumpster there." The officer's face dripped sweat, her voice tight with fear. Jack wondered if this was her first firefight

"On me," he told the soldiers. They moved up the alley as a group, weapons clenched in tight grips. When they reached the dumpster, one trooper lifted the lid while Sykes checked inside. A grim shake of the sergeant's head reported that it was empty.

Jack panned his pistol's flashlight over a window just past the dumpster. One of its large panes had been broken, making an opening wide enough for someone to get through. Shards of broken glass littered the ground beneath it. Jack peered through the window and into the factory beyond. The assembly lines were dark. Their target could be hiding within, but something didn't feel right to Jack. He pulled away from the window and checked around the dumpster again.

Sykes watched him, confused. "Sir? Are we going after him?"

Jack ignored him. He kicked some boxes aside. Hidden behind them was a familiar grate in the ground—an access point to the tunnels.

Jack cursed under his breath. "He went down here. Sykes, get this open." He spoke into his radio again, "Citadel One to Echo Five. Target has entered the tunnels. Secure this entrance and make sure he doesn't double back. All other squads in the vicinity, keep looking. He may come up in another location."

Once Sykes had the grate open, Jack crouched next to the opening and looked down into the exposed hole. Just wide enough for a man to climb down the wall-mounted ladder, it went down about fifteen feet before opening up into the main tunnel. Jack motioned for Sykes to go down first, then followed himself. He skipped the last few rungs, dropping a couple of feet to land in a crouch on the tunnel floor. Their flashlights cut through the darkness, shining on the ragged walls of the tunnel that stretched out in front of and behind them.

As the first civilian colony on Mars, in the days before engineers had perfected the protective domes, Waycross had initially been built underground. When deposits of silver and gadolinium were discovered in the area, the city became a mining boomtown. Miles upon miles of mining shafts encircled the colony and criss-crossed beneath it. When the current domed city was built, even more tunnels were added for the electrical, water and sewage grids. The elaborate underground network had become the rebellion's lifeline.

"Which way?" Sykes asked, his light panning across the loose dirt (technically regolith) on the tunnel floor. There were plenty of footprints, but no way to tell which were recent.

Jack wandered a few meters in each direction. Without tracks to follow, finding their man was going to be a long shot. He had a several minute head start, and no doubt knew the tunnels far better than they did. They didn't have the resources to check every tunnel branch.

"This one," Jack decided, picking one on nothing more than gut instinct.

Sykes didn't question him, and they set off down the twisting tunnel. Before long, they'd lost all orientation with respect to the world above.

Without warning, gunshots boomed in the corridor. Jack dove for cover behind a rocky outcropping. Leaning out, he fired blindly in the direction of the muzzle flashes. He'd only hoped to keep the gunman's head down, but heard a pained cry and a thud. A lucky shot. Jack rushed forward, his wrists crossed to brace both his pistol and his light.

His flashlight illuminated the gunman in the middle of the corridor, clutching a bleeding left shoulder. His pistol was on the ground, inches from his hands. As Jack approached, the gunman lunged for it. He had to know he had no chance, and just wanted to provoke Jack into shooting him.

Closing the distance in two quick strides, Jack stomped on the terrorist's outstretched hand. "You're not getting the easy way out."

The gunman was in his mid-twenties, with close-cropped black hair. His dark brown skin glistened with perspiration, a goatee-ringed mouth twisted in pain. Jack leveled his pistol at the man, who stared back at him with quiet hatred.

Jack stepped aside so Sykes could pass him. "Secure him."

Sykes did so, then took a step back. "Get up." When he got no response, Sykes stepped in and gave the man a sharp kick to the ribs. "I said up, you bastard." As the prisoner got to his knees, Sykes mumbled, "Be faster to put a bullet in his skull now. Damn coward doesn't deserve a trial."

"Believe me, a trial is the least of his worries right now." That seemed to appease Sykes, and for the first time, the prisoner looked rattled. Jack keyed his radio mic. "We got him."

CHAPTER 3

ALEX GARRISON KNELT ON THE cold floor of the tunnel, looking up at the Peacekeepers who'd captured him, and knew he was completely screwed. He wasn't afraid of dying, but had always imagined himself one day going out in a blaze of glory. The thought of instead spending the rest of his days in a jail cell left an icy fear gnawing in his stomach.

He'd made it into the tunnels with a good head start, but must have taken a wrong turn in his haste. Next thing he knew, he ended up on top of the Peacekeepers pursuing him. And now they had him.

"Get moving." The sergeant hauled Alex to his feet and gave him a rough shove.

Alex stumbled, grimacing as the shove sent a wave of pain through his shoulder. He'd had worse from a broken collarbone playing hyperball in high school, but it still hurt like hell. His ribs were also sore, thanks to the soldier who'd kicked him. They called the rebels cowards, but didn't hesitate to beat up an injured, unarmed man. He focused on that anger, using it to push away the fear.

The Peacekeepers herded him down the tunnel to the access ladder. Paying attention to their chatter, he deduced their names —Decker was the one in charge, and Sykes the burly sergeant. Decker went up first. Sykes cut off the ties and gave him another shove toward the ladder.

"You can climb. I'm not dragging your sorry ass up there."

They were alone now, and his hands were free. Alex took a half-step forward, reaching for the ladder, but then shifted his weight and lashed out with a backward kick. His boot connected solidly, knocking Sykes flat on his ass. Alex dove atop him, trying to wrestle the soldier's rifle from his hands. After a brief struggle, he jerked the weapon free.

His elation at was short-lived. Alex saw motion out of the corner of his eye, but he didn't get out of the way fast enough. Decker had slid back down the ladder. His pistol connected with the back of his skull with a sickening crack, and Alex went down in a heap.

"Persistent bastard." Alex thought he might have detected a hint of grudging respect in the officer's voice, but maybe that was just his concussion talking. The world spun crazily, and he felt himself slipping away.

The first thing Alex noticed when he regained his senses was a rhythmic red light painting the walls and ground. As his vision came back into focus, he saw that an ambulance had pulled up across the street, its emergency lights flashing. Alex lay flat on the ground, new zip-ties cutting painfully into his wrists. Something—probably someone's boot—pressed against the small of his back. His head throbbed from where Decker had clubbed him, and it only got worse when he craned his neck to see.

"Who called the medics?" Decker's voice demanded from behind him.

One of the other Peacekeepers piped up. "I did, sir. Your radio report said that there were injuries."

Decker moved into view, frowning. Did he not think Alex merited medical treatment? He scowled at the paramedics. "You two again."

The two paramedics crossed the street, a man and a woman. They might have been mistaken for Peacekeepers in their navy blue uniforms, save for their bright orange medical bags and the silver Waycross Fire Department badges pinned to their chests.

The woman glared at the captain, her voice dripping sarcasm as she said, "We wouldn't want you to miss a chance to arrest us again."

"You don't know when to quit, do you?" Sykes sniped back.

Her partner cleared his throat, interrupting the glaring contest. "So… was anyone else hurt?"

Sykes muttered something unpleasant under his breath, but it was Decker who spoke. "One dead at the end of the alley there."

The male paramedic looked at his partner and said, "You want to go pronounce him?"

"You can do it. I'll get him." She pointed to Alex.

The paramedic frowned at the injured rebel. "Cait, I really think—"

She interrupted him before he could finish his sentence. "I've got it, Vince. Here, take this." She handed him a box that Alex recognized as a heart monitor. As a still-scowling Vince took the monitor, she assured him in a quieter tone, "I'll be fine—don't worry."

Vince cast one last dark gaze at Alex before heading off to the tunnel. Alex almost laughed. Injured, bound, and under guard by a half-dozen trigger-happy Peacekeepers, what was he going to do?

The woman spoke again to Sykes, sounding more annoyed. "I need you to move, Sergeant, so I can treat him."

"How about we just toss him in the back of the truck for you, and you can be on your way?"

Eyes narrowing, the woman snapped at him. "How's about you just back off and let me do my job."

Captain Decker cut in. "Let him up, Sykes."

Sykes backed away from Alex, posturing the whole time. Slowly, so as to not provoke any retaliation, Alex rolled onto his back and then sat up. His ribs ached even worse now, after laying on them, but the bleeding from his shoulder seemed to have slowed.

The paramedic knelt beside him, opening her trauma bag. She seemed tall, though his current position made it difficult to gauge exactly. There was something striking about her—good-looking, with a trim, athletic form. Wavy strands of blonde hair escaped from a braid to frame her pale face.

She introduced herself as Caitlin and asked, "What's your name?"

Conscious of the Peacekeepers around him, Alex replied with a lie—the first name that popped into his mind. "Ty."

"All right, Ty, let's take a look." She unzipped his coveralls down to his waist and then cut open his sleeves and T-shirt to expose his entire chest, arms, and shoulders. "Looks like the bullet went straight through. It probably didn't hit any major vessels."

"I suppose you're going to tell me how lucky I was," Alex scoffed.

Caitlin arched an eyebrow, noting the assembled soldiers with a nod of her head. "'Lucky' wasn't my first thought, no."

Alex snorted. "Well, we're agreed on that." She continued her assessment, checking out the rest of his chest. When her probing fingers found one of his tender ribs, Alex gasped. Caitlin looked more closely at the bruises developing along his side and frowned. "Punched?" she guessed.

Alex shook his head. "Kicked." She cast a disgusted glance at the Peacekeepers behind him. As she continued to work, Alex realized there was no fear in her gray eyes when she looked at him; no disdain; no hatred. Just a quiet compassion, and a hint of curiosity. He knew that his best chance for escape would be in the ambulance, alone in the back with a guard and a paramedic. With the medic on his side, he would only have to deal with a single Peacekeeper.

Maybe his luck was beginning to change.

[[—✳—]]

By the time Vince returned from pronouncing the other soldiers dead, Caitlin had bandaged her patient's wound and started an IV. He refused the morphine she offered, which surprised her. Most people would be demanding painkillers for an injury like that. They loaded him onto the stretcher and into the back of the ambulance. As Caitlin climbed into the back, she noticed Vince's worried frown. She smiled at his over-protectiveness. Dangerous patients were an occupational hazard. She had a small scar across her eyebrow from a few years ago, when a hallucinating diabetic had clocked her with a lamp because he thought she was "the enemy" in some unnamed war. She appreciated Vince's concern, but she didn't need babysitting.

Besides, part of her was fascinated by "Ty". Was he really a rebel? Had he been involved in the explosion? Other attacks? These were questions she could never ask a patient. Instead, she peppered him about his past medical history and symptoms. He answered each question with the barest amount of information possible. Often, patients gave one-word responses out of an uncooperative anger, but his seemed quite calculated in their brevity. It was as if he was worried he might give something away.

"So who's coming with us?" Vince asked the Peacekeepers as he closed the ambulance's left rear door. He left the right one open while he waited for the soldiers to figure out who they were going to send as an escort. There was some controversy over this, though Caitlin couldn't hear much from inside the back of the truck.

Caitlin sat on the smaller bench seat, on the driver's side, and took out her datapad to jot down notes about her patient. She smirked at the first field on the patient information form— patient name. "Ty." She echoed the name he'd given when she asked him earlier. "Not your real name, is it?"

It was an off-hand remark, and she honestly didn't expect him to answer. "It's Alex." Startled, she glanced up from the datapad, and saw him staring intently at her. Still in that quiet voice, he continued, "Caitlin, please, you have to help me."

Caitlin's response was automatic. "You're going to be fine. We'll bring you to the Medical Center and they'll—"

"That's not what I mean. You know what they're going to do with me, don't you? Torture… interrogations… if I'm lucky they'll kill me before I betray my friends. Otherwise I'll end up in a Peacekeeper prison for the rest of my life." There was a palpable desperation in his voice.

Caitlin's lips drew together in a thin line, knowing the awful truth of what he was describing.

"You can stop all that. I need your help. Please." His dark eyes were wide, imploring her. For the first time, she saw fear etched on his face.

Caitlin swallowed hard, her gaze snapping toward the back door to see if anyone had heard him. Vince was still talking to the Peacekeepers, but she couldn't hear what they were saying. She murmured back to Alex, "I'm sorry—there's nothing I can do." It was easy to dismiss his request as impossible. It meant she didn't have to think about what he was asking her to do.

Alex wasn't deterred. "Yes there is." His voice dropped to a low whisper, so she had to strain to hear him over the ambulance's air conditioning system. "Cut off these ties." He twisted to reveal the plastic zip-ties around his wrists. "Please, Caitlin. There's not much time."

It was impossibly dangerous. She should have told him again that she couldn't help him, but found herself caught with indecision. She had always been sympathetic to the rebel cause; the events of tonight had only given her a few more reasons to hate the Peacekeepers. Even so, she had never crossed the line between quiet resentment and open defiance. She cast an uncertain glance toward the rear doors, beyond which were a half-dozen Peacekeepers who'd arrest her in a heartbeat for even considering this. Any moment, one of them would climb up into the truck to escort their prisoner to the hospital. Logic and reason told her to forget Alex had said anything.

Wordlessly, Caitlin took her trauma shears from the pouch on her belt. Alex leaned forward to give her better access, and she snipped the tie loose.

"Thank you," Alex breathed, his eyes conveying a depth of gratitude she'd only ever seen from patients whose lives she had saved.

Caitlin could only manage a quiet nod in return; she didn't trust herself to speak. She sank back against her chair, heart pounding so hard she figured the Peacekeepers outside could hear it. Alex pocketed the zip-ties and leaned back against the stretcher, keeping his arms behind him as if he were still tied up. It made sense that he wouldn't want to try his escape right now, with Peacekeepers everywhere. He'd wait until they were on the way to the hospital.

Caitlin had just put the scissors back in her belt pouch when a heavy footstep on the back railing sent a jolt down her spine. A glowering Sergeant Sykes entered the ambulance. Caitlin fought to quell a surge of panic, feeling as though someone had squeezed her heart. Had he seen her? Sykes didn't say a word; he just plopped his bulky frame down on the opposite bench seat. Caitlin watched him carefully, daring to breathe only after it became clear that he wasn't rushing in to arrest her.

Vince closed the other rear door, and a moment later the ambulance started moving. Caitlin called in a radio report in to the hospital to let them know the ambulance was on its way. Then she started writing her treatment notes—anything to keep her busy, and to keep her hands from shaking. She didn't know when Alex might make his move and didn't want to do anything to give away the game. It almost felt like watching a horror movie, knowing that the monster was going to leap out at any moment to assault the oblivious victim. And, just like in the movies, she jumped when that moment came.

Alex gave no warning before he launched into action; not even a glance in her direction. His hands came out from behind him. In an instant he had unclipped the strap holding him to the stretcher.

Sykes stood up, reaching for his pistol. "What the hell?"

Vince glanced into the rear mirror and slammed on the brakes. Everyone lurched forward. Sykes had to grab hold of the bench seat to keep from losing his balance. Alex was on the sergeant then, wrestling for control of the gun.

"Grab him!" Sykes shouted.

Caitlin didn't want to help the sergeant, but the situation would look even more suspicious if she just sat back and did nothing. She had to at least make it look good. Climbing over the stretcher, she grabbed Alex's shoulder and arm in a light grip. Without looking, he drew his arm back sharply and slammed an elbow into her face. Caitlin fell sideways onto the stretcher, her cheek stinging.

Moving faster than one would expect from an injured man, Alex landed a few punches. He somehow managed to twist the gun out of Sykes' grip. Two gunshots rang out, deafening in the confined space of the ambulance. Sykes slumped backwards against the bench seat. Clutching his chest, he glared up at the rebel. They all assumed that Alex would put another bullet in his head to finish the job, but the shot never came. There was only a quiet thud as Alex stepped forward and clubbed Sykes with his pistol, knocking him unconscious.

Caitlin stared at Alex, relief mingling with confusion on her face. The question on her lips died when the ambulance's rear door flew open.

"Cait!" Vince stood there, wielding a fireman's halligan tool like a club. Relief washed over his face seeing she was all right. It quickly turned to fear as Alex swung his pistol in Vince's direction.

"No!" Caitlin shouted, fear flooding through her. She couldn't let Vince get hurt. She jumped to her feet, standing between them, holding out her hands in a 'stop' gesture. "Look, just go," she pleaded to Alex. "We won't stop you."

Alex sized up Vince, perhaps gauging the likelihood of him trying to play the hero. Feeling the same concern, Caitlin shot a warning glance in Vince's direction. Vince didn't move, common sense winning out over macho pride. Finally. Alex lowered his pistol and moved to the side door. As he opened the door, his eyes met Caitlin's. He didn't say a word, but she could sense his gratitude. Then he was gone—out of the ambulance and into the night.

Vince was at her side in an instant, asking if she was all right. Caitlin tried to pay attention to his barrage of concerned questions, but wondered instead about Alex. Would he get away this time? Where would he go?

But most of all—*Did I do the right thing?*

CHAPTER 4

JACK STOOD IN THE BACK of the ambulance, fuming at the empty cot. They'd had him. They'd had him, and Sykes had let him get away. Jack had already let out a string of rage-filled obscenities that had the crime scene technicians scurrying out of range. They should at least get the prisoner's fingerprint and DNA samples off the cot. That was something.

And next time, he'd guard them his own damn self.

Jack crouched in the narrow gap between the cot and the bench, studying the zip ties that had fallen atop the crumpled sheet. Even Jack knew a few tricks for breaking zip ties to escape, but the break in these looked unnaturally smooth. Almost like they'd been cut. Had Sykes missed a knife? Or had the man somehow used something on the stretcher?

Leaving the truck with more questions than answers, Jack made his way over to the Medical Center. Someone directed him to Sykes' room, and he barged right in.

The young doctor by Sykes' bedside draped a stethoscope around her neck and said, "Sir, you really can't be in here. You need to wait."

Jack flashed his ID badge, cutting her off in mid-sentence. He gestured toward the soldier on the gurney. "Is he going to live?"

"Yes, his vest stopped both bullets. He'll be sore for a few days, but he'll be fine."

"Good, then I can kill him myself," Jack muttered.

The doctor raised her eyebrows and seemed about ready to say something.

Sykes, sitting up on the gurney, waved her off. "Give us a minute, would you, doc?"

Frowning, the doctor nodded. "I'll be just outside." It came across as a warning, which Jack found amusing.

Once the doctor had gone, Jack fixed a scowl of his own on Sykes. He said nothing, waiting for an explanation. Sykes sat up a little more, wincing as he did so. Jack could see the red outline of fresh bruises on the center of his chest where the bullets had struck his protective vest. Right over the heart. Sykes was lucky he'd been wearing the vest—luckier still that the terrorist hadn't finished him off with a bullet in the brain. For a man who had gone to such lengths to kill a few Peacekeepers, why leave a live enemy behind him?

"I don't know how it happened, sir. One minute he was on the stretcher, tied up, the next he got up and charged at me." The sergeant clenched his jaw at the admission.

"How did he get out of the ties?"

"I don't know, sir. I was watching him pretty close. He must have been one hell of an escape artist."

Or he'd had help. "What was the paramedic doing during all this?"

"Writing something on her datapad. She tried to grab him, but he clocked her." Sykes scoffed. "Useless. We should've had the other guy ride in back. He and I could have taken that asshole."

"Maybe that's the way they wanted it," Jack mused. Too many coincidences were stacked up for his liking. He started for the door, offering no explanation to the confused Sykes. He spotted Caitlin talking to Sykes' doctor near the administration area. A fresh bruise forming on her cheek would probably be a nice shiner by morning.

Jack stalked over and grabbed her arm. "We need to have a word, Ms. Farland."

"Hey! Get the hell off of me." Caitlin tried to yank her arm free.

Jack ignored her protests, holding tight. He pulled her toward the second, unoccupied, trauma room. Only when they were inside did he let go of her.

Her momentum carried her another step or two, and then she spun back to face him. "What the hell do you think you're doing?"

"You've got some explaining to do," Jack snapped.

"You first." Caitlin's eyes blazed with anger. "You can start by explaining how your Sergeant let a prisoner escape *and* get his gun. He might have killed us!"

She was trying to put him on the defensive, but Jack refused to play. "And yet he didn't. I wonder why that is?"

"Maybe he's not the heartless killer you'd like to think he is."

Eyes narrowing, Jack snarled, "That bastard and his friends killed a half-dozen good men tonight. I know exactly what he is. How did he get free?"

"How should I know? Maybe he's Houdini."

"Houdini often had an assistant."

Caitlin rolled her eyes. "Jesus, you can't be serious! You think I want a prisoner loose in the back of my ambulance?"

Jack had a knack for reading people, but he had a hard time seeing anything behind Caitlin's sarcastic bluster. His instincts told him she'd been involved somehow, even if he had nothing concrete to back them up. "You were the only one alone with him."

"For sixty seconds! With a half-dozen Peacekeepers standing just outside! Maybe you think *I'm* Houdini."

Even Jack had to admit that the scenario sounded improbable, but his suspicions lingered. "I think you're a smart-ass with one hell of a knack for being in the wrong place at the wrong time."

"In case you haven't noticed, Captain, the fire department has been short-staffed for years. So, I expect we'll be seeing more of each other. And believe me—I'm no happier about it than you are."

Jack was tempted to take her in on principle. The Internal Security Act allowed him to detain anyone suspected of aiding the terrorists for seventy-two hours without a warrant. It would almost be worth the paperwork just to crush that attitude of hers. He resisted the temptation, knowing he had nothing concrete to charge her with. He only had his hunch.—for now.

"Oh, I'm sure we'll see each other again." There was no mistaking the threat implied in his voice. He'd be keeping an eye on her.

[[—✳—]]

Caitlin watched the captain go, her heart thudding in her chest. For a moment there she thought he was going to arrest her on the spot. She hid behind her genuine anger, hoping it would be enough to throw him off. Thank God he'd bought it. Relief washed over her, tempered by the sobering reality of just how close she'd come to going to jail. She brushed her bangs back with a trembling hand, and then paced across the trauma room in a vain attempt to calm herself. How could she be so stupid—risking everything for a man she didn't even know? It was the most terrifying experience of her life. And, God forgive her, the most exhilarating.

After a few minutes, she regained her composure and left the room. She'd have to walk back to the fire station. The Peacekeepers had claimed their ambulance as a crime scene, and it was doubtful they'd get it back before morning. In the back of her mind was a nagging worry that they might find evidence that she'd helped Alex.

Stepping through the sliding doors into the cool outside air, Caitlin saw a bright light to her left. A news crew from the Martian Chronicle was interviewing a Peacekeeper. She averted her eyes from the blinding spotlight without looking at the group.

She caught the tail end of the Peacekeeper's sentence: "The suspect escaped from custody, assaulting his guard and the two paramedics who were treating him…"

Caitlin turned away in disgust without listening to any more. Alex clips her with an elbow, probably by accident, and now they're saying he 'assaulted two paramedics'. Typical.

She didn't get more than a few steps before a familiar voice called out from behind her, "Cait! Hey, Cait, wait a second."

Caitlin sighed and looked back at the news crew. The camera and spotlight now aimed at the ground, and the Peacekeeper being interviewed looked irritated as the reporter abandoned him.

"What do you want, Tom?"

Tom MacIntyre somehow looked great, even at two in the morning. He'd slicked back his dark hair to combat the errant tufts that always plagued him when he first woke up, and his handsome face showed lines of worry.

"Are you all right? Vince told me what happened…" He reached toward her bruised cheek, but stopped short with a sad frown when she shied away from his touch.

"Yeah, fine," she replied coolly, "Don't let me keep you from your interview." She motioned back toward the captain. It stung a little that he would rather get a scoop than check up on her.

"Come on, Cait, I'm just doing my job," Tom protested, coming across somewhere between apologetic and indignant. "I was waiting for you. Vince told me you were okay; he said you shooed him away while they were checking you out. I didn't think you'd want me there either."

"He's my partner; you're my husband," Caitlin pointed out, though deep down she had to admit he had a point. Tom knew her too well. "Look, just forget it, okay? I've got to get back to the station." She took a few steps backward as she spoke, then turned away.

Tom paused just long enough to make a 'wait one' gesture back toward Harry, the camera operator, before he started following. "You sure you're okay?"

"Yeah, I'm just tired." She rubbed her forehead, a headache beginning to brew behind her eyes.

Tom didn't take the hint, as usual. "Vince said they harassed you at the fort? You guys should file a complaint."

Caitlin scoffed at the suggestion. "Yeah. I'm sure that's going to end well." Tom had only been on Mars for five years, and he was still naive about the politics. Even if she thought it would do any good, she couldn't afford to draw more attention to herself.

"Come on, Cait, I know it's not much. But nothing's going to change if we just sit back and keep taking this crap from them."

She couldn't help but wonder if his 'change the world' attitude would hold up if he knew what she had done to help Alex. Probably not. He would worry, and lecture her for acting rashly. And he might not be wrong. Either way, after the verbal sparring with Decker, Caitlin didn't have the energy to get into it with Tom as well.

"I'll think about it."

He knew better, but didn't press her. As the run-down brick fire station came into view, Tom began, "So… I thought I might stop by tomorrow morning and pick up a few things."

"I'll be at the station until noon, so you can just let yourself in."

He looked disappointed, but tried to make light of it. "Sure, just figured I'd make sure you hadn't changed the locks on me." He chuckled half-heartedly, but the smile faded when he saw she wasn't laughing.

Caitlin rubbed her forehead. "Tom, please. It's been a long night, okay? Can we not do this now?"

"Sure," he replied, stung by the dismissal. He touched her arm. "I'm glad you're okay." He seemed to want to say more, but instead turned away in awkward silence.

Caitlin watched his departing back before heading into the station. The bank of garage doors on the first story stood open, and she heard the familiar shrill beeps as one of the engines backed into the bay alongside Park and Tierney's ambulance. The rest of the crew was probably still back at the fire scene.

She expected to find Vince in the office, getting started on the paperwork. They had a long night of paperwork ahead of them —an incident report and a fistful of patient care reports. Instead, she found him sitting on a bench in the downstairs garage, a troubled frown on his face. He rose when he spotted Caitlin, and said ominously, "We need to talk."

CHAPTER 5

ALEX HUDDLED IN THE SHADOWS of the tunnel, drawing the remnants of his coveralls around him for warmth. Mars may be a desert, but it had more in common with Antarctica than Arizona. Outside the dome, the frigid temperatures and thin carbon-dioxide atmosphere would kill an unprotected human before anyone even noticed they were gone. The dome's environmental engineers fought a constant struggle against the unforgiving environment, keeping the dome at a chilly 20 degrees Celsius. Underground, without the dome heating system to help, the temperature dipped even lower.

He peered down the tunnel, the darkness broken only by street lamps filtering through an occasional access grate in the ceiling. Without a flashlight, Alex couldn't see the marker stones and symbols that the rebels used to find their way around the maze of shafts and caverns. He had to navigate by memory and hoped he wasn't going around in circles. At least no one seemed to be following him. He was tempted to avoid the tunnels after the Peacekeepers caught him there the first time, but traveling above ground at night, with the streets nearly empty, was even riskier. The cold and the pain in his shoulder sapped his strength, but he forced himself to continue on.

After an hour, just when he thought he might be lost, Alex spotted a familiar marker in the light from a grate. A few turns later, he climbed up an access ladder and emerged in an alley behind the low-rent apartment building that held his team's safe house. Nobody paid him any mind as he went inside and up the stairs to the fourth floor—it was the kind of neighborhood where people didn't get involved in each others' business. Alex knocked, two quick raps followed by two longer ones.

"Alex!" Samantha Chen's eyes went wide as she pulled open the door and ushered Alex inside. Though barely younger than Alex, Samantha's short stature and youthful Asian features made her look much younger. She was very much the little sister of the group, and also a world-class hacker and electronics expert. "Are you okay?"

"I'm fine. It's not that bad." Alex crossed to the center of the room and sat down in one of the metal folding chairs ringing a small table. The hideout was spartan, but as often as they moved around, it wasn't worth the effort making the place more comfortable.

"I'll message Noah," Samantha offered, moving to the MarsCom unit. Noah was a junior resident at the hospital who helped them out when they needed medical attention. The ER docs raised eyebrows at unexplained gunshot wounds.

"Hold on. Let me see." An older man strode out of the kitchenette. A stocky man in his fifties, Ben Holstrom had been leading rebel cells since he was Alex's age. The years had taken their toll on him; his hair had gone gray years ago, and he had more than his share of wrinkles. Ben peeled back the bandage to examine the wound. "It'll keep till morning. We don't need Noah to draw more attention than necessary." Despite his businesslike tone, Alex could see the concern in the old man's eyes.

Ben replaced the bandage and asked, "What happened? We worried when you didn't make the rally point—"

Samantha cut in, worry creasing her brow, "And then the news feed said they'd captured someone."

"I ran into a PK squad by the Cross plant and they caught me in the tunnels," Alex explained. "I managed to escape on the way to the medical center, but it was close."

Thinking about it now, Alex had the sobering realization of just how close. Were it not for Caitlin's help, he'd be languishing in a Peacekeeper holding cell right now, awaiting interrogation. He decided not to mention the details to Ben and Samantha. Even though he trusted them with his life, any one of them could fall into enemy hands at any time. He'd proven that tonight. The fewer people who knew about Caitlin, the safer she'd be.

"One of these days you're gonna run out of lives, man." Julio, the last member of their cell, grinned as he emerged from the back bedroom. The Hispanic man was a few inches shorter than Alex, but his athletic frame gave him an imposing stature. Alex knew that underneath Julio was a gentle soul. Julio came over and stretched his arm out for a bro handshake, clapping Alex on his good arm. "Glad you made it back."

Ben grunted in agreement. "You sure you weren't followed?"

"I'm sure."

"Sam, stay on the street cams just to be sure," Ben ordered.

The young hacker grabbed her tablet and went to their couch. Tucking one leg under her in a torturous yoga position, she went to work.

Julio refilled Alex's water bottle and brought it over. "Looks like you can use this." Then he asked Ben, "You think we should call off the mission Saturday? Maybe Alex should lie low for a while."

Samantha looked up from her screen long enough to chime in, "The Peacekeepers will have extra security at the rally. And they'll be itching for a fight."

The Martian Liberation Society, the non-militant side of the Martian independence movement, had planned a rally for independence this coming weekend. It shared a close relationship with the more militant Free Mars Militia, to which Alex and the others belonged. The Society kept its hands clean, at least officially, playing a sort of "good cop" to the FMM's "bad cop". In turn, the FMM relied on the Society for funds and manpower. In fact, most of the army's recruits came from Society members. Alex himself had been one, when his dreams of being a history professor had been shattered after his graduate thesis was declared too "controversial". It had been an academic death sentence; no other college on Mars would accept him, and he was damned if he was going to go to Earth just to get his diploma. He had stayed, disillusioned, until eventually Ben recruited him.

"A fight is exactly what we plan to give them," Ben reminded them. "We knew that hitting the Fort before the rally would stir up the PKs, but we've worked too long to set this up to throw it away now. These people need a wake up call. They're willing to wave a flag or stand in a parade, but they won't stick their neck out unless someone gives them a push."

Alex nodded, finding himself caught up in the fervor of Ben's words. "So we get the Peacekeepers to push them. A little tear gas, a few arrests. Get people stirred up." Despite the close call earlier, he found himself with renewed confidence that it had all been worth it.

"Still seems like a big risk." Samantha chewed her lip.

"Risk is part of the game," Ben said, his tone marking an end to the discussion. All democratic ideals aside, this was a military organization and Ben had the final decision. "We stay the course."

Alex nodded. Despite all the close calls and perils of the evening, he couldn't deny the thrill of staying one step ahead of the Peacekeepers. Like Ben had said, it was part of the game.

[[—✳—]]

Caitlin followed Vince into the supply room, one of the few places in the fire station with any real privacy. Vince shut the door behind them and crossed his arms. He didn't say anything at first, just stared at Caitlin with an accusing expression.

She lifted her hands in a questioning gesture and prompted, "What?"

"You helped him escape, didn't you?"

Caitlin averted her eyes, unwilling to lie to his face. Even if she had, Vince would see right through her. They had known each other for too long.

Vince's face reddened. "God, Cait, what were you thinking? Have you completely lost your mind?"

Caitlin had been asking herself that same question for the last hour. "He asked for my help."

"He's a terrorist!" Vince raised his voice a little before catching himself and bringing it back to a hushed volume. "He could have killed both of us!"

"But he didn't," Caitlin pointed out. "He didn't kill Sykes either, even though he had the chance." She guessed Alex was trying to protect her. Maybe he didn't want her to face an accessory to murder charge if the Peacekeepers found out she helped him.

"That doesn't change the fact that he and his buddies killed a bunch of people tonight. He's a murderer."

"Just because he doesn't wear a uniform, that doesn't make him any less of a soldier than the Peacekeepers," Caitlin retorted.

Vince sighed, scowling and throwing up his hands. "Cait, not all the rebels are like your father. You can't paint them all as some kind of noble..."

"This has nothing to do with my Dad." The words lost their conviction as soon as they'd left her mouth. Maybe it had everything to do with him. She hadn't thought about her father when Alex asked her to help him, but maybe his comment about prison had hit a little too close to home. Maybe subconsciously she was just doing what she wished someone else had done for her father all those years ago.

She still had nightmares, sometimes, about the night the Peacekeepers came for him. Strong hands dragging her, screaming, out of bed. Her father kneeling on the floor with his hands behind his head. The soldiers pummeling him with rifles when he tried to reach her, hitting and kicking and punching him over and over again. The next thing Caitlin remembered was being in the hospital, with a concussion and six stitches in her head where a rifle butt had connected. They said she'd leapt onto the back of a soldier, screaming and kicking for all she was worth. Caitlin had to take their word for it; she couldn't remember. She knew only that her father was gone—first to trial, and then to prison on Luna—and she was alone. She was twelve years old.

Caitlin set her jaw stubbornly. "He didn't deserve what those bastards would have done to him." She was talking about Alex, though the comment could have applied to her father as well. "I'm glad I was able to help him. I'd do it again."

Vince shook his head, his angry scowl still remaining. "What you do doesn't just affect you, Cait. They're going to question me next, you know. And I'm going to have to cover for you."

"I'm not asking you to—"

He didn't let her finish. "You don't have to. I'm not going to rat you out."

Caitlin sighed, realizing he was right. "No, I know you wouldn't." They were more than partners; they were best friends. For a time, before either of them were married, they had been more than friends. Vince would never betray her, but she regretted putting him in a position where he had to lie for her.

"I've got a family, Cait. I can't afford to get mixed up in this crap, okay? Next time you cross a line like that, don't drag me with you."

Caitlin wasn't planning for there to be a 'next time', but she nodded all the same. "I won't. I'm sorry, Vince."

Vince nodded in satisfaction. He opened the door and said, "We'd better get started on the trip reports." He glanced back at her when she didn't follow him. "You coming? You'd better not be expecting me to write them all by myself." He offered a half-smile, and she knew they'd be okay.

Caitlin smiled back. "Wouldn't dream of it," she said, and followed him back into the station.

CHAPTER 6

ALEX AWOKE WITH A START, a vague feeling of alarm tugging at his subconscious. He sat up quickly, his senses on edge. The sudden movement caused a sharp pain to ripple through his shoulder, and he sucked in a sharp breath. He could hear raised voices, followed by a thump. Grabbing his pistol from the nightstand, he crept cautiously toward the doorway of the small bedroom. The second bed was empty and already made; Ben must have been up for a while.

As Alex reached the door, the voices became more distinct. "Damn it, Julio, you going to be in there all day?" Samantha sounded more irritated than alarmed. Relaxing, Alex opened the door and peered down the hallway. Samantha stood outside the door to the bathroom, slapping her hand against it to get Julio's attention. "Other people live here, too, you know!"

Shaking his head in annoyance, Alex flipped the safety back on his pistol and stepped out into the hallway. "What the hell are you guys doing? You want to attract attention to us? Knock it off."

Samantha turned to him, chagrined. "Sorry, Alex." She then raised a hand in exasperation. "Julio's hogging the shower, *again*." The young woman wore a long T-shirt over a pair of leggings, rumpled from having slept in it. Loose strands of black hair splayed out from a hasty ponytail.

Alex rolled his eyes. "This is like a bad dorm flashback." He and Samantha had been on the same dormitory floor at Lowell University, though he had been two years ahead of her. With a sigh, he rapped on the door and said, "Come on, man, save some water for the rest of us." He was rewarded with silence as the water shut off. "There. Happy?"

Samantha's bright smile of triumph was answer enough, but it faded when her eyes drifted to the bandage taped to Alex's shoulder. She stared at it, wincing. "Does it hurt much?"

Alex offered an awkward one-armed shrug. "I've had worse." In truth, it still hurt like hell, but he wasn't going to admit to it. Samantha wouldn't think any less of him, but Julio would never let him hear the end of it. He was as bad as Alex's brother, always competing to see who was the bigger tough-guy. "Noah's going to stop by later and check it out. It'll be fine."

The bathroom door opened, revealing a still-damp Julio with a towel wrapped around his waist. A faint color rose to Samantha's cheeks, but she tried to cover it by smacking Julio's arm and ducking past him into the bathroom.

"You couldn't have put some pants on first?" Alex said dryly.

Julio just gave him a 'what can you do?' shrug in return, grinning. "Didn't see her complaining." They all knew that Samantha harbored a one-sided crush. Julio didn't lead her on, not directly, but he might have done more to discourage her.

Alex rolled his eyes. "Where's Ben?" He couldn't imagine the old man standing for all that racket.

"Went out for groceries," Julio replied, disappearing into the bedroom to get dressed.

Alex went in the other direction, into the living room. With only a single bedroom, this apartment was too small for the four of them. Alex banged his shin on the edge of Samantha's portable cot. After swearing up a storm, he took a moment to fold it up and put it out of the way.

Alex rummaged in his backpack for a clean T-shirt, smothering a wince as he maneuvered his injured shoulder into it. He grabbed a meal bar for breakfast and pushed Julio's gaudy yellow blanket out of the way to make room on the couch.

Munching on his meal bar, Alex browsed to the news sites on their MarsCom tablet. As expected, the bombing had made headlines on the Martian Chronicle. Alex skimmed the article. Nine soldiers killed between the bombing and firefight, and a tenth in critical condition. Alex felt a sense of grim satisfaction at the damage they'd done—another small victory in a long war—but he took no joy in it. He hoped he'd never see the day when he was *happy* about taking a life.

They mentioned two paramedics being injured during the escape attempt, and Alex frowned. He didn't remember anyone being hurt while he was there. Had the Peacekeepers done something to Caitlin and her partner after he'd escaped and tried to blame it on him? Had they somehow found out that Caitlin had helped him? He dismissed the thought as soon as it entered his mind. If that had happened, it would be all over the news.

Thinking of Caitlin made Alex curious. Mars was full of rebel sympathizers, but not many of them would stick their neck out like that for a total stranger. He waned to know more about the woman who had helped him. He brought up the search bar and entered her name. The first hit, the Waycross Fire and Rescue site, told him only that she was a firefighter/paramedic who worked there. He already knew as much.

The second hit was an article from the Martian Chronicle dated five years ago. A firefighter had rescued a four-year-old boy from an apartment fire, despite being injured when the floor collapsed. A photo accompanying the article showed the same Caitlin that Alex knew. The third article was a footnote from a society page: Caitlin had married Chronicle reporter Tom MacIntyre—the same reporter from the rescue article—later that same year. Alex switched off the computer, feeling like a pathetic stalker.

It took only a moment for reality to set back in. Who was he kidding? Even if she wasn't married, he was a criminal, living on the run. They'd both be better off if they never saw each other again.

[[—✳—]]

The morning sun painted the sky a pale purple, casting long shadows from the buildings inside Fort McChord. Despite the early hour, the fort already bustled with activity. Soldiers packed the mess hall for breakfast, and groups of them ran around the parade ground as part of their morning exercise routine. Jack could see the ruins of the main gate through his office window.

Troopers overnight had erected a makeshift barricade in front of it. Grim-looking soldiers in full battle gear patrolled the area around the spot where their friends had died. Jack felt a nagging sense of guilt as he watched them. It had been his job to keep these attacks from happening, and he had failed. Now ten good soldiers were dead or at death's door, including one of his own.

For seven years, Jack had made it his personal mission to stop these terrorists. He hated them. It wasn't just because of their methods, although that was reason enough. He hated everything they stood for. Two hundred years ago, the only things living on Mars were long-buried bacteria. Trillions of dollars had gone into the Mars project. Earth dollars. Earth food that fed the original colonists. Earth plastisteel that built the original domes. Earth spaceships bringing Earth people to live on this barren, lifeless world. And now that everything was running smoothly, these ungrateful Martians wanted to turn their backs on the people who had gotten them this far. Why? To work fewer hours; to pay less taxes? They disgusted him.

Jack rubbed his eyes. After working all morning, he was no closer to finding the bomber than last night. He had scanned the mug shots and police records for anyone matching "Iy's" name or description, but came up empty. The forensics unit crawled through the wreckage of the guard house. The fast-moving nature of the fire suggested an incendiary bomb, which would help them narrow down the origin of the explosives. The wreckage would be filled with clues—the type of bomb, the placement, the timer. Every piece of debris was evidence that would help them find the men responsible.

Movement by the door caught Jack's attention. Though his rank entitled him to a private office and a secretary, Jack had no use for such things. He had instead claimed one of the briefing rooms for his team, and set it up as a sort of war room. At the moment, it was more like a ghost town. Edwards's empty desk was a gnawing reminder of their loss the night before. Sergeant Cruz was off on an infiltration assignment in Lowell, following a lead that one of the rebel groups there was amassing arms for an uprising. Corporal Kitatani went back to Earth for convalescent leave after being shot during the arrest of a rebel cell leader last month. Lieutenant Dubois declined to volunteer for another tour on Mars, and had transferred out a few weeks ago. Jack wasn't sorry to see him go; he didn't have the stomach for counter-intelligence work. His replacement was supposed to be arriving today.

Sykes entered the office, carrying a file folder under one arm and a tray in the other. "Breakfast, sir." A frown crept across his face as he set the tray on Jack's desk. Sending him on menial errands like getting breakfast and fetching reports was just the sort of punishment to drive Sykes crazy. The sergeant handed over the folder, and said, "There's a digital sketch of our suspect. Fingerprints and DNA from the ambulance turned up a few matches, but no ID."

Jack took a bite out of his bagel as he flipped through the report. Ty, or whatever his real name was, had been linked to two other hit-and-run attacks on Peacekeeper squads, and a bombing attack against a troop shuttle at the spaceport. Nothing linked the fingerprints back to Ty's real identity. Jack set aside the report, frustrated to learn that Ty had eluded them at least three times before. God only knew how many other attacks he had been a part of.

"Nothing from the street cams?" Jack asked. He and Sykes had both gotten a good look at their suspect, but an artist's rendition paled compared to photos and video.

"Not yet. It looks like the rebels hacked them. The Net Security guys are on it. I also got the preliminary report from the engineers about the blast," Sykes continued, taking a seat in one of the office chairs. "Looks like they placed the bomb in a sealed-off maintenance shaft running under the gate. It had been a few months since the inspection teams checked to make sure it was still secure."

"I'll talk to Colonel Isakovich," Jack said. "We'll get his men to check all the other maintenance shafts and tunnels under the fort."

Sykes scowled. "Damn tunnel rats. If command would just give us the men, we could sweep the whole tunnel system and cut the rebellion off at the knees." He shook his head. "Turn up anything interesting on our missing prisoner?"

Jack turned his computer monitor so Sykes could see the screen. "Not yet, but I looked up our friend Ms. Farland. Turns out her file is flagged."

The sergeant raised his eyebrows. "The paramedic? What color?"

The Federation central database contained dossiers on every Martian colonist, with everything from birth and bank records to criminal history. Files of individuals with known or suspected rebel ties were flagged with a colored threat level. Red for "most wanted" terrorists, like the bomber Jack was after; orange for those convicted or suspected of rebel activities; and yellow for suspected sympathizers and those with ties to known rebels.

"Yellow," Jack replied. "Her father's serving life in Luna Prison for bombing a supply depot back in '64. And her uncle is Max Farland."

Sykes' brows rose. "The Syndicate guy?"

"They haven't been able to pin anything on him, but yeah. Him." Jack would have liked to take a crack at Old Max, but organized crime was outside the purview of the counter-terrorism taskforce. He suspected the Syndicate had been smuggling weapons to the rebels, but so far they had no proof.

"Huh. So do you think she's involved?"

Jack shook his head. "Not in the bombing." The background with her father explained her attitude, and their story about the ambulance assignments checked out. As much as he wanted to suspect a conspiracy, everyone from the fire chief to the emergency dispatcher assured him that she and her partner had every reason to be there. "But I think she knows more than she's telling about the prisoner escaping. Maybe she helped him, or maybe she just turned a blind eye while he worked his magic with the zip-ties."

The sergeant frowned. "Should we bring her in?"

"Not yet," Jack said after considering it for a moment. Sykes seemed about to protest, but Jack waved him off. "We don't have enough to charge her with anything, and there's no sense tipping our hand. We'll keep an eye on her. If she did help our guy escape, he might contact her again. Or she might lead us to him."

Jack opened the file folder Sykes had brought, and flipped to the digital sketch of their bombing suspect. "In the meantime, I want you to take this around and lean on all our contacts. Find out who this man is." Jack stared at the image, fixing it in his mind. "I want this one, Sergeant. He slipped through our fingers once. Not again."

Sykes nodded. Taking the sketch, he headed out of the office. Almost as soon as he'd gone, another man knocked tentatively on the doorframe. Jack saw a young officer standing there in his

Class A semi-formal blues. He was tall and slender, with close-cropped black hair. "Excuse me, I'm looking for Captain Decker."

"I'm Decker." In his usual civilian clothes, Jack could hardly blame the officer for not knowing who he was.

The officer recovered quickly from his surprise, then stepped forward and offered Jack a folder. Standing at attention, he said. "Lieutenant Matthew Hale reporting for duty, sir."

Jack recognized the name of Lieutenant Dubois's replacement. "Have a seat, Lieutenant." Jack set the folder aside. It was a formality; it would contain a copy of Hale's file and orders, which Jack had already received. Hale had spent three years in a military intelligence unit within the United Canadian American States' Army before volunteering for the Peacekeepers. "Welcome to Mars."

"Thank you, sir. I'm looking forward to working with you."

"You won't have too much time to settle in before you're in the thick of it. We're spread thin here, and there's been a sharp rise in the number of incidents over the past three months. Including one last night."

Hale nodded. "Yes, sir, I was looking over the situation report on the shuttle. It sounds like the rebels may be building up to a major offensive."

"Insurgents," Jack corrected. Hale gave him a puzzled look, so he elaborated. "We don't call them rebels here. It lends legitimacy to their cause, makes them sound like they're noble freedom fighters. Call them insurgents, guerrillas, terrorists… whatever. Just not rebels."

The young lieutenant looked chagrined. "Sorry, sir."

"Don't apologize; learn," Jack said. "I don't stand on ceremony, so don't feel like you have to 'sir' me every sixty seconds. And tomorrow, lose the uniform. We're detectives as much as soldiers here, so we need to blend in."

"Yes, si—" Hale caught himself with a wry grin.

Jack smirked and handed him a tablet. "Here's everything we have on the incident last night. I want you up on every detail by the end of the day. We lost one of our team, and we're going to make those Free Mars bastards pay."

CHAPTER 7

CAITLIN WATCHED WITH A RESIGNED expression as the eight ball glided into the side pocket.

"Oh for three? You're slipping, Farland." Firefighter Kim Zhang offered a self-satisfied grin from the other side of the pool table and rubbed some more chalk on the tip of her cue.

Despite the literary associations of its name (which came from the owner, not the author), Hemingway's Pub was an unassuming place, geared toward the wage-slaves of Waycross' many factories. It prided itself on having all the "old world" charm of an Earth roadside bar, right down to the pool tables, dart boards, and little snack trays scattered everywhere.

Caitlin scowled at Zhang's gloating, which only earned her an amused chuckle in return. She forked over a pair of ten credit coins.

Zhang scooped them up. "What do you say—double or nothing?"

"No thanks." Usually Caitlin could hold her own in the game —even against Zhang, the fire company's resident pool shark— but tonight her heart just wasn't in it. This was her day off, a brief respite while she switched from night shifts to days. She had allowed herself to be dragged along to the bar, but didn't feel much like partying. She couldn't stop thinking about what happened last night, or second-guessing herself. Had she done the right thing? Or had she just turned loose a heartless murderer?

Caitlin slid her pool cue back into the rack on the wall and Zhang started looking for a new victim. "What about you, Vince?"

Slouched against the wall, Vince had been watching the game with a practiced eye. When they played doubles, Caitlin and Vince were nearly unstoppable. "No thanks," Vince demurred, "My wife will never let me hear the end of it if I let you clean me out."

Disappointed, Zhang set her sights on the other two members of their little group. "Andy? Chris?" But Park and Tierney had found something else to occupy their attention.

"Hey, guys, check this out." Tierney pointed to the MarsCom terminal positioned at the end of the bar.

A news feed showed recorded footage of the firefighters in action. "Emergency crews responded to Fort McChord last night after an explosion destroyed the guardhouse outside the main gate."

Tierney grinned at the announcer's voice-over, young and vain enough to get a kick out of watching himself on television. Caitlin couldn't care less. She'd had her fill of news coverage after rescuing a young boy from an apartment fire a few years back. It had been her fifteen minutes of fame, and it couldn't end fast enough for her. The only silver lining to all the attention was catching the eye of one charming, handsome reporter in particular. Barely a year later, she'd married him.

"Nine soldiers were killed in the explosion and a tenth died earlier today from injuries suffered in the blast. Peacekeeper MPs arrested a man believed to be responsible for the attack after a brief chase just blocks from the scene. The unidentified man escaped while being transported to the hospital." The names and faces of the dead soldiers paraded across the screen, trying to look tough in their official military photos. Not a one looked a day over 21.

The anchor continued, *"Two paramedics treating the prisoner were also assaulted."* Caitlin shook her head in disgust at the Peacekeeper spin-doctoring. *"Peacekeeper command issued the following digital sketch of the suspect and advised the public to consider him armed and extremely dangerous."* The screen showed an artist's impression of Alex.

The newscast switched to another story, and everyone lost interest.

"I'll never understand what these guys think they're going to accomplish by blowing up innocent people," Tierney remarked.

Zhang, practicing by herself at the pool table, agreed with a grim, "Hear, hear."

Out of the corner of her eye, Caitlin saw Vince shoot her a warning glance, but it was too late. One of her buttons had been pushed. "Funny, I don't remember seeing any 'innocent people' out there last night—just a bunch of soldiers in uniform." Vince winced, his face a silent *here we go again.*

Tierney rolled his eyes. "Come on, Cait, you know what I mean. Bombs in the night? Snipers? Sabotage? They're cowards. They have no honor."

"Right, because it's so much more heroic to drop a smart bomb from a Peacekeeper jet three miles from its target."

"That's different," Tierney insisted. "They're *soldiers*, fighting for a *government*. The rebels are no better than thugs, dragging civilians into the line of fire."

Caitlin frowned, frustrated. "The rebels stopped hitting civilian targets decades ago."

"What about those two women in Lowell a couple months ago? They sure as hell weren't soldiers. Right, Vince?"

Shaking his head, Vince held up a hand. "Leave me out of this." Vince never got involved in their political debates. He jokingly referred to himself as a political agnostic, a rarity in the polarized world of Martian politics. Mostly he was pragmatic enough to acknowledge the argument couldn't lead to anything good.

Zhang, on the other hand, jumped in to support Tierney. "He's right—there were those girls, and the old man in Owen's Point back in August. How can you sit there and claim the rebels don't hurt civilians?"

"I'm not saying that. And I'm not excusing it either." Zhang's smugness at her admission was short-lived when Caitlin clarified, "I've seen the aftermath of this too, you know, from *both* sides. Stray Peacekeeper rounds hit innocent people too sometimes, and that's just as bad. But none of that is what happened last night. The base is a military target."

"That's crap, Cait," Tierney challenged. "They're terrorists."

Caitlin sighed and shrugged, knowing that talking sense into Tierney was a lost cause. "Well, there's that old saying: One man's terrorist is another man's freedom fighter."

"That's just an excuse to help the terrorists sleep at night. What—did your father tell you that one? Let's consider the source." Tierney snorted.

It stung, and Caitlin's face froze. Tierney's Peacekeeper sympathies ran as deep as Caitlin's support for the rebels, but he'd never made it personal before. A hush fell over the group, and even Tierney seemed to realize he'd gone too far.

Caitlin snapped, "Considering the source, I'd say he knows a hell of a lot more about it than you do." She picked up her glass, which was still two-thirds full, and said, "I'm going to get another drink."

Caitlin tried to ignore the murmured conversation as she walked away from the group. She knew they were talking about her, and she didn't want to care. What did it matter what they thought, anyway? She sat down at the bar, nursing her half-full beer in a sullen silence.

It wasn't long before Vince's large frame perched onto the stool next to her. "Tierney's an asshole. Don't let him get to you." He nudged her arm companionably.

"It's not just him…" Caitlin trailed off, losing her thought in midstream. Her eyes had locked on the doorway, over Vince's shoulder. After the look on her face, Vince swiveled around to see for himself. Tom had just walked in with a redhead. He took her coat in a gentlemanly fashion, revealing a gray business suit with a shorter-than-necessary skirt beneath. They walked toward a table.

Scowling into her glass, Caitlin muttered, "This night keeps getting better and better."

Tom couldn't have heard her, not from across the crowded bar, but something made him look in their direction. He met Caitlin's gaze, and his face clouded with embarrassment. He leaned in to say something to the redhead, and then abandoned her to join Vince and Caitlin at the bar.

"Hey guys," he greeted, trying to sound nonchalant. When Caitlin just scowled at him and Vince offered the barest of nods, Tom changed tack. "Look, it's not what you think. She's a source. I'm doing a story on Ares Tech."

Caitlin arched an eyebrow. "So you decided to take her out for drinks." She noticed that he was still wearing his wedding ring.

"No," Tom insisted. "She wanted to meet in a public place. I figured we weren't likely to run into any Ares bigwigs here." He had a point. Tom finally gave in to exasperation, "You don't believe me? Come on over, I'll introduce you. You can sit in on the interview if you want."

Shaking her head, Caitlin sighed. "I believe you, Tom." And she did, deep down. "That's not the point."

"Then what is the point?" Irritation crept into Tom's voice. It seemed like he was keeping it to a normal volume by sheer force of will alone. "To keep punishing me for one mistake?"

"One mistake?" Caitlin's voice pitched up incredulously. "You had an affair, Tom. For *months*."

"I know! And I've apologized a million times. I've tried to make it up to you. How long are you going to keep holding this over me?"

"Oh, I don't know. Ten years? That sounds fair, don't you think, Vince?" Caitlin had intended it to be an off-hand remark, but the bitterness in her voice surprised her. Vince wisely stayed out of it, pretending he didn't hear.

Tom set his jaw, as he always did when he was upset. "Well, when you make up your mind, you know where to find me." Stiff-backed, he turned and walked back to his non-date.

Caitlin watched him go, her satisfaction tempered by a nagging guilt. He had hurt her, and a part of her took pleasure in striking back. But that part was overshadowed by the part that already regretted her words. Caitlin frowned into her glass. "Do you think I'm being too hard on him?"

Vince didn't reply at first, which Caitlin took as a bad sign. "You know I'd never defend him…" Caitlin winced, anticipating the 'But'. "But it's been what—six months? How long do you plan to go on like this? You can't expect him to stay in a hotel forever waiting for you to make up your mind."

Caitlin's frown deepened, and she traced a finger along the edge of her glass.

Tilting his head, Vince studied her face. "You still love him, don't you?"

It would be easy to say no; to say that she was so angry that she despised him. But if that were true, it probably wouldn't hurt so much. Caitlin offered a silent nod.

"Then you can either try to work things out—maybe therapy or whatever—or you have to let him go."

"It's not that simple."

"I'm not saying it's easy, but those are the choices," Vince insisted, his tone gentle but firm. "And the sooner you accept that, the sooner you can stop wallowing and move on with your life." Vince squeezed her shoulder and left her alone with her thoughts.

Looking across the bar, her eyes fell on Tom's table. The woman kept fidgeting with her napkin and looking around, as if she expected someone to sneak up on her. Tom had his datapad out to record his notes. It looked like an interview, just as he'd said, but still Caitlin felt jealous. She didn't want to be there sitting with Tom, but she didn't want the other woman to be there either.

After a few minutes of impolite staring (which, thankfully, neither of them seemed to notice) Caitlin stopped torturing herself. She drained the last of her beer and settled the bill. Near the door, she stopped to look back at Tom once more. This time he looked up, and their eyes met. She saw a brief flicker of annoyance cross his features, but when he saw the sadness in her eyes, his expression softened. He understood her; he always did, and that's what made it hard to stay angry with him.

CHAPTER 8

VINCE BACKED THE AMBULANCE SLOWLY in the bay, between the ladder truck and the empty spot where the second ambulance would park. It was just past noon, and Caitlin and Vince were returning from their third ambulance call of the day. Park and Tierney, in the station's other ambulance, had a similar tally.

Caitlin, for one, was glad for the distraction. Between the incident with Alex and the confrontation with Tom, her brain wouldn't stop spinning.

"You going to sit in the truck all day?" Vince asked from the driver's seat.

Caitlin realized that while she was daydreaming, he had turned off the engine and filled out the mileage log. She shook off her blank stare and gave him a weak smile. "I figured it would save time when the next call came in."

No sooner had she uttered the words than the fire klaxon echoed in the garage. "Medic Five-One: Code 2 dispatch at the Commons. Elderly female fainted, but is now conscious and alert."

Vince reluctantly put his seatbelt back on. "Good going, Cait." Everyone teased him for his superstitions about calls. If things were slow, he'd knock on wood anytime someone mentioned how quiet it was, then blame them when the next call came in. Caitlin didn't put any stock in such nonsense.

Caitlin radioed the dispatcher to call them en route. Then something occurred to her. "I think that independence rally started a bit ago in the Commons."

"Is that today?" Vince frowned. Usually the rallies consisted of nothing more than speeches and flag-waving, but sometimes things got out of hand. The worst case happened six years ago when a demonstration turned into a full-blown riot. Several people were killed. The Federation had banned public protests for nearly a year following that mess. The Peacekeeper propaganda machine used such incidents to paint the entire independence movement as a bunch of violent radicals. Pro-rebel reporters like Tom were few; the major news services on Mars, all affiliates of Earth networks, portrayed a mostly-one-sided view of the conflict. Even people like Vince associated independence rallies with violence.

Caitlin smirked, seeing a chance to push Vince's buttons a little. "Well, with any luck, there won't be any trouble there today."

Vince gave her a dirty look, probably trying to think of something wooden he could knock on. She chuckled, and went back to watching the road.

They parked at the edge of the Commons, a wide-open square, paved with cobblestone, at the very heart of the city. A white gazebo stood in the middle of the square, the only building for a hundred yards in any direction. Beside it, a rocket-shaped statue marked the spot where the first Martian colony ship touched down over a century ago.

Today, the gazebo served as a stage for those speaking at the rally. A woman's voice boomed over the speaker system. "Thirty percent of Mars' population works in the mining industry, and employees reported over a thousand safety violations last year alone. Four hundred miners died in accidents, the highest number in ten years. And what has the Federation done about it? Nothing! Why? Because they care more about Mars' natural resources than its people. They need our gadolinium, our platinum, our steel. They don't need us."

The crowd roared its assent. There must have been over a thousand people packed into the square. Many waved signs supporting the independence movement's favorite topics: "No Taxation Without Representation", "Free Mars Now", and "Protect Our Miners."

Caitlin frowned at the speaker's words. "I wish they wouldn't emphasize those statistics." Vince shot her a questioning look, and she went on, "It's so abstract, so impersonal. Four hundred people doesn't sound like so many, but each of them is a father, or a wife, or—"

"Or a mother? Cait, you take these things way too personally."

Caitlin scoffed. "How else am I supposed to take it? She died so some Earther corporation could skimp on safety costs."

"It was fifteen years ago."

Sixteen, Caitlin corrected silently. "But nothing's changed since then. Conditions in the mines are even worse. The safety oversight committee is run by the Federation, and the only thing they care about is getting their quotas filled. Turning a blind eye is their favorite pastime." They'd certainly looked the other way after her mother was killed. Seven miners died in an "accident" attributed to flagrant safety violations. There was a brief scandal, promises of investigations and tighter controls, and then business as usual.

Vince couldn't argue with that, so he just offered a half-shrug in agreement. Grabbing the radio mic, Caitlin let some of her frustration creep into her tone. "Dispatch, this is Medic Five-One. Can't you get a better location on our patient? There are a thousand people here." She sighed impatiently, waiting for the dispatcher to figure out where they needed to go. As her eyes drifted over the sea of protesters, she almost wished she could be out there with them.

[[—＊—]]

Jack scanned the faces of the protestors, watching through the digital zoom of his binoculars. Surveillance always gave him a little thrill, tracking his targets while they remained oblivious to his presence. Like a hunter tracking his prey. His binoculars drifted past a man holding his son on his shoulders, and Jack wondered what sort of father would bring a child to hear this abhorrent rhetoric. Next to the father, a young couple nuzzled their heads close together so they could talk over the din of the loud speaker. Hundreds had gathered, packed so densely in places that they stood shoulder to shoulder. More filtered in, drawn by the commotion or the speeches. Jack shook his head in disgust.

Jack's team had set up an observation post on the second story of a convenience store overlooking the park. Hale fiddled with his tablet, testing the feed from the cameras they'd placed in the windows.

"You really think you're going to get anything off that, Lieutenant?" Sykes wondered, looking over his shoulder.

Hale didn't look up from the tablet. Images of faces began scrolling across the screen. "If there's anyone on our watch list out there, the facial recognition software will let us know. So far, it's just the speakers. No surprise there." Their database had files on most of the Martian Liberation Society leadership.

The woman in the gazebo wrapped up her speech about miner's rights to thunderous applause, many in the crowd pumping their fists in agreement.

Sykes snorted. "Miners' rights, my ass. Nobody's holding a gun to their heads and making them go down into the mines."

"Why don't they just go on strike if the conditions are so terrible?" Hale wondered.

"They can't," Jack explained. "Mining is considered a critical industry."

"I wish they would," Sykes said. "Just give me five minutes, and I'll show them 'unsafe conditions'." He snickered, but Hale just frowned.

Jack glanced at the young officer. Sympathizing with the enemy led to a slippery slope. "Don't forget that the agitators are good at propaganda," he said flatly. "Twisting numbers until it paints the picture they want. Quoting studies written by researchers with an agenda. It's how they push people into extremism. Stay focused."

Hale nodded, "Yes, sir." He returned his attention to the screen. A few minutes later, he said, "Captain, we've got a hit on facial recognition. Northeast corner; grid seven." He paused. "Holy crap. It's him."

Jack rushed over. Hale had zoomed in on a group of protestors. A sidebar on the screen showed two images—their sketch of "Ty" from the night before, next to a headshot of a man in a blue ball cap, beard, and glasses. Jack might have missed the resemblance on casual inspection, but the computer saw through it. He sucked in a breath.

"Sykes, with me," Jack barked, already heading for the door. Over his shoulder, he called to Hale, "Don't lose him."

[[— ✳ —]]

Having finally located their patient—an older woman who fainted in the press of the crowd and refused to be taken to the hospital—Caitlin and Vince carried their gear back to the ambulance.

Caitlin had just opened one of the exterior compartments when she heard Tom's voice behind her. "Hey Cait." Turning, she faced him with a less than welcoming expression. Disappointment crossed his face for a moment before he continued awkwardly, "I was covering the rally and I saw you guys pull up. Everything all right?"

Caitlin offered him a brisk nod. "Yeah—it was just a refusal. Where's Harry?" She rarely saw Tom without his cameraman these days.

"Back getting some crowd shots." Tom motioned in a vaguely northern direction. Looking back at Caitlin, his brow furled and he seemed about to say something. Instead, he took a few steps closer and leaned against the side of the ambulance. She watched him with raised eyebrows until finally he blurted out. "Cait, I know I've messed everything up, and there's nothing I can do or say to fix it. But please, give me another chance. I promise things will be different this time." He stared at her with a somber intensity.

Caitlin couldn't meet his gaze. His soft, earnest words were such a contrast to his usual confidence. She knew he meant it. But he'd also meant it when he spoke his marriage vows four years ago, promising to forsake all others. How could she be sure?

Her silence must have seemed like a bad sign, so Tom eased off a little. "Just think about it, okay? We can talk about it later. Over dinner, maybe? Tonight?"

Looking down at her hands, Caitlin's eyes focused on her wedding ring. She'd made vows of her own, promising to stand by him. Tom had thrown away the last few years, but she wasn't ready to give up on the rest of their lives together. "I can't tonight." Tom looked crestfallen, thinking she was blowing him off, but brightened when she said, "Tomorrow?"

"Tomorrow," he agreed, grinning. His expression showed a mix of joy and relief, and he reached out tentatively to touch her cheek. This time, she didn't shy away. The light brush of his fingers was comforting, and she smiled.

The moment was fleeting—a brief respite before the world intruded on them again. Tom's com beeped at him, demanding his attention. He answered it, listened for a moment, and then frowned. "Okay, I'll be right over." After hanging up, he explained to Caitlin. "That was Harry. Someone just got arrested for spitting at the Peacekeepers. I'd better go see what's going on."

Caitlin frowned as well. "Be careful."

"I'll see you later," Tom said. He started off across the square.

Caitlin watched him until the crowd swallowed him from view. She turned back to the ambulance and stowed the trauma bag in the proper compartment. Vince waited for her in the driver's seat. She opened the passenger door, but then stepped up onto the running board. The extra two feet let her see over the heads of the crowd.

Vince looked over in concern. "You okay?" When Caitlin nodded, he said, "We should get back to the station."

"Tom said that someone was arrested. There may be trouble." Arrests meant Peacekeepers, and Peacekeepers and restless independence supporters made for a volatile combination.

"All the more reason to go. They'll call us back if they need us. The station's only a few blocks away." If something happened, Vince didn't want to be anywhere near it. Looking out over the crowd, Caitlin saw the impassioned faces of the independence supporters. A cluster of Peacekeepers kept a watchful eye with their riot gear and assault rifles, and she wondered if maybe Vince had the right idea.

CHAPTER 9

ALEX LISTENED TO THE SPEECH over the loudspeaker. "I'd like to thank all of you for coming out here today. In the wake of such incidents as the bombing two nights ago, it is easy to get distracted from our cause. By being here today, you are showing the world that there is another way. A way that doesn't involve violence or death. A way that ultimately will bring peace and independence to Mars."

A way that doesn't work, Alex added to himself, even as the onlookers cheered the words. He had been that naïve once. The Federation let the colonists indulge themselves in these little rallies and protests. It let them feel as if they were accomplishing something, but the Federation would never just gift Mars its independence. There was too much at stake: Resources. Money.

Power. They wouldn't give that up. Not unless Mars forced them to.

"Everyone's in position," Alex murmured to Ben, mouth close to his ear to be heard over the din. "Bottles and rocks, like we discussed; no guns." Alex had been very clear on the latter point. The Peacekeepers had two full squads—twenty men—ready in full riot gear at the corners. Half were armed with assault rifles; the others with stun batons and riot shields. Starting a firefight with them would be suicide. "Julio's keeping an eye on them."

Alex steered clear of the soldiers, worried that he might be recognized. Every time someone glanced his way, he felt a pang of fear. He wouldn't have come at all, except that he had recruited most of the participants in the operation today. Switching faces at the last minute would have spooked them. So far, his disguise—eyeglasses, a fake beard and a Waycross Knights ball cap—had held up.

A sudden commotion to the north drew their attention. Alex heard shouting, but none of it distinct enough to make out over the background noise. He strained to see what was happening, but there were too many people in the way.

Ben glanced at his watch. "It's too early." The men they had recruited to start trouble weren't supposed to do anything for another ten minutes. That should have been enough time for Ben and Alex to get clear of the square.

Alex spoke into the microphone attached to his collar. "Julio, what's going on over there? Someone jump the gun?"

"No, not one of ours," Julio replied in his earpiece. "Some dumbass got arrested. I think we should execute now, though. Take advantage of the distraction."

Ben nodded, and Alex keyed his mic again. "Go for it. Good luck. We'll see you at the rally point."

Alex headed for the edge of the square, weaving his way through the spectators, but then skidded to a halt. Standing not ten feet away, wearing civilian clothes, was the big British Peacekeeper from the ambulance. Alex jerked back, averting his face.

"What is it?" Ben didn't know the sergeant by sight.

"Peacekeepers," Alex hissed. "Let's get out of here." Alex pushed his way past a couple and rushed off in the opposite direction.

[[—∗—]]

Jack pushed his way through the crowd in the square. In his earpiece, Hale's voice guided him to the right sector. "Confirm you still have eyes on the target?" Jack asked.

"Affirmative," Hale answered, sounding tinny over the radio. "Grid six. Heading west. Should be approaching at your five o'clock, Captain."

Squinting into the crowd, Jack saw no sign of their quarry. "Fan out," he told Sykes, waving to his left.

Hale's voice cut in again. "Sir, I'm picking up some chatter on the military police channel from the squad at the square. I think you should hear it."

He patched it through, and Jack heard the familiar voice of Captain Cerulli, in charge of the MP division. "Command, this is Delta One. We've got trouble brewing her at the northeast corner of the commons. One in custody, but the crowd is pushing in." There was a grunt of surprised pain, and the sound of shattering glass. Cerulli growled, "They're throwing bottles at us. Command, request backup and medics."

The command center at Fort McChord responded that reinforcements would be on the way.

"Should we lend a hand?" Sykes' voice came over the radio, on their private frequency. He sounded too eager; no doubt itching to bash some heads.

"We're not here for riot control. Let the MPs do their jobs for once." Jack spotted a bench and stepped up onto its corner, ignoring the angry glare from the woman sitting on the opposite end. From that vantage point, he could see Cerulli's squad under siege. They held back the tide of protestors using riot shields and stun batons, but at least one Peacekeeper went down under a hail of blows from a plastic sign. Someone toting a bulky shoulder camera with the Martian Chronicle logo had a front-row seat to the violence.

Ignoring the melee, Jack scanned the crowd for someone in a blue ball cap. There were several, none of them matching the target's appearance. "Damn it, Hale, where is he?"

"Captain, looks like he made Sergeant Sykes. He's changed direction, heading straight for you."

Jack jumped down off the bench, reaching inside his jacket to rest his fingers on his pistol. He pushed through the crowd, making no apologies. As he hurried north, he heard a series of quiet thumps. Moments later, white smoke billowed from several spots in the area.

Tear gas.

The protestors yelled and scattered. Eyes watering, Jack scanned the faces that rushed past him. A few meters ahead, their target came into view. His eyes locked on Jack's, spotting him at the same instant. Jack swore as the man abruptly changed course and started heading south.

"Out of the way! Move!" Jack shouted at the people blocking his path, cursing and pushing through. He drew his pistol, which cut a path in front of him as people shrieked and scurried aside.

There was a second man with the target—an older guy with gray hair and a beard. The old man spun toward Jack, one hand drawing a pistol from the folds of his jacket. Jack raised his own weapon and reflexively squeezed the trigger. The first shot struck some hapless protester who was passing between them, but Jack fired again even as the man was falling. The second shot struck the old man, knocking him backwards into his comrade.

Those nearest Jack panicked, screams cutting through the tear-gas haze. Someone careened into Jack in their frenzied flight, nearly knocking him over. Jack regained his balance, but the two rebels had vanished into the crowd.

"They're shooting!" The frantic voice of one of Cerulli's Peacekeepers echoed in Jack's ear. Unable to tell where the shots were coming from, the soldiers thought the protesters were shooting at them.

Jack reached for his radio to switch channels. "Delta One, this is Citadel One. Stand down. You're not—"

His warning came too late.

Captain Cerulli's voice echoed in Jack's ear, his fury clearly audible on the radio. "Open fire!"

Jack shouted to Sykes to take cover, and barely hit the deck himself before the first shots rang out.

CHAPTER 10

IT WAS A CHAIN REACTION. First one shot, then another, then the continuous staccato beat of rifles firing fully automatic. The bullets cut a swathe through the crowd, and the screams of pain and terror nearly eclipsed the noise of the gunshots. Those not felled by the shooting knocked over and trampled each other in their panic.

Caitlin saw it all from her vantage point on the ambulance's running board, eyes wide with shock. She stayed there only a moment before jumping back down to the ground.

"Cait, get down!" Vince shouted.

The repetitive clang of stray bullets striking the side of the ambulance punctuated the urgency of his words. Caitlin ducked under the large side mirror. A bullet shattered the glass inches from her face, the shards stinging her forehead. She scrambled around the front of the truck. Vince grabbed her in a bear hug and pulled her down into an awkward crouch behind the front tire. They huddled there together, sharing the meager cover.

Caitlin grabbed the radio microphone attached to her lapel. She keyed it and spoke breathlessly into the speaker. "Medic Five-One to Dispatch: Emergency message." She struggled to keep her voice level. "We have shots fired at this location. Large number of victims. We'll need everyone you have, and put LMC on a mass casualty standby."

A bullet struck the hood, causing Caitlin to flinch and look up. "Scene is not safe. Repeat: not safe."

The dispatcher acknowledged the understatement of the century, and a flurry of radio traffic broke out as the call went out to all the emergency personnel in the city and the staff at Lafayette Medical Center. Caitlin felt so helpless.

After a few minutes that felt like an eternity, the shooting tapered off. Dozens of terrified people rushed past the ambulance. One man stumbled around the back and collapsed into a seated position near the rear tire. He had his left arm draped across his chest. Blood soaked through the sleeve of his white shirt.

"Help me!" he cried.

Vince twisted to look at her, letting go of Caitlin for a moment. "Just stay down, sir." He wouldn't leave their position of cover until the shooting had stopped. It was the first rule they drilled into your head in paramedic school: don't become a patient yourself. "Keep pressure on the bleeding."

Caitlin heard a cry of pain from in front of the ambulance, and looked just in time to see another fleeing man get shot in the back. He fell forward limply, hitting the ground less than six feet from the ambulance. Caitlin hesitated only a moment before dashing to the fallen man's side, all the rules forgotten.

Vince reached for her when he realized what she was doing, but he wasn't quick enough. His hands caught her sleeve, but didn't get a good grip and she pulled away. "Cait! Cait!!"

Caitlin tried to keep low, conscious of the bullets still flying at the crowd. She yelped and ducked as one struck the cobblestones just a few feet away, ricocheting off with a puff of dust. Caitlin grabbed the injured man under his shoulders and dragged him back to cover.

Vince helped her once she had reached the corner of the ambulance. Terror and livid anger mingled on his face. "Are you all right?" was his first question. Once he saw that she was, he snapped, "Are you out of your goddamn mind?"

"He was right there," Caitlin said, panting. She brushed back her bangs, which were now plastered to her forehead with sweat. Her heart pumped so hard she could feel it hammering against her chest. "I couldn't just leave him there to bleed to death."

Vince just shook his head. "Don't ever do that to me again!"

It wasn't a stunt Caitlin planned on repeating. She cut open the man's shirt and saw a neat bullet hole in the left chest. He was still breathing, for the moment. Vince tried to check the man's lung sounds—a lost cause given how noisy it was in the square—while Caitlin pressed a hand against his chest to stop the bleeding.

A voice from behind distracted her. "Please, you have to help my granddaughter!" A gray-haired woman dragged a younger one around to the safe side of the ambulance.

"Go. I've got this," Vince told her.

Caitlin hurried to help the injured woman down to the ground. The grandmother didn't seem hurt, but the college-aged one didn't respond when Caitlin tried to rouse her. Two gunshot wounds had turned her abdomen into a bloody mess. Caitlin checked for a pulse, but felt nothing. Instincts pulled at her to begin resuscitation, but in a multiple casualty incident, with the medics outnumbered by the patients fifty to one, they had to focus on the ones they had a chance of saving. 'Do the most for the many' was the main rule of triage.

Caitlin drew her hand back and met the older woman's searching gaze. The woman's teary-eyed reaction showed she knew the answer even before Caitlin spoke. "I'm so sorry. She's gone."

The woman cradled her granddaughter's head in her lap. Her lip quivered, and tears streamed down her face, but she didn't make a sound. Caitlin patted her arm in a weak gesture of support.

The man sitting near the back tire gasped at the body. "Oh, God. Is she dead?" Seeing Caitlin's grim nod, the other man paled, looking horrified. "I think I'm going to be sick."

Caitlin sat back on her heels, sighing. She knew this wouldn't be the only fatality they saw today. Catching Vince's eye, she could see him also steeling himself for what lay ahead. Yet as she listened to the continued gunshots, she thought of Tom, out there somewhere amid the fighting, and prayed he was all right.

[[—∗—]]

Alex ran through the square, dragging the unconscious Ben along with him. He didn't really pick a direction to go, but allowed himself to be swept up along with the fleeing crowd. So many had fallen, and yet the gunfire continued. Bullets passed by, close enough for him to feel, but somehow they all missed. Behind him, a loud whoosh and screams marked someone in the crowd hurling a Molotov cocktail at the Peacekeepers.

The prudent thing would have been to seek cover until the shooting stopped, but Alex couldn't risk it. He had to get Ben out of here, before the soldiers got organized and sealed off the area. He was pretty sure Sykes and Decker were too busy dodging their own guys' bullets to chase him, but that distraction wouldn't last forever.

Alex still couldn't believe this had happened. The Peacekeepers had never opened fire on a demonstration before. Tear gas, stun batons, and old-fashioned beatings, sure, but never anything like this. Alex felt a cold shock that had started when the first bullets flew. This was all their fault.

With every rapid breath, Ben made a gasping sound like someone coming up for air after being underwater. The old man's features were pale, his lips already turning blue. Alex knew Ben wouldn't make it back to the safe house. He needed help now.

Alex spotted the ambulance over the heads of the people in front of him, its side pock-marked with bullet holes. Flinching when a bullet whizzed by his ear, Alex sprinted the last few meters to the ambulance. As he came around behind the truck, he found a makeshift treatment area. All the compartments on the safe side of the ambulance were open and empty, their contents dumped into half-hazard piles on the cobblestones. At least a dozen people were sheltered by the vehicle—some moving and talking, others just moaning, and a few covered in bloodstained sheets. In the middle of it all, two paramedics struggled to manage the chaos. Alex blinked, then felt a surge of relief when he saw Caitlin and her partner.

Vince knelt near the front of the truck, starting an IV on a seriously injured patient. He hadn't noticed Alex, which was probably for the best. Caitlin crouched by the rear tire, placing a dressing on the forehead of a bleeding woman. Alex hauled Ben over toward her.

The paramedic took a small medallion from a satchel slung over her shoulder. After fiddling with it for a moment, she slipped it over the woman's head. It pulsed with a dull yellow light. Looking around, Alex saw medallions on most of the other patients. Some were red, but most were yellow or green. The color seemed to correspond to the seriousness of the injury. Caitlin pressed the woman's hand against the dressing. "Hold this tight, okay? It'll slow the bleeding. You'll be fine."

Caitlin stood up and turned around, letting out a startled gasp when she found Alex standing right behind her. She didn't recognize him at first, but then her eyes widened and she whispered, "Alex!"

A bullet struck the top of the ambulance with a loud clang, causing them both to duck. Snapping out of her surprised daze, Caitlin helped Alex lower Ben to the ground.

Alex watched her while she worked, her brow furled with intense concentration. Suture strips held a fresh cut above her eyebrow closed, and her face was smudged with dirt and dried blood, some of it her own. She listened to Ben's breathing with her stethoscope. "His lung's collapsed."

That didn't sound good. "Can you do anything for him?"

Caitlin nodded, and cut open Ben's shirt. She taped a dressing of what looked like aluminum foil over the bubbling gunshot wound in Ben's chest. "Roll him on his side for a minute," she said. Alex did so, and she did the same for the exit wound on his back.

Caitlin opened a package from her satchel and took out a device that looked like a valve with a needle attached. As she worked, she asked tautly, "Did your people start this?"

Alex swallowed, a hollow feeling in the pit of his stomach. He couldn't deny it. "It wasn't supposed to turn out like this." He didn't know why he was so desperate for her to understand. "The Peacekeepers fired first. Our men didn't even have guns." Except Ben, and he didn't even get a shot off.

Her eyes flicked up to him briefly, as if to gauge his sincerity. Then she nodded, the accusatory look fading from her face. Feeling along Ben's ribs, she found a spot an inch or so below his collarbone. She cleaned the spot with alcohol and then stuck the needle into Ben's chest. Alex winced as Ben groaned. Caitlin left the needle in, and the valve protruded from Ben's chest like a small straw. She padded around it with bandages and taped it in place.

Within seconds, Ben was no longer gasping for air, and had gotten some of his color back. He still hadn't regained consciousness, though. "Will he be all right now?" Alex asked.

"It'll do until he gets to the Medical Center." Caitlin started to put one of the medallions around Ben's neck, but Alex stopped her.

Shaking his head, Alex said, "I can't take him to the hospital. We have to get out of here before the PKs catch us."

Caitlin's expression was grim. "He needs surgery to repair his lung. He could die without it."

"But he might not."

Frowning, Caitlin shook her head. "There's no way to know, but the risks—"

"—are worth it," Alex finished, without hesitation. Ben would agree. "Better dead than rotting in a Peacekeeper cell." A hint of sadness swept across Caitlin's features when he said that. "Don't worry, I'll make sure he's taken care of."

Caitlin gave a reluctant nod, and helped Alex get Ben up.

"Thanks," Alex said, before hurrying off with Ben's arm draped across his shoulder. The word seemed inadequate for his gratitude. This was twice now she'd helped him. He wouldn't forget.

[[—＊—]]

Caitlin watched Alex go, chewing her lower lip. Once again, she'd taken a chance helping him, and once again she didn't entirely know why.

Vince came up beside her. "That was him, wasn't it?" He looked at Caitlin, and his frown deepened at her quiet nod. "You're playing with fire, Cait. I hope you know what you're doing."

So do I, Caitlin thought.

The square had quieted, except for the cries of the injured. Caitlin took a quick peek around the front of the ambulance. A haze had settled over the area, a mixture of tear gas and smoke. The dome's air filters worked overtime to clear the air, but some still drifted toward the ambulance and made Caitlin's eyes sting. She had seen a few people moving around near the gazebo, and hoped one of them was Tom. Part of her wanted to believe that he would come to the ambulance if he were able, to let her know that he was all right. The other part knew that he was most likely in the thick of it, trying to cover the story of a lifetime.

She and Vince were now juggling twenty patients in their little treatment area, and she couldn't help but wonder how many more they'd find out there. And was one of them Tom?

Caitlin couldn't take it any longer. She grabbed a trauma kit. "I'm going to go start triage in the square."

"The hell you are!" Vince growled. "We're staying here until we're damn sure it's safe."

Caitlin gestured toward the other side of the ambulance. "The shooting's stopped. I think it's as safe as it's going to be." She took a breath and said plaintively, "Tom's out there. I have to find him; make sure he's okay."

Vince frowned. "Fine. I'll go."

"Would you stay here if it were Adelle out there?" He had no answer for that, and she touched his arm. "I'll be all right. Now that the fighting's over, the Chief will be on his way." They had been staged a block away, waiting for the all clear. "You can manage things here, and come and find me once he takes over."

Vince didn't like it, but he saw the determined look in her eye and knew he couldn't stop her. He grabbed a flak vest and fire helmet from one of the side compartments and handed it to her. Neither was meant for protection against Peacekeeper assault rifles, but they were better than nothing. "Be careful."

Caitlin nodded, took a deep breath to steel herself, and ventured out from the cover of the ambulance.

Not even her quick peek around the truck had prepared her for the carnage she found when she ventured into the square. She felt weak, gasping as if someone had knocked the wind out of her. Bodies lay everywhere—broken; sprawled atop each other. Blood pooled around them on the cobblestones. Caitlin stopped counting at ten, but there were several times that many. A few people stood with shell-shocked looks on their faces.

Picking up her microphone, she swallowed hard and tried to find her voice. "Medic Five-One to dispatch: There's at least… God, there's at least a hundred people down."

She stared for a long moment, barely registering the dispatcher's response. The Peacekeepers had been stationed in the north, and Caitlin guessed that's where Tom would have gone to investigate the arrest earlier. She set off in that direction, stepping carefully over and around the people in-between. She scanned the faces, looking for the one she hoped desperately not to find among the injured.

"Go over to the ambulance if you can," she called out to the injured. "If you can't walk, stay where you are. Help will be here soon." A cluster of people started toward the ambulance—some hobbling, and some helping each other along.

Caitlin approached the northeast corner, where the shooting started. This was where the most seriously injured would be, and where she would start her triage. The Peacekeepers stationed here had withdrawn, joining up with their comrades somewhere off to her left. A handful of people were still on their feet; some searching for loved ones, others trying to help the wounded with basic first aid. Caitlin coughed from the smoke still hanging in the area. A small fire burned off to her right, where it appeared some fuel had soaked into the ground from a Molotov cocktail.

Caitlin stopped short when she spotted the familiar blocky shape of a professional-grade vid camera. Its owner lay on his side, facing away from Caitlin.

Caitlin hurried to him. "Harry? Harry, can you…" She stopped in mid-sentence. Harry couldn't hear her. Tom's eager young cameraman had taken a bullet in the temple, ending his dreams of one day being in front of the camera instead of behind it. Caitlin closed her eyes, shuddering. If Harry was here, Tom had to be…

Finally she saw him. "Oh, God… Tom."

CHAPTER 11

CAITLIN DROPPED TO HER KNEES beside Tom. His face was a ghastly white, his lips gray. A dark splotch of blood marred the center of his sky blue dress shirt. She tried to rouse him, shaking him and calling his name, but he didn't respond. Tossing her helmet aside, she bent over him and placed her ear over his mouth. He wasn't breathing.

She recoiled in horror, letting out a pained sound. For an instant, all her medical training abandoned her. She keyed the microphone on her radio and cried, "Vince! I need you at the northeast corner!"

Although she still couldn't think straight, her instincts took over and she started CPR. She closed her mouth over Tom's cool lips, breathing for him. "Please, don't do this, Tom," she whispered between breaths.

Vince rushed over from across the square. "Cait, what…" He seemed puzzled to find her doing CPR, but then recognition flashed in his eyes. "Jesus."

"He's not breathing, Vince," Caitlin said, her voice broken. She pressed rhythmically against Tom's chest, her exam gloves coming away dark with blood. When Vince just stood there, Caitlin cried, "Help me!"

That snapped him out of it. He moved to the other side and cut open Tom's shirt with his trauma scissors. There were two bullet wounds on the left side of the breastbone, just over the heart, but surprisingly little blood. Caitlin knew that didn't mean much; the bleeding could all be internal. Vince attached the heart monitor leads and switched it on. Caitlin glanced at the waveform on the monitor, hoping that it would be a rhythm they could shock—anything that might give him a chance. But it showed a flat line.

"It's asystole, Cait," Vince said gently. She heard him, but the words didn't sink in until he put a hand on her shoulder and repeated, "Cait…"

Caitlin finally looked up, and saw the terrible truth written all over his face.

She stopped doing chest compressions, sinking back on her heels. On an ordinary day, they would pull out all the stops, hoping for a miracle—intubate him to keep his brain alive; take him to the hospital for emergency surgery. Today? It wouldn't do any good. The medical center had to prioritize resources for those who had a chance. *Do the most for the many.* The rules of triage hit her full force. Her vision blurred, and she choked back a sob.

Vince took a small medallion from the jump bag and clasped it around Tom's neck. It gave of a faint black light, marking Tom as beyond help. Shuffling over, Vince drew her into a hug. "Cait, I'm so sorry," he whispered by her ear.

Caitlin buried her face against his broad shoulder. Her throat felt like someone had tightened a vise around it. Tears left tracks down her soot-stained cheeks, but she didn't weep. She felt numb. This couldn't be happening. She had just talked to him a few minutes ago. They were going to have dinner tomorrow. She didn't know how to reconcile those thoughts with the image of her husband's bloody body.

Vince held her, saying nothing until repeated queries over the radio demanded his attention. After replying to the Chief's status update, Vince said, "Cait, I'm sorry—the Chief's pulling up. I'll be back as soon as I can."

Caitlin barely noticed him go. She couldn't take her eyes off of Tom. Hands shaking, she stripped off her exam gloves and reached out to touch Tom's cheek.

She sat there for a minute or two before the screams of the wounded cut through the fog around her brain. She couldn't wallow in her own grief while so many needed help; Tom wouldn't have wanted that. Taking a deep breath, she dragged a sleeve across her face and pulled herself together.

Caitlin squeezed Tom's hand one last time and then crawled back to Harry. Seeing his crumpled form threatened a fresh round of tears, but she held onto her composure by a thread and slipped a black-lit triage medallion around his neck.

She was about to move away when her eyes locked on Harry's camera. He must have been filming when they shot him. Was he filming Tom? The thought made Caitlin recoil. Part of her didn't want to know. Didn't want to have that image etched into her brain. But that video was a testament to the murders of Tom, Harry, and all the other people littering the ground around her. Caitlin knew what a stranglehold the Peacekeepers kept on the news services—Tom had complained about the government censors often enough. The idea of them twisting Tom and Harry's final work for their own ends sickened her.

Caitlin snuck a glance around to make sure nobody was watching, then ejected the camera's memory card. She stared at the key-sized rectangle in her hand for a long moment, tempted to smash it to bits right then just to keep them from having it. But she couldn't bring herself to do it. That card also contained Tom's last moments—interviewing people in the square, doing what he loved. She slipped it into her shirt pocket, underneath her flak vest. She'd figure out what to do with it later. For now, there were people to help.

Forcing herself to her feet, Caitlin moved on to the next victim.

[[—*—]]

Jack crouched behind a refreshment cart that had been overturned during the mass exodus from the square. Only once the firing had stopped did he consider emerging from cover. Peering over the top of the cart, he saw that the two Peacekeeper squads had formed a protective square to guard against attacks from all sides, like old-fashioned tin soldiers. Bodies littered the square, some moving; most not. Those able to run had already done so. Only a few still hobbled away. The soldiers finally held their fire, ready for an assault that would never come.

Jack coughed, spitting to get rid of the bitter taste in his mouth from the tear gas. When he looked back up, he spotted Sergeant Sykes dashing toward him in a low crouch.

"Good to see you alive, Sergeant," Jack murmured as Sykes joined him.

"Same here, Captain. No thanks to those trigger-happy assholes over there." Sykes hadn't emerged from the incident unscathed. Blood dripped down his face from his right earlobe. "Lost my radio," he growled, holding up a mangled earpiece.

Jack felt a fury of his own brewing up within him. Those bumbling idiots had likely cost him his quarry. They'd been so close!

"Captain!" Lieutenant Hale rushed toward them from across the street. His eyes tracked the bodies he passed, wanting to help, and by the time he reached Jack and Sykes his face was white. "My God…" The young officer turned away and vomited behind the refreshment cart.

Sykes rolled his eyes at the heaving lieutenant, then shook his head. "What now, Captain? The target's long gone or dead."

Jack sighed. "Now we clean up this damn mess." He keyed his own radio. "Citadel One to Delta One. Three friendlies coming to your position from the south. Do not fire. Confirm?"

Jack waited for Cerulli to confirm that they were coming across, then headed over to join the other soldiers. Storming up to Cerulli, he growled, "What the hell is the matter with you? You open fire on an unarmed crowd?"

"*Unarmed*, my ass! We were taking hostile fire."

Jack lifted his eyebrows, eyeing the soldiers behind Cerulli. A few nursed minor cuts and burns, two had more serious lacerations from broken bottles, and another was being treated by the squad medic for burns from the Molotov Cocktail. None had gunshot wounds.

Cerulli followed Jack's gaze, reading his inference. "Go to hell, Decker. I was defending my men."

"I'm assuming command of this incident," Jack said flatly.

Cerulli scoffed. "You've got no jurisdiction here."

"I have the authority to convene an investigation into any insurgent activity."

"The hell you do," Cerulli spat back. "This is an infantry operation. When we need some papers shuffled, we'll let you know."

"Your men were attacked, which makes this a terrorist incident. That puts it squarely in my damn jurisdiction," Jack snapped. Cerulli ground his teeth, realizing he was outplayed. "Have the incoming units create a perimeter around this entire square. No one in or out. And I want your guys to scour the area and confiscate any recording devices. Cellcoms, cameras, all of it."

Cerulli nodded stiffly and went to pass along the orders to his men. Lieutenant Hale, still looking green, asked, "Why collect the coms? Whatever video there is will be all over the net in an hour."

"Not once Net Security is done," Jack replied. "I want you to liaise with them. Keep this from spreading, and scour all the footage. I want identities of the agitators, and any clue about where our target and his injured friend might have gone. Oh, and alert the Med Center to keep an eye out for him. Chances are he's too smart to turn up there, but you never know."

Sykes came up next to Jack, holding a field dressing to his ear. "What do you need me to do, sir?"

Jack waited until Hale had moved out of earshot before muttering to Sykes, "We can't let it get out that Cerulli mowed down unarmed civilians. We need evidence that his men were taking hostile fire from the square."

Sykes furrowed his brow. "And if that evidence doesn't exist?"

"We'll make sure it does."

CHAPTER 12

IT TOOK CERULLI'S MEN NEARLY half an hour to sweep the square. By that time, additional squads had arrived from Fort McChord and set up a protective perimeter that extended beyond the square for a block in all directions. Curious bystanders gathered outside the barriers, along with the inevitable news crews, but they couldn't see much from where they stood. This allowed the Peacekeepers a measure of privacy essential to their cleanup operation. Not just a cleanup, Jack corrected himself, a cover-up—a way to justify the deaths of dozens of civilians. He told himself he shouldn't care; these protesters had chosen their side. They supported the enemy. But even so, they didn't deserve to be slaughtered like cattle.

They'd set up a command post near the gazebo. Captain Cerulli stood nearby, speaking harshly to a young private. "There has to be more than this. Look again!" The Captain's voice took on an angry desperation. He held two clear plastic evidence bags, each containing a handgun.

"Sir, we've checked twice," the private explained, "That's all there is."

Jack held out his hand for the evidence bags, and Cerulli handed them over. He donned exam gloves and took the weapons out of the bags. One looked like the pistol the insurgent had carried. They both had full clips, so neither had been fired today.

"Didn't check too closely, did you." The gruff comment came from Sergeant Sykes, who walked up with two larger evidence bags in hand. Each bag contained four or five more pistols, all individually wrapped and tagged. The Sergeant handed them to Jack. "I also found some spent shell casings - they're marked over there."

Sykes caught Jack's eye and flashed a blink-and-you'd-miss-it smirk. The pistols had come from a rebel weapons cache captured by Jack's team a few days ago. Sykes had fetched them from the evidence locker at the fort. They'd have to fix the records later, but that wouldn't be a problem. The shell casings were a nice touch.

Cerulli stared at the weapons, baffled. Whatever his suspicions, he at least had the common sense to realize that these weapons would save his ass.

The private cleared his throat, then. "We also found this, sir." He picked up a professional camera bearing the Martian Chronicle logo.

Jack cursed under this breath. He remembered seeing the news crew earlier, but had forgotten about them in the chaos. He stepped over to Lieutenant Hale, working nearby at a portable computer. "Switch to the Chronicle's live feed. Are they broadcasting anything from the riot?"

Jack tapped his foot while Hale checked, and was relieved by the response. "No, sir. They've got people beyond the barriers, saying they hope to be able to reestablish contact with the crew in the square. They're promising an exclusive look at the riot from ground zero, but nothing yet."

"Good. I'm going over there." Jack opened the slot on the side of the camera to take its memory card. His fingers felt nothing, and when he looked, he saw that the slot was empty. "Damn it! The memory card is gone." He walked back over to the private. "Show me where you found this."

"Yes, sir." Leaving Cerulli at the command post, Jack and Sykes followed the private to a spot in the northeast corner. The private looked around for a moment before he spotted the evidence tag marker blinking on the ground. "Here, sir. This fellow had the camera."

Jack searched the cameraman's pockets, and found nothing. He checked a few of the people nearby, pulling back the sheets covering them to see their faces. If the cameraman was here, the reporter might be nearby. Finally he found him. Jack recognized the man's face from the news Mac-something? He wasn't sure of the name. They searched him, but still found no memory card.

"Damn it. Someone must have taken it." Turning once more to the private, he asked, "Did you see anyone else in this area?"

The private looked helplessly baffled, "Umm, I don't know, sir… there was a lot going on. There were a few injured folks, some other guys from my squad, the medics…"

Sykes and Jack looked at each other, thinking the same thing. Jack spoke first. "Did you see any of the medics over here, in particular?"

The private shrugged. "There were a couple of them."

Jack motioned to Sykes. "Take him and check the medics. I want that memory card."

Sykes nodded. "What are you going to do, Captain?"

Jack, already walking away, called back over his shoulder. "I'm going to go pay a visit to the Martian Chronicle."

[[—∗—]]

Shock left a hollow ache deep inside Caitlin. She had been to multiple casualty incidents before—a few bomb blasts, a building collapse—but never anything of this magnitude. And never anything that struck so close to home. Caitlin tried to keep her mind occupied by focusing on her patients, but the only one she really cared about was already gone.

"Are we out of saline?" Vince's voice jolted her out of her thoughts, and Caitlin wondered how long she had been staring at the open trauma bag.

"No, I found some." Caitlin took the bags and returned to work, but she could sense Vince's eyes following her as if he were afraid she would fall apart at any moment. Maybe she would.

She heard Vince curse under his breath, and turned to see what was wrong. He shook his head, muttering, "Great. What do they want?"

A pair of Peacekeepers approached. Both carried assault rifles, but only one was in uniform. The other Caitlin recognized as Sergeant Sykes. Caitlin knelt down beside her next patient, a middle-aged woman with a gunshot wound to the thigh. As she worked, she tried to watch the soldiers out of the corner of her eye. They beelined for her, and Caitlin tensed.

"That's one of them." The private pointed at her.

Sykes sneered. "Why am I not surprised. Stand up and turn around."

Caitlin stood, balling fists at her side. "What do you want?"

Ignoring her question, Sykes waved to the private. "Search her."

Vince stepped forward. "You've got no right to do that."

"You want to end up on the ground again, mate?" Sykes growled, getting nose to nose with Vince. Vince wasn't a small man, but Sykes seemed to loom over him.

Behind them, a couple of the other firefighters and medics had also gotten to their feet. The Peacekeeper private, spooked by the movement, lifted his rifle. Visions of the broken bodies in the square hit Caitlin full-force. Imagining her friends and co-workers joining them, a cold rage flooded through her.

"Enough!" she roared, shoving the soldier's rifle aside. "Look around! Haven't you bastards done enough killing for one day?"

Body trembling, she waited for him to shoot her or arrest her.

No one moved, then she heard Chief Daniels' voice rumbling behind her. "What in God's name is going on over here?" The tall Black man may not have had Sykes' muscles, but his booming voice and steely presence took charge of almost any situation. This one was no exception.

Everyone looked at each other, but it was Vince who answered, "They want to search Cait."

"Why?" the chief demanded.

"Someone took the memory card from the Chronicle's video camera. Our troopers saw some of your medics in the area. Including her."

Caitlin's stomach dropped into her boots, the memory card a heavy weight in her breast pocket. If they wanted it, it couldn't be for anything good. And if they caught her with it…

Chief Daniels' gaze flicked her way, and Caitlin shook her head. "I don't know what he's talking about." She lied like her life depended on it. Which it probably did. "Why the hell would I take something like that?"

The chief leveled a stern look at Sykes. "You heard her. My medics were in the area doing their jobs. Jobs they need to get back to. We're done here, Sergeant." From his tone, no one could mistake it for a suggestion.

Sykes bristled at Daniels' defiance, but arresting the fire chief was probably above his pay grade. "This isn't over," he warned, before the two Peacekeepers stalked away.

Caitlin watched them, clenching her hands to keep them from shaking. She heard the chief telling everyone to get back to work, then he came up behind her.

"You and Vince can take the next run over to the Med Center and stay to lend them a hand. They're swamped."

"I'm fine, Chief," she insisted. He meant well, but she couldn't deal with his sympathy right now.

"It's not about that," he said, though they both knew it was. "We've got things under control here. You two will do more good at the hospital."

Caitlin said nothing, and the chief moved off. She stared out at the square. Zhang and one of the other firefighters were out there, making sure they hadn't missed anyone. The coroner had arrived, already making arrangements to transport and store all the casualties. Peacekeeper MPs were photographing and cataloging evidence.

Evidence. The word was a bolt of lightning in her brain, reminding her of the memory card in her pocket. She couldn't keep wandering around with it. Sykes would be back to hassle her about it again. Crouching down beside their jump bag, Caitlin shuffled around some gauze pads to look busy. When she was sure no one was looking, she took the memory card from her shirt pocket and slipped it into a little-used compartment on the med scanner.

She was just zipping the jump bag closed when Vince called to her. "Cait, time to go."

Caitlin didn't want to leave, feeling a tug to stay here with Tom and the other victims.

Sensing her reluctance, Vince came over. "There's nothing more you can do for him, Cait. We have to help the people we can." He picked up the bag, then squeezed her shoulder. "Come on."

Caitlin let him steer her over to the ambulance and climbed into the back. As she watched the square receding through the back window, all she could think of was Tom's body lying under a flimsy hospital sheet. All alone.

CHAPTER 13

THE CARTER BUILDING TOWERED OVER the western city center. Ten stories might not count for much on Earth, but it was the tallest building in Waycross. Jack passed through the deserted lobby, heading straight for the glass door bearing the Martian Chronicle logo. A bored rent-a-cop sat behind his desk, his eyes glued to his tablet. He barely looked up as Jack passed. Sykes and Hale had things under control in the square; the important thing now was keeping this debacle under warps.

The plump receptionist gave Jack an odd look when he entered the Chronicle offices. Sweaty, his face smudged with soot, he was a mess. With strained politeness, she asked, "Can I help you, sir?"

Jack reached into his inside jacket pocket for his identification, and saw the receptionist's eyes widen when she noticed his shoulder holster. He flashed his badge and said, "Is Rachel Griffiths working today?"

"Yes. I'll call her down…"

Jack interrupted as the woman reached for her touchscreen. "Is she in her office?"

The woman frowned at his tone. Reluctantly, she said, "She's probably in the news center. It's through that door, up…"

"I know the way." As the leading news service on Mars, the Chronicle's archives rivaled that of the Peacekeeper database. They had footage from virtually every independence rally and terrorist act in the history of Mars, and Jack leveraged them often in his investigations.

Jack strode across through the lower level and up the stairs. While the ground floor of the Chronicle held cubicles and offices, the upper floor was where the real work got done. He passed a group of people speaking excitedly. From the snatches of conversation he caught, no one seemed sure what had happened in the square, only that shots had been fired. Jack passed a store room where a crew readied some AV equipment, and a large television studio with a flashing "On Air" light outside the door. Through the glass, he saw two anchors sitting behind a wooden desk, their faces grim. Jack turned when he heard someone clearing their throat behind him.

"Captain Decker." The voice belonged to Rachel Griffiths, producer of the Chronicle's Waycross division. She wore a business suit without the jacket, her skirt showing off her long legs. Black hair spilled over her shoulders, falling into her face as she regarded Jack.

"Ms. Griffiths." Jack inclined his head in a brisk greeting.

"I've been expecting you. Your Lieutenant called earlier and put a hold on our broadcasts. No one's released any information about what happened, and the Medical Center won't let us in to interview the victims." Rachel sounded annoyed. "What's going on?"

Most of the journalists resented interference from Peacekeeper media affairs, but censorship was a necessary evil in a world where public opinion could be so easily swayed by the media. Rachel, at least, was one of the good ones; a loyal citizen who bore no love for the insurgents.

"You had a crew in the square this afternoon. I need to see everything you have from them."

Rachel motioned for him to follow her into one of the editing suites, a small booth with a bank of monitors along one wall and a complex control panel. Rachel sat down in front of the controls. "We've been trying to get back in touch with them. Their uplink cut off right when the riot started." A slight tremor in her voice betrayed her worry, a stark contrast to her otherwise cool demeanor.

Jack watched her touch the screen and debated whether to tell her. "They're dead."

The color drained from Rachel's face, and she covered her mouth with her hand. "No..." She said nothing else for a long moment, before finally she whispered, "Are you sure?" Jack nodded, and she gasped, tears welling up in her eyes. "Oh God... there has to be some mistake."

Jack gave her a minute to compose herself. It surprised him that she was taking it so hard; he had never thought of her as the overly emotional type. He directed her attention back to the monitor. "I need to see that footage."

Rachel nodded, still sniffling, and brought up the recording. She played it on the large central monitor. The first part was all crowd shots and color interviews. At the first sight of the good-looking reporter, Rachel's face crumpled. The interviews seemed to go on forever, even on fast-forward. Impatient, Jack told Rachel to jump ahead to a few minutes before the end. The atmosphere had transformed. Instead of the slow pans of the crowd and well-framed shots of the reporter, the screen showed a chaotic scene of people screaming and running, the clatter of gunfire audible in the background. The camera jerked to the right, just in time to see several people go down under the hail of bullets, and then the playback suddenly ended.

Beside him, Rachel sucked in a breath. "My God."

Jack ignored her. "Go back further. Find the beginning of the riot."

Rachel did so, rewinding until the scene was calm again. Jack watched the soldiers arrest the protester, then saw the first bottle fly. There was a lingering shot of a Peacekeeper writhing on the ground, blood from his neck gushing through his fingers. The camera swung away just as the squad's medic rushed to the fallen soldier.

"Save that shot. We can use that," Jack said.

Rachel, still looking pale, used the editing software to copy that brief segment of the recording to a separate file. Jack saw no sign of guns among the crowd in the footage, just a few people throwing rocks and bottles. He guessed the rebels had planned this ahead of time; it seemed too well-organized to be a coincidence. "Get that, too." Jack had Rachel save the footage of the crowd closing in on the Peacekeepers.

The cameraman moved for a better angle. "Play that part again at half speed. Zoom in there." Jack clenched his jaw as he realized that the camera had caught him firing at the rebels. He was clearly facing in the opposite direction; nobody would believe he was shooting *at* the soldiers.

Captain Cerulli, believing they were taking fire from the crowd, yelled at his men to shoot back. The image bounced for a moment before it came back into focus on Cerulli, leveling his pistol at a man in the crowd. There was a perfect shot of him pulling the trigger, killing a demonstrator armed only with a broken bottle. Rachel flinched, wincing at the image. The camera panned back for a wide shot, just as everything went to hell.

"That's enough." Jack cursed under his breath, switching off the feed.

"No one fired on the Peacekeepers," Rachel realized, her voice a stunned whisper. "My God."

Jack frowned. This was exactly the reaction they had to avoid, at all costs. "Who else has seen this vid?"

Rachel thought for a moment before replying. "Just two of our techs, who were here when we first got the uplink. But they only saw part of it. We stopped going through it when Net Security called."

"I want their names. No one speaks of this, do you understand?" He knew that Rachel would keep her mouth shut, but he would take steps to ensure that the others also remained silent. "You can use the parts we edited in your broadcast. Save the complete file to a card for me and then erase the original."

Jack made sure Rachel wiped out all traces of the file. They had plenty of evidence to show that the crowd had turned violent and the soldiers feared for their lives. With the weapons Sykes planted, they could even claim that the protesters fired first.

And no one would be able to prove otherwise.

[[— ✳ —]]

Alex sat on the couch in the safe house, a quiet fury building inside him as he listened to the Chronicle's 'news' broadcast.

"One Peacekeeper was killed when an independence rally turned violent this afternoon in Waycross," the anchor reported, *"The protesters reportedly attacked the Peacekeeper security force with bottles, rocks, and even Molotov cocktails. The soldiers attempted to quell the riot with stun batons and tear gas, and were fired upon by armed insurgents within the crowd. Several Peacekeepers and protesters were injured."*

The images on the screen painted a ridiculously one-sided view of events: the crowd throwing bottles, besieging the soldiers with fists and clubs. A close-up showed a soldier with a ghastly neck wound, and then a military medic zipping up a body bag.

The Chronicle's version of events had been picked up all over the net. Alex didn't expect them to admit that the Peacekeepers had fired first, or that the majority of the crowd had been unarmed civilians involved in a peaceful protest. But to completely bury the fact that over a hundred people had been killed or injured? That was a new low, even for them. Alex switched off the MarsCom in disgust and started pacing.

The door to the back bedroom opened, and a young man stepped out. Noah Ross, the doctor they had on call, stripped off his examination gloves and bloodstained smock, and went straight for the kitchen to wash his hands. Alex couldn't contain his impatience. "How's Ben?"

"He's stable for now." Noah frowned. "He won't let me take him to the Med Center, so there's not a lot more I can do for him.

I'll check back when I can. Just watch him for fever, worsening trouble breathing."

"You're not staying?"

"They've called in all hands to help with the casualties from the riot. You're lucky I was able to slip away at all."

Alex reluctantly nodded. He knew Noah had a job to do, but the images of Ben gasping and turning blue in the square still haunted him. "Thanks for coming out."

Not long after Noah had left, Alex heard their signature knock on the door heralding Samantha's return. She had gone to the Medical Center a few hours earlier to look for Julio. No one had heard from him since the rally. Samantha held out hope, but Alex knew Julio would have found a way to check in if he were able. He couldn't help but assume the worst. Seeing her face, etched with pain and sorrow, Alex's suspicions were confirmed.

Their eyes met, and Samantha said in a tiny voice, "I found him." Tears spilled over her cheeks.

Alex crossed the room, taking her in his arms. He held her, stroking her dark hair while she cried. Light-hearted and cheerful, Julio lived life with a passionate zeal. He and Alex had been as close as brothers. Samantha loved him differently, always hoping their friendship might develop into something more. Alex had been rooting for them to get together, but now that chance had been stolen by the Peacekeepers. It only made him hate them more.

"What went wrong, Alex?" she asked plaintively. The expression on her face broke his heart. "How could this happen?" Alex had no answer for her. He had been asking himself the same thing for hours. "I should have been there," Samantha lamented with a sob. As usual, she had been back at the safe house on a computer, coordinating things from afar.

"Then you'd probably be dead, too," Alex said, more harshly than he had intended.

Samantha wiped away the tears, and in behind the sorrow he saw a quiet fury brewing in her eyes. "We have to make them pay for this, Alex."

"We will."

CHAPTER 14

THE FACES OF THE PATIENTS at the medical center started to blur together. So many lives shattered, so many lost. Caitlin went through it in a daze, staying on her feet solely through caffeine and force of will. Finally a cadre of doctors flew in from the nearby city of Tantewei, allowing the medics a reprieve. They headed back to the fire station.

Now Caitlin leaned against the shower wall, her shoulders shaking with sobs. Alone for the first time since Tom had died, she was no longer able to fend off the overwhelming sense of loss that had dogged her all day long. Water coursed over her face, washing away the blood and tears. She stayed until she had cried herself out, but the hollow ache remained.

Emerging from the shower, Caitlin dried herself and started putting on her street clothes. Her dirty uniform lay in a crumpled heap on the floor nearby. The dark fabric hid the bloodstains pretty well, but if she looked closely enough, she could see them—a physical reminder of the carnage of the afternoon.

She nearly jumped out of her skin when someone knocked on the locker room door. The door opened a crack, just enough for Vince to call to her without having to shout through the door. "Cait? You okay in there?"

Caitlin rubbed her forehead, a dull throb behind her eyes. A myriad of possible responses ran through her mind, everything from biting his head off to lying. In the end, she just settled down wearily on the bench and admitted, "Not really."

"I'm coming in," Vince warned, presumably to give her a chance to stop him if she wasn't decent. Caitlin hastily pulled her T-shirt over her sports bra, though a part of her realized it was silly to be self-conscious. Vince had seen her in less. But that was a long time ago; they were both married now. *No*, Caitlin corrected herself silently: He was still married. She was a widow. She still had a hard time wrapping her head around that.

Vince sat down on the bench beside her and draped an arm around her shoulders. She could tell he wanted to say something, but he didn't seem to know where to begin. Caitlin found his presence comforting, even in silence.

Finally she spoke, "We should have brought him to the hospital."

Vince looked at her, his eyes conveying a sad sympathy. "It was a traumatic arrest. He probably bled out in seconds. It's the first rule of triage. Even if we brought him in, they wouldn't have worked on him. Not in a mass cas incident."

His words had little impact; her heart didn't want to listen to logic. "All this time we were separated, I just wanted him to suffer. I wanted to hurt him, the way he'd hurt me." Her voice quavered, her eyes watering again. She blinked back the tears and whispered miserably, "There's no way to take it all back."

"I wish I knew what to say, Cait. 'I'm sorry' just seems so inadequate."

"It's okay," Caitlin told him. She didn't know what to say either. She was silent for a long moment, and then admittedly quietly, "I'm glad you're here."

"Come stay with us tonight," Vince said. "I called Adelle—she doesn't want you to be alone, either." He cut off her brewing excuses. "Come on. You can have Zac's room, and he can make a fort in the living room."

Caitlin was tempted. Vince and his family were all she had. She imagined four-year-old Zac charging her for a hug the moment she stepped into the door, shouting, "Aunt Cait!" as he always did. Maybe his irrepressible cheerfulness would be good for her, but she just couldn't face it right now. Slowly, she shook her head. "I think I'd rather just be alone." She had been living alone for the last four months; she could handle another night. "But I appreciate the offer."

"You sure?" When Caitlin nodded, Vince said, "All right. If you change your mind, or if you need anything, just call. Any time." He squeezed her gently, then got up to go.

"Vince." Caitlin's voice stopped him at the door, and he turned back. "Thanks." Vince offered a subdued smile and left the locker room.

Caitlin took a little while longer to compose herself and then ventured downstairs. Most of the other firefighters had gathered in the living room, swapping war stories about what they had seen and done that day. The conversation grew quiet when she walked in; word had traveled fast about Tom. Most of the guys came over to offer their condolences, some more heartfelt than others. Chief Daniels gave her a hug and told her to take as much time off as she needed. Caitlin suffered through the platitudes as long as she could before finally making her excuses and leaving.

Walking into her empty apartment, Caitlin regretted turning down Vince's offer. The lights on the Christmas tree turned on automatically when she entered, taunting her with their cheery blinking. She threw her jacket on the back of the kitchen chair, not bothering to hang it up, and crossed to the living room. Reminders of Tom assaulted her, remnants of the life they'd had before everything fell apart. Pictures of them, a souvenir rock from their trip to the summit of Olympus Mons last spring, a Saint Michael statue Tom had given her shortly after they met.

Seeing Tom's picture on the mantle threatened to drive her to tears again. She stared at the photograph, taking in the gentle lines of Tom's handsome face and his beautiful blue eyes until her vision blurred. He was smiling, his arm around Caitlin as they sat on the couch. Caitlin thought back to that happier time and wondered how things had gone so terribly wrong.

Tearing her eyes away from the photograph, Caitlin turned on the MarsCom unit to ward away the oppressive silence. The Chronicle's news feed came up automatically, and she felt a swell of grief when she saw the headline across the bottom of the screen: *Riot Turns Deadly.* Caitlin started to switch to something else, but the anchor's words sent a wave of shock right through her.

"A Federation spokesperson issued a statement blaming Martian extremists for the brutal attack, which left one Peacekeeper dead and two hospitalized…"

"Son of a bitch," Caitlin breathed. She had known the Federation would spin the truth, but this? How could they possibly think they could get away with it?

As she stared at the screen, she realized they already had. Taken out of context, Harry's footage made the Peacekeepers look like heroes, fending off the crazed protesters. A cold anger filled her.

Grabbing her jacket, she stormed out of the apartment.

[[—✳—]]

After taking care of things at the Chronicle, Jack had spent several hours overseeing the investigation in the square before being summoned by the garrison commander. He made his way over to Fort McChord's administration building, past the command center to Colonel Isakovich's office. The outer office was empty when Jack arrived; Isakovich's secretary, a civilian contractor, had no doubt gone home for the day. Jack knocked on the inner office door, and a gruff voice told him to come in.

"Captain Decker reporting as ordered, sir," Jack said formally. Andrei Isakovich, unlike himself, actually put stock in a lot of the antiquated military rituals. He had enlisted in the Russian military as a young man and worked his way up the ranks. With over a decade on Mars in Peacekeeper service, the word around the base was that he had no intention of retiring.

Isakovich told him to have a seat. Jack did so, marveling at the oversized oil painting of Olympus Mons on the colonel's wall.

"I've been watching the Chronicle's newscast," Isakovich began in his impeccable English. "I understand you're responsible for that little work of fiction?" When Jack nodded, Isakovich frowned. "You've exceeded your authority, Decker. Major Plata and the Public Information Office are demanding to know why they weren't consulted on this."

Jack struggled to keep his composure. This maddening political nonsense was why the Peacekeepers were making so little progress in the war against the insurgents. "There wasn't time to get them involved, sir. We had a crisis that required immediate attention. With all due respect, I don't think Major Plata fully grasps the gravity of the situation." He didn't think Isakovich did, either. "The Chronicle had footage showing that our men fired, unprovoked, on the crowd."

Isakovich frowned, his bushy eyebrows coming together. "We have a dead trooper and two more in the hospital, Captain. I think that constitutes provocation."

"The one who died was killed by a Molotov Cocktail, *after* the soldiers opened fire."

"Cerulli's report indicated that the crowd opened fire first."

"He's lying," Jack said flatly. He reached into his jacket pocket and took out his copy of the Chronicle's footage. "You'd better see for yourself, sir."

Isakovich took the memory card with obvious skepticism, and slotted it into the MarsCom unit on his desk. As the vid played, Isakovich's eyes narrowed. He shut it off and demanded, "Who else knows about this?"

"A few people at the Chronicle, and my Sergeant. None of them will be a problem."

Isakovich nodded, appeased. "Good. Make sure it stays that way."

Jack hesitated, wondering whether he should tell Isakovich the rest of it. "There is one wrinkle, sir. The storage card from the camera in the square is missing. We have to assume that it has a copy of this footage on it, and that someone took it deliberately."

"So? Plata has his people on it. They will deal with anything from the riot that turns up on the net."

"It's not that simple, sir," Jack said. Isakovich raised a dubious eyebrow, and Jack explained, "Most of the people who saw what happened up close are dead or at death's door. We have their coms and cameras, and anything that got out would be low quality and easily discredited. But the Chronicle camera? That's professional video from a trusted source. And it would be corroborated by the pieces of footage we already released. If the Earth news picked it up, it would be hard to contain."

"And it would make clear that we had not released the full video." The colonel frowned in realization. "That is a hell of a wrinkle, Decker. If this gets out and people learn that there was a cover up…"

"I'll handle it, sir. My men are already on it."

That didn't do much to appease Isakovich. "You do whatever it takes, Captain. Make sure that video is contained."

CHAPTER 15

WHAT AM I DOING HERE? Caitlin hesitated at the bottom of the stairs, looking up at the apartment building's glass entrance. Her original intention had been to march right into the Chronicle office downtown, but she thought better of it before she got there. They weren't going to just oppose the Peacekeeper censorship on her say-so. She needed a different approach. Taking a breath, Caitlin went up the stairs and pushed through the revolving doors.

The building was a far cry from her own, with marble tile and a night watchman in the lobby. Plush chairs surrounded a coffee table in one corner of the room, reminding Caitlin of a hotel. "I'm here to see Rachel Griffiths," Caitlin told the watchman, giving her name.

He picked up a phone on the desk and called Rachel's apartment. "Ms. Griffiths, there's a Ms. Farland here to see you." There must have been a long silence, for the guard said in confusion. "Ms. Griffiths? You there?" Another pause, and then he said with a faint frown, "Yes, ma'am. Good night." Caitlin had already braced herself, convinced the guard would say that Rachel didn't want to see her. Instead, he said, "You can go up. Room 315."

Caitlin thanked him and took the elevator to the third floor. She listened to the quiet beeps as the elevator passed each floor, wondering what she was going to say. She had met Rachel only a few times before, mostly at Chronicle office parties. Rachel was the type of woman Tom's father would approve of. An Ivy League graduate from a well-to-do family back on Earth, she was wealthy and sophisticated. Caitlin, in comparison, had gone straight from high school into the fire academy. She didn't even know what Ivy League meant until Rachel had condescendingly explained it to her.

Rachel had always been interested in Tom. Caitlin had seen it immediately in the way she looked at him; the way she laughed and touched his arm when he said something funny. Tom had teased Caitlin for being jealous, assuring her that he would never go astray. He probably meant it at the time. But last year things got complicated. Park was seriously injured and his old partner killed in a fire. The department, short two medics, had pulled everyone into mandatory overtime to pick up the slack. Caitlin put in more than her share, to help out the medics with families. She thought nothing of it when Tom started working late at the office. She wasn't even around to notice most of the time. It never occurred to her that he was cheating on her with his boss.

And now Caitlin needed that boss's help. It had taken a lot of effort to swallow her pride and come here, and it took even more to knock on that door. Rachel took her sweet time coming to open it. When the door finally opened, Caitlin saw that Rachel was not looking her best. Her dark curls were flat and lifeless, her eyes and nose red from crying.

Rachel regarded Caitlin for a long moment before she said, "I didn't expect to see you here."

"That makes two of us. Can I come in?"

Rachel shrugged and went back inside, leaving the door opened. Caitlin followed, glancing around the apartment. It was quite posh, with impractical white carpet and expensive paintings adorning the walls. A bottle of amber liquid sat on one of the glass end tables in the living room, half-empty. Rachel went over and refilled her glass. She didn't offer one to Caitlin.

"You know about Tom," Caitlin said, half-question, half-statement.

Rachel nodded, her expression sad. "Yes." She took another drink, and then murmured, "I'm sorry."

It was just a meaningless platitude like all the others, but Caitlin couldn't just nod and accept it gracefully. "Sorry he's dead? Or sorry for having an affair?"

Rachel frowned, staring back over the rim of the glass. "What do you want, Caitlin?"

An accusing edge crept into Caitlin's voice. "Why is the Chronicle going along with this cover-up? Two of your own people were killed out there today. How can you let them get away with this?"

"They're the government," Rachel said. "They get away with whatever they want."

Her attitude only fueled Caitlin's outrage. "Only if people sit back and let them. You're in a position to stop that!"

Rachel scoffed bitterly. "Leave the naïve idealism to people like Tom. We both know it doesn't suit you."

Stiffening, Caitlin snapped, "You don't know anything about me." But Rachel had a point: Caitlin was the one always telling Tom that you couldn't change the world with words. Now here she was—trying to do just that.

"I know enough," Rachel said, taking another drink. Caitlin wondered how many times Rachel and Tom had sat in this living room, talking about her, chuckling over her failings. The thought sickened her. "It's over, Caitlin. The Peacekeepers have put a lid on this story. They've taken the vid footage. They'll take any other evidence they find. There's nothing you can do."

Caitlin refused to accept that. "What if you had another copy of the vid?"

Shaking her head, Rachel said, "All the backups were erased. The only other copy would be from Harry's camera, and I'm sure the Peacekeepers..." She trailed off, staring at Caitlin, realization dawning in her eyes. "You have it. That's why you came."

There was no point in denying it, even though Caitlin hadn't intended to tell Rachel. She nodded. "You could still run the story. Tell the world what *really* happened. It's what Tom would have wanted." Much as she hated to admit it, Caitlin wasn't the only one with a personal stake in all of this.

"I'd lose my job," Rachel replied flatly. "I could go to jail. There's no way Tom would have wanted that."

"Then I guess you didn't know Tom as well as you thought you did." Caitlin could tell from Rachel's silent glare that she had made a mistake even trying, but it didn't matter. If Rachel wouldn't help her, she'd find another way.

[[— ✳ —]]

Alex walked into the bedroom. It reminded him of a hotel room, with two twin beds spaced on either side of an end table. One could hardly tell that Noah had been using the place as a makeshift emergency room just a few hours ago. He had cleaned it up well. Ben was on the bed closest to the door.

Alex pulled up a chair beside him. "Hey," he greeted quietly.

Ben's face was pale, but his eyes were open and alert. "How many dead?" he asked, not wasting any time on pleasantries.

"They haven't released any figures," Alex replied, shaking his head. Nor would they, judging from what he'd seen on the news. "Dozens. Maybe fifty." He paused, his jaw set tightly. "Julio didn't make it."

He watched Ben's expression harden, his mouth turning downward in a frown. "Damn." Ben sounded more disappointed than upset, and Alex wasn't sure quite how to take that. Although Ben was always more distant than the rest of them, they all thought of themselves as a family. He expected more of a reaction. Then again, Ben had probably seen a lot of friends die for the cause through the years. Maybe it didn't hit him as hard any more.

"They're saying we fired first," Alex said. "They're even parading around a bunch of weapons they supposedly picked up at the scene."

"Did you issue a statement denying it?"

Alex scoffed. "Why? They'd never publish it."

"Do it," Ben said firmly. "One of the Earth news services might pick it up."

"All right. I'll have Sam post something," Alex agreed, though he wasn't convinced it would do any good. The Federation controlled most of Earth, and even the independent nations weren't eager to cross the most powerful force on the planet. "In the mean time, we're going to send the PKs a message that they can't get away with this. We'll hit a patrol tomorrow, and plan more operations for later in the week."

Ben frowned. "Use your head, Alex," he scolded. "You and Sam can't take on an entire patrol by yourselves."

Alex bristled, even though Ben had a point. "We can't just sit back and do nothing."

"Right now, the best thing we can do is get the word out about what happened." Ben coughed, wincing as the simple movement brought a wave of pain. Alex frowned, worried, but Ben quickly recovered. "This is exactly what we need to sway public opinion in our favor."

The enthusiasm in Ben's voice took Alex aback. It was almost as if he had been hoping for something like this to happen. Or maybe expecting it. Alex recalled the gun that Ben had taken to the rally, and wondered what might have happened if the Peacekeepers hadn't fired first.

How far would Ben really go for the cause?

[[—✳—]]

The clock ticked past 0100 in the darkened office, just after the "timeslip" period that accounted for the extra 39.5 minutes between the Martian day and the Earth day. Jack frowned at the computer screen, watching the footage from the square for the dozenth time. Sykes had come up empty with the medics, so Jack was looking for something—anything—that might give him a clue about who might have taken the memory card. So far, all he'd gotten was a bad case of eye strain.

"Hale, anything on that search?" he called over to Hale.

Hale had run the camera footage through a facial recognition program, looking for anyone in their terrorist database. "I just sent the data over to you, sir. No match on our main suspect—Ty, or whatever his real name is. But the guy who was with him—he turned up." Jack brought up the file on his computer, even as Hale gave him the highlights. "Benjamin Holstrom. Mars native, out of Tantewei. Wanted in connection with a dozen bombings and other attacks in the early seventies. They nearly caught him about ten years ago, but he managed to get away. He's stayed under the radar since then."

Jack scanned the file. The photos were ten years old, but Jack was certain it was the man he'd shot in the square. "Keep digging. See if we can turn up any associates."

"Yes, sir." Something in the inflection of Hale's voice made Jack look at him.

"Something else on your mind, Lieutenant?"

Hale frowned, twirling a stylus in his fingers. "Why are we helping Captain Cerulli cover his ass?"

Jack leaned back in his chair, arching an eyebrow. "Cerulli's an officer."

"He's a murderer."

At the other desk, Sykes snorted. "The guys we were chasing? They're the murderers." His face twisted in a snarl, and he jerked a finger at a desk across the room. "They're the reason that desk is empty right now. Why Edwards' wife is figuring out how to ship his body back home to Earth. Why his kid's going to grow up without a dad."

"And we should keep chasing them for that," Hale said. "That doesn't change what Cerulli did. Those people at the rally were innocent."

Sykes muttered, "They picked their side."

Jack spoke before Hale could respond. "Cerulli made a bad call, but don't fool yourself into thinking things are black and white here. If we hang him out to dry, all we do is give the insurgents more airtime, more propaganda, more recruits. Where's that get us? More empty desks and letters home to grieving families."

Hale's frown deepened. "So he just gets a pass?"

Jack shrugged. "The Colonel will deal with him. His career's over." Hale still didn't seem convinced. Before Jack could say anything more, his com chirped to indicate an incoming call. Jack tapped the screen to answer. "Decker here."

"Hello, Captain. It's Rachel Griffiths from the Chronicle."

"Ms. Griffiths." Puzzled by the late call, he asked, "What can I do for you?"

"I have some information that might be useful to you. Someone came to see me tonight, wanting me to run the full story behind the riot in the Commons. I told her I couldn't, of course, but I don't think she's going to take no for an answer."

"I'm not sure what—"

Rachel interrupted him. "I believe she has a copy of the footage from Harry's camera. I think she's going to try to use it somehow."

Jack's face froze. "Who?"

"Caitlin Farland. She's a paramedic with the fire department." Rachel continued to explain, but Jack's brain was already spinning with the information. "Her husband… he was our reporter at the square." Rachel's voice caught, and Jack remembered her reaction when he had told her the crew was killed. He guessed that there had been something going on between them, which would explain why Rachel was so willing to sell Caitlin out.

"Thank you, Rachel. I appreciate the tip. I'll be in touch."

Jack hung up and pushed back his chair. "Hale, keep searching. Sykes, grab your gear." He rose, taking his pistol from a desk drawer and sliding it into its holster. "I know who's got the memory card."

CHAPTER 16

CAITLIN LAY ON HER COUCH, staring at the ceiling. She should have known better than to expect journalistic integrity from a woman who had tried to steal her husband. It satisfied her to hold the moral high ground over Rachel, but it didn't help her current situation.

The first step was to retrieve the memory card. In her haste to leave the fire station earlier, Caitlin had completely forgotten about it. It would be safe in the trauma bag until morning; nobody had opened that compartment since their last annual inspection. But even if Caitlin could convince another of the local reporters to run the story, it would never get past Rachel. She could try contacting reporters in another town, but ultimately she would face the same government censorship.

Would any of the reporters in those cities be willing to stick their necks out for the truth? She could post the vid on the public MarsCom net, but even if someone saw it before the censors took it down, she would have about as much credibility as the conspiracy theorists claiming that the Martian Face outside Cydonia had been built by aliens. The more Caitlin thought about it, the more discouraged she became. Maybe Rachel was right; maybe she should just let it go.

Her com beeped, alerting her to a new message. She wondered who would be calling at this hour. Vince had left a message earlier, while she was at Rachel's, but he wouldn't be calling back so late. Caitlin considered ignoring it, but curiosity finally got the better of her. She picked up the phone and allowed herself a small smile when she saw the sender: Luna Federal Correction Facility.

With a transmission lag between Earth and Mars, she knew it would be a pre-recorded message rather than a live call. Caitlin hit play, and her father appeared on the screen. His yellow prison coveralls always made him look sickly, but moreso today than usual. Despite the stubble of a half-grown beard, Caitlin frowned at the dark bruise on his cheek. The Peacekeepers weren't even bothering to hide their beatings any more.

Daniel Farland offered a thin smile. "Hello, Cait. I know it's late there, but the Peacekeepers are so fond of their rules. Phone time is at 1400 sharp—never mind what time it is for the person you're calling." He shook his head, scowling. "I heard about the bombing on the news. You stay safe out there." Daniel talked about a few of the other prisoners, but it was just something to fill the time. Meaningless conversation in a vain attempt to connect with a daughter he hadn't seen in over a decade. He never talked about the important things, like how he got that bruise on his face, or why he looked so tired all the time. To be fair, neither did she. He ended his message as he always did. "I wish I could be there with you, Caity. I'll talk to you soon."

The screen went blank, and Caitlin switched off the terminal. There was no use in replying tonight. It would take the message thirty minutes to reach him, on top of the thirty minutes it had taken his message to get here. His phone time would be long over. Just once, she wished they could have a real conversation. No screens, no lag—just sitting down and talking. But even after all this time, they still had her father in maximum security. No visitors. Limited screen time. She wished she could ask him what he thought she should do about the video from the square. She sighed, the loneliness overpowering.

Sighing, Caitlin turned off the lights and decided to get ready for bed. Sleep wouldn't come easily, but she should at least try. She headed to the kitchen to get a glass of water, and had just grabbed a glass from the cabinet when an odd clicking sound in the living room drew her attention. Caitlin frowned, moving to the edge of the kitchen island. Nothing seemed amiss, but the sound happened again. It seemed to be coming from the front door. Caitlin squinted against the darkness, then her eyes widened in shock.

The door was opening.

$$[[-*-]]$$

"What's the plan, Captain?" Sykes asked, his voice betraying his eagerness. "Smash and grab?" He checked his pistol.

Jack looked up at the apartment building. The shabby low-rent complex made his job easier; there were no elaborate security systems or guards to worry about. Down the block stretched similar run-down buildings, separated from one another by narrow alleys. It reminded Jack of a rabbit's warren, cramped and twisted.

He counted windows until he found the one on the fifth floor belonging to Caitlin Farland's apartment. The window was dark, as were most of the others at this hour. If they went in hard, as Sykes suggested, they would draw a lot of attention. Attention Jack could live without.

"We don't know who she told about the card," he murmured. "She may have given a copy to someone. We start breaking down doors, we might tip off the others and send them into hiding." He shook his head. "No, we keep this quiet."

Hiding his disappointment, Sykes asked, "So we sneak in and arrest her?"

Jack glanced up at the window again. "We get her, get the card, and then make sure she didn't give it to anyone else. Case closed. Nobody even needs to know we were here. When we're finished, it'll look like a random break in." And Caitlin wouldn't be alive to say otherwise.

"Copy that." Smirking, Sykes took a silencer from the pocket of his jacket and screwed it onto the barrel of his pistol. Jack did the same, and led the way across the street. He had expected to have to pick the lock of the building's front door, but it turned out someone had wedged a rock to keep the door from closing all the way. Glancing at the intercom unit, Jack realized why: the speaker dangled uselessly from a smashed casing.

The Peacekeepers went through the door and up the stairs to the fifth floor. Creeping down the hallway, they stopped outside of apartment 502 and bracketed the doorway. Jack listened at the door for a moment, but couldn't hear anything. He nodded to Sykes, who went to work on the lock and deadbolt with his auto lockpick. After a minute and two satisfying clicks, Sykes slowly turned the handle and opened the door.

Jack went in first, holding his pistol in both hands. He didn't expect to have to use it; personal firearms were outlawed on Mars, even for home protection. But with a father in jail for blowing up a supply depot, Caitlin just might be the type to have an illegal weapon.

Giving the quiet living room a cursory glance, Jack headed for the hallway. He paused to check the bathroom before proceeding cautiously into the bedroom. His eyes went first to the bed. The covers were pulled back, as if in preparation to sleep, but there was no sign of Caitlin. Jack cursed under his breath. Where the hell was she?

He had his answer when a loud rush of air, followed by a clang and a shout of pain, came from the direction of the living room.

$$[[-*-]]$$

Caitlin ducked down behind the island, her heart pounding wildly. Someone was breaking in! Her eyes darted around, trying to find something she could use to defend herself. She was in the kitchen, for God's sake, it shouldn't be that difficult. But the knives were in a drawer, and even the pots and pans were put away. She couldn't get to any of them without attracting attention. She clutched her glass in sweaty palms, realizing it was her only weapon.

Shrinking against the cabinets, Caitlin strained to hear what was going on. Two men entered. They didn't speak, but she could hear the quiet rustle of boots on carpet as one moved down the hall toward the bedroom. The other cautiously crossed the living room. They both moved purposefully, too organized to be a bunch of hopped up kids looking for some quick cash from a break-in. This was something different.

The second burglar got closer. It wouldn't take him long to find her. Caitlin took a breath to steel herself, as she did when facing a fire. The fear receded, giving way to determination. Slowly opening one of the lower cabinets, she grabbed the small fire extinguisher she kept near the stove. The intruder paused, and Caitlin felt a rush of panic. Had he heard her? A moment later the footsteps resumed, this time heading straight for the kitchen. Caitlin pulled the pin out of the extinguisher, wincing as it made a quiet squeak. Her fingers tightened, heart thudding in her ears.

She waited until the last possible moment, then stood up quickly and squeezed the trigger. It discharged with a tremendous whoosh, sending a cloud of dry chemical dust right into the face of the intruder. He howled in a mixture of surprise and pain, twisting away and trying to cover his face. The man raised his hand, and Caitlin realized with a jolt of terror that he was holding a gun. He pulled the trigger blindly, and the gun gave a quiet thump. Caitlin felt the searing slash of a bullet graze her forearm, even as a detached part of her mind wondered what sort of burglars carried silenced pistols.

Grabbing the extinguisher by its neck, she swung it like a stubby baseball bat. It struck the side of the intruder's head with a hollow clang. He staggered, but still didn't go down. Caitlin hit him twice more until finally he collapsed, his pistol skittering across the floor. She scooped it up and leveled it at him, but he didn't stir. Looking for the first time at the intruder's face, Caitlin gasped. Even with his upper body covered in white residue, there was no mistaking the familiar face of Sergeant Sykes.

Caitlin knew at once what they were after. Rachel must have told them about the footage. That backstabbing little… Her fury took a back seat to the more pressing need to flee. The second Peacekeeper came down the hallway, his pistol visible in the dim light. Without thinking, Caitlin raised her stolen weapon and fired. The bullets went wide, striking the plaster wall separating the hallway and the living room, but they still had the intended effect. The soldier dove back into the hallway, seeking cover.

Caitlin dashed into the living room, firing two more shots to keep the Peacekeeper's head down. How many bullets did this gun have? She shrieked as a bullet whizzed past her ear, shattering a lamp behind her. Ducking, she practically fell through the open front doorway. The stairs were at the end of a long, open hallway. She'd never make it. Her only chance was the window at the closer end of the hall, beyond which was a fire escape. Caitlin hammered at the window, clearing out the glass. Cursing her lack of shoes, she stepped over the broken shards and climbed out onto the fire escape.

"Drop the gun, Farland." Captain Decker's voice came from behind her. Caitlin didn't have to look to know that there was a gun trained on her back. The ladder going down was just inches away, but there was a hatch covering it. She'd never get it open in time.

When she didn't move, Decker repeated the command, more harshly this time. "I said drop it!"

Caitlin looked out over the steel railing that ran around the fire escape, at the street a dizzying five stories below. Suddenly she knew how to escape. She held up the gun and bent forward slowly, as if she was going to do as Decker asked. But at the last second, she vaulted over the railing and found herself in free-fall, her stomach lurching as she plummeted toward the ground.

CHAPTER 17

CAITLIN'S BREATH CAUGHT IN HER throat, stifling a scream as the ground rushed up to meet her. Even though Martian gravity was only a third of Earth's, it still felt like an insane distance to fall. She hit the cobblestones feet-first, then folded into an inelegant tuck and roll. The jarring impact left her feeling as though she'd been hit by a truck. She lay on the street, gasping for breath.

Up on the fire escape, Decker fiddled with the hatch to the fire escape ladder. Caitlin recovered enough to scramble for Sykes' pistol. The captain ducked back through the window just as she fired, bullets clanging harmlessly off the metal cage of the fire escape.

Caitlin rolled to her feet, and a sharp stabbing pain shot up from her right ankle. Gritting back a cry, Caitlin took a few tentative steps. The ankle could still bear weight—barely—it just hurt like hell. She wouldn't be able to outrun Decker, and frantically searched for another way out. North of Second Avenue, buildings just like hers were packed closely together, separated by only small alleys. If she could put enough distance between her and Decker, she could probably lose him in the maze. Tucking the pistol close against her ribs to hide it, she hobbled into the alley.

She followed the twists and turns through the maze of alleys, quickly losing her bearings in the warren. A few times she paused to catch her breath and listen for signs of pursuit, but all she could hear was her own ragged breathing and pounding heart. The fear of being captured spurred Caitlin onward, but eventually her endurance ran out.

Sagging against the wall of the alley, Caitlin slowly sank to the ground and buried her face in her hands. *God, what have I gotten myself into?* At the riot, when the bullets started flying, Caitlin had been more afraid than she ever had before. But that was nothing compared to the terror that gripped her now. She had no idea what to do.

She tried to take a deep breath to calm her racing thoughts. Decker hadn't come to arrest her; that much was obvious. She remembered the Peacekeepers coming for her father. Six of them, in full riot gear, kicked down the door and charged in, shouting and knocking things over. Decker and Sykes had snuck in during the middle of the night like burglars, with silencers on their pistols. She was only defending herself. If she turned herself in to the Peacekeeper MPs... Caitlin dismissed the thought almost as soon as it entered her mind. She had shot at them. It would be her word against theirs—a terrorist's daughter versus two Peacekeepers.

Caitlin wiped her forehead with her sleeve, the sweat stinging the gash on her forearm from Sykes' bullet. She stared at the wound, a numb disbelief washing over her. A gunshot. It didn't feel real. Blood oozed from the cut, but she had nothing to dress it with. She was dressed for bed, in a long-sleeve fire department T-shirt and sweat pants. She didn't even have any shoes, just a pair of socks that were now caked in the reddish-brown dust that sometimes eluded the ventilation systems. She had no money, no way to contact anyone—not that there was anyone to contact. Vince was the only one she could trust, and she couldn't bring this trouble down on him and his family.

Caitlin picked up Sykes' pistol, studying it. Her father had taught her a little about guns, though she'd never fired one before tonight. She checked the clip and saw that there were six bullets left, plus one in the chamber. Making sure the safety was on, she tucked the pistol into the back waistband of her pants. As she shivered in the cold dome air, Caitlin knew she couldn't stay out on the street all night.

She could think of only one person who could help her now. She just had to figure out how to find him.

[[—✳—]]

Jack took the stairs three at a time, racing down breathlessly. When he reached the ground floor, he flung open the door to the lobby and charged out into the street. By the time he got there, Caitlin had gone, and there were no signs of which way she'd gone. Both of the nearest alleys were empty.

"Shit!" Jack snarled. He looked up at the apartment building, eyeing the fire escape Caitlin had jumped from. He should have just followed her over the ledge, and ended this then and there. But even knowing about the lower gravity, he just couldn't bring himself to jump out of a five story window. It went against thousands of years of evolutionary instincts. Now she was armed and on the run. He couldn't call in the infantry to seal off the area without explaining what he and Sykes were doing here. They were on their own.

Sykes was still out cold on the kitchen floor when he returned, the empty fire extinguisher lying next to him. Shaking his head in disgust, Jack dumped a large glass of water on Sykes' face. He couldn't help but feel some small measure of satisfaction as the sergeant awoke, coughing and sputtering.

"Get up, Sergeant," Jack said through clenched teeth.

Sykes sat up, holding his head, a dazed look on his face. Blood trickled from a cut on his forehead, and he brushed off the dust from the fire extinguisher. "Christ, I'm bleeding. What happened?"

Tossing the glass back into the sink, Jack fixed Sykes with a withering glare. "You tell me."

Sykes slowly pulled himself to his feet, using the counter for support. He looked around, still dazed. "I thought I heard something, so I came over to see..." His eyes drifted to the fire extinguisher, and he just shook his head. "I'm sorry, sir, I don't know how it happened."

"Goddamn it, Sykes. You let a damn paramedic get the drop on you!" Jack tried to keep his voice down, to avoid attracting any more attention from the neighbors than they might have already.

"It won't happen again, sir." Sykes drew himself up straighter, and looked around. "Are we going after her?"

Jack shook his head, scowling. "She's long gone by now." He paced across the living room. "I think I winged her. There was some blood on the fire escape."

"Should we put a watch on the hospital?" Sykes asked.

"No, she's not that stupid. I don't think she'd try the fire station either, but that's her home turf. She might risk it." Jack turned from the window, mulling over the possibilities. "She left here in a hurry. She might not have taken the storage card with her. Toss the place. If it's here, we'll find it." As Sykes started searching the apartment, Jack found a com unit on the coffee table. Who would she turn to if she was in trouble? He scrolled through the notifications, seeing three calls in the last 24 hours. Two were from her partner.

Quirking a smile, Jack pulled out his own com and made a call. It took a few rings, but eventually the sleepy voice of Lieutenant Hale answered.

"Hale, I need you to do two things," Jack said. "Have the MPs set up surveillance on the fire station. If Caitlin Farland shows up, notify me but take no other action. She's to be considered armed and dangerous."

"Yes, sir," Hale replied, now fully alert. "What's the second thing?"

"I need a trace on another paramedic. Vince Castellano. I want his address and everything else you can get on him."

[[—✳—]]

The Flux was one of Waycross' most popular dance clubs. On a typical night, the line to get in stretched halfway down the block. Its pounding music could be heard as a dull throb even through the brick walls. Caitlin had only been inside once, and she still got a headache just thinking about the flashing strobes and near-deafening industrial rock. It was not a place she would return to under normal circumstances, but tonight was anything but. She approached cautiously from the rear, keeping alert for Peacekeeper patrols.

A muscular black guy in a dark suit and tie stood by the rear door. He held a radio in his hand, probably for communicating with the other club staff.

"I think you're in the wrong place, darling," he said gruffly, surveying her appearance with a frown. It was hardly suited to the club scene.

Caitlin folded her arms across her chest for warmth, the pistol an uncomfortable presence against her back. "I'm looking for Max Farland. Is he still the manager?"

The man's eyes narrowed. "Who's asking?"

"His niece. Caitlin. Is he here? It's important." The young man told her to wait, and muttered something into his radio. Caitlin could only make out her own name, and Max's. She waited nervously, looking up and down the street.

After a few minutes, the door opened and another man in a similar suit appeared. "Come on up." Relieved, Caitlin followed him through the door. She expected it to be noisier inside, but there must have been some kind of soundproofing for the back areas.

As soon as the door closed, Caitlin felt powerful hands grab her shoulders from behind. She let out a startled cry as she was slammed against the wall. She tried to struggle, but her attacker twisted an arm up behind her and cut off any resistance. The man quickly grabbed her pistol and pressed it hard against her temple. "You think we're stupid? Who sent you?"

"Nobody sent me!" Caitlin protested frantically, gasping as he applied more pressure on her arm. "I told you…"

He pulled the hammer back on the gun, and it cocked with an ominous click. "I'm only going to ask you one more time."

Caitlin closed her eyes, breathing fast. She was wracking her brain for something she could say to convince them when a voice spoke from the nearby stairs. "Paul!" It was a sharp command, and immediately got the attention of the man holding a gun to her head. "Old man says to let her go."

"You serious?" Paul asked, incredulous. Apparently so, for Paul reluctantly lowered the weapon and released her. Paul kept her pistol, motioning to the stairs with it, "You heard the man. Go on up."

Caitlin skittered away, rubbing her arm. She followed the other man up the stairs, down a long hallway, and through an office door. There, sitting behind a simple oak desk, was her Uncle Max.

The years had taken their toll on Max. His balding hair had turned completely white, and he'd put on a good twenty pounds. "Caitlin." It was as much a statement of surprise as it was a greeting, and his unsmiling gaze lacked the warmth she remembered from her childhood. "Well, I'll be damned. It's been a long time."

"It has." Caitlin swallowed, remembering their last meeting. Judging from Max's tight-lipped gaze, he remembered it as well. "It's… good to see you," she managed awkwardly.

"Cut the crap, Cait," Max said evenly. "You show up here, after all this time, carrying a gun and looking like something the cat dragged in? What the hell is going on?"

Taking a breath, Caitlin ran a hand through her hair. "I'm in trouble, Max. I need your help. I need to get in touch with someone…" Glancing at the bodyguard, or bouncer, or whoever he was still standing in the back of the room, she chose her words carefully. "Someone in your and my dad's line of work."

Max's eyes narrowed, his mouth turning downward. "That'll be all for now, Hasan," he said, dismissing the bodyguard.

"You sure, boss?" When Max nodded, Hasan frowned unhappily, but left the room and closed the door.

"I'm not involved in that any more, Cait. I'm a legitimate businessman now."

"So legitimate you need a small army downstairs?" Caitlin asked dryly. "Come on, we both know you're not just running a nightclub here."

"You can't believe everything you see on the news nets. You should know that." Max's alleged ties to the Syndicate, Waycross' organized crime network, had been the subject of several news articles a few years ago. Nothing had come of it; there was never enough evidence to charge him, but the rumors had persisted.

Sighing, Caitlin tried a different tack. "You promised me once that I could come to you if I needed anything."

"And after that, you told me to go to hell, and haven't spoken to me in years!" Max snapped. "I'd say that eliminates any obligations I might have had."

Caitlin winced. "I'm sorry, Max. I shouldn't have said what I did. I was young. I was angry. Dad was in prison…"

"And you thought it should have been me instead," he said bitterly.

Caitlin didn't deny it. It hadn't seemed fair at the time, that her father was arrested when all the rest of them got away.

Especially Max, the leader of their cell. "Look, I can't change what happened before. But I really need your help now." Desperation crept into her voice, "Please, Max. I've got nobody else to turn to."

Max said nothing for a long moment, then finally sighed. "What do you need?"

Caitlin let out the breath she'd been holding. "I need to talk to one of the rebels. He's been on the news the last few days—from the bombing. His name is Alex." Max's eyebrows shot up, and Caitlin could have sworn there was a flash of recognition there. "You know him, don't you?"

Max didn't answer the question directly, instead saying, "Even if I did, what makes you think he'd talk to you? He seems to have enough trouble of his own."

"He will," Caitlin said, unwilling to acknowledge the other possibility. "He owes me. Do you know how to find him?"

If Max was curious about why a rebel owed her a favor, he didn't ask. Maybe he decided he was better off not knowing. "I can't promise anything, but I might be able to get him a message. It's the best I can do." He handed her a notepad and pen, and she scribbled a note to Alex. As she did so, Max asked, "Where will you be staying?"

Caitlin paused, looking up from her writing. "I was hoping you might have someplace."

"Cait, look, I'd like to help you..." Max began, and Caitlin's heart sank. "But it won't take the PKs much work to link you to me. I can't be caught helping you. I'm sorry."

The rejection stung, but she wasn't surprised. Max hadn't taken her in after her father went to jail either, trying unsuccessfully to convince her that she'd be better off with some strangers. "Do you think you could at least find me a jacket? Maybe a pair of shoes?"

Max gave her a quick once-over, and then nodded. He called Hasan back in and spoke to him quietly for a moment before the big man departed again. He returned in short order, carrying a dark, hooded cloth jacket. As she slipped it on, she found that her pistol had been tucked into the front pocket. Caitlin murmured her thanks. She still had no shoes, but she doubted they kept some just lying around the nightclub.

She handed Max the note for Alex, and in return he pressed a folded wad of bills into her hand. Caitlin didn't have to count it to tell that it was a respectable sum of money. "Take care of yourself, Cait."

Caitlin nodded. Venturing back outside, she tightened her new jacket and glanced up at the dome overhead. It was a clear night, and the stars were out in force. She prayed silently that Max would be able to get her message to Alex. She was running out of options.

CHAPTER 18

THE QUIET APPROACH HADN'T DONE too well for Farland's place, but this time it worked like a charm. The Castellanos lived just a few blocks away, in an apartment way too crowded for a family of four. Jack and Sykes got in without incident, despite a brief scare when the family cat jumped off the back of the couch and scampered into the rear of the house. Jack quickly swept the living room and kitchen while Sykes guarded the door. Then they both moved down the hallway, splitting up to take the two bedrooms.

Jack crept into the master bedroom. The door was open, Vince and his wife sleeping soundly beneath a striped comforter. Sykes joined him a moment later, shaking his head. There was no sign of Caitlin anywhere. Had she come and gone already, or had she anticipated that they would come here? Only one way to find out.

Moving swiftly, Jack clamped his hand over the wife's mouth and jammed the pistol in her face. She shrieked, the noise muffled by his gloved hand. She tried to scramble away, but Jack dragged her off the bed. He whispered in her ear. "Not a sound."

Vince awoke with a jolt, but Sykes belted the paramedic hard across the jaw and had him in zip-ties in an instant.

"What the hell is going on?" Vince asked, dazed but not unconscious. "Adelle? Adelle, are you all right? Let her go, you bastards!" Vince tried to struggle, but Sykes kept him pinned to the bed.

Jack zip-tied Adelle's hands behind her and left her at the foot of the bed, motioning for Sykes to drag Vince over. When the sergeant shoved the medic to his knees, Jack fixed him with a cold glare. "Where is she?"

"Where's who?" Vince spat back. He sounded honestly baffled.

"Caitlin Farland. Has she contacted you?"

The expression on Vince's face changed, surprise mingling with concern. "What? Why?"

"Focus, Vince. It doesn't matter why." Obviously Caitlin hadn't been here. Maybe she was smarter than he'd given her credit for. That just meant he'd have to jump to get a step ahead of her. "You're going to help me find her."

"The hell I am."

Adelle shook her head, tears streaming down her face. "Vince!"

Jack looked at her, then back to Vince. The raised voices had disturbed Vince's youngest, shrill cries rising from the bassinet in the corner. "Your loyalty to your girlfriend is touching and everything, Vince, but you need to start thinking about your family here. Pretty wife. Sweet little boy. Brand new baby. You've got a lot to lose."

"You leave them out of this." Vince tried to lunge up at Jack, but Sykes shoved him back down and kicked him in the thigh for good measure. The medic grimaced, muttering something unflattering in Spanish.

"Oh, they're in this. They're in this because of you, Vince. Because of her. Give me a name. Someone she'd go to. Someplace she'd feel safe."

Vince's jaw worked, chewing over his response like it left a bad taste in his mouth. "I don't know."

"Bullshit," Jack challenged. He gave Sykes a nod, and the sergeant kicked him again. "Come on, Vince. You guys go back a long way. I have your com records. All those calls, texts, visits, social media posts. I know you know something."

Still Vince stayed silent, his chin lifted defiantly. Jack flicked a glance to the medic's terrified wife, addressing both of them, "Here's how this is going to go. We're going to haul you both in for aiding and abetting a wanted fugitive. I've got enough here to make a solid case for a judge. I'm sure they'd be particularly interested in hearing about how you let a terrorist escape from the back of your ambulance." A muscle in Vince's cheek twitched. "Child services is going to take your kids. Even if you manage to beat the charges, good luck getting them back with that cloud hanging over your record."

"Vince, please… tell him something," Adelle pleaded, tears streaming down her face.

Jack lowered his voice, speaking almost soothingly. "It doesn't have to be like that, Vince. Think about your family. Caitlin is going down. Don't let her take you down with her. Tell me how to find her."

The medic shook his head, his face twisted in anguish. Finally his shoulders slumped. "Father Cranston," he mumbled. "That's where she'd go. St. Michael's church."

[[—✳—]]

Alex approached the park at the corner of Archer and Third. Traffic on the streets of the residential district had picked up in the last half hour, as party-goers started to make their way home after last call. He'd met Max Farland a few times, in the course of arranging arms deals, but never out of the blue like this.

Spotting two Peacekeepers coming down the street, Alex quickly ducked behind a wall. His hat-and-glasses disguise would pass a casual inspection, but he didn't want to push his luck. When he checked back to see if the soldiers had gone, Alex saw a familiar figure approaching from across the park. He left his hiding place to meet Max.

Max had been an active rebel operative in his youth, but the years had robbed him of his idealism. He left the rebels and went underground, resurfacing a few years later in organized crime. Old Max still had a soft spot for the rebels, who used him as an information broker and black market contact.

"Alex. So good to see you again."

"You, too. How's business?"

"Booming, my friend." The older man smiled. "You and your friends have been causing so much trouble for the Peacekeepers that they hardly bother with us."

Alex smirked, but then turned their attention to the matter at hand. "I got your message. What's so urgent?"

Max took a folded sheet of paper from his pocket and handed it to Alex. "Someone came to see me tonight. She asked me to give you this."

Curious, Alex unfolded the paper and read the message scrawled inside in a hasty script.

Alex,

I have proof that the Peacekeepers are covering up the massacre at the square. They're after me to get it. I need your help. Please meet me at St. Michael's church tonight.

Caitlin Farland

Alex shook his head, baffled. "Caitlin… the paramedic?" He hadn't connected her last name to Max's until just now. "Wait… you're related?"

"She's my niece. Her father and I were in the same cell a long time ago."

"Her father's with the rebels?"

Shaking his head, Max said, "Not any more. He's doing time in Luna."

Alex blinked. He had no idea Caitlin had rebel connections. It put things into a different perspective. He now knew why she had been willing to help him. But something still didn't add up. "Why me, Max? Why didn't she just come to you?"

"Things got complicated between us, after my brother was sent away." Max frowned sadly, but then he shook his head again. "Besides, I can't afford to stick my neck out for anyone. Not anymore. It's bad for business."

Business or no, Alex didn't see how Max could turn away his niece like that. But it would have been rude to say so. "Thanks, Max. I'll see you later."

"Take care, Alex. And good luck. I think you might need it."

Alex paused, glancing at the note once more before pocketing it. "I think you're probably right."

$$[[-*-]]$$

Ten blocks wasn't that far, normally, but on a sprained ankle it felt like ten miles. Caitlin stopped to catch her breath in a downtown alley. She realized that she was only a block from the fire station, and the surreality of it all hit her hard. This morning she had gotten up and gone to work, running calls just like any other shift. Now her life was unrecognizable.

She felt a wave of relief when she saw the white steeple of St. Michael's church. She wasn't Catholic, but the church had always been a haven for her. Father Cranston and the nuns ran a group foster home next door, and Caitlin lived there for a few years after her father was arrested. Even after she had moved out on her own, Caitlin had always come back to the church whenever she needed a respite. Right now, it was the only place she could think of where she would feel safe.

The door was locked, but Father Cranston had always kept a spare key around. She eventually found it under a loose cobblestone, and let herself in. The lights in the stain glass windows high above cast a faint light, but most of the church lay in shadow. Caitlin moved past the rows of dark pews, toward the back office.

Out of the darkness, a figure emerged from behind a pillar right in front of her. She couldn't see his face at first, in the shadows, but the sinister British accent was all too familiar. "About time you turned up."

CHAPTER 19

CAITLIN GASPED, BACKING UP AND reaching for her pistol. She got it out of her pocket, but not before Sykes closed the distance and grabbed her arm. Her finger squeezed the trigger reflexively, and the gunshot shattered the peaceful quiet of the church. The bullet took a chunk out of a nearby pew before embedding itself harmlessly into a wall. The next thing Caitlin knew, she was hitting the floor at Sykes' feet, flat on her stomach with her arm in some kind of joint lock.

"I'll take that back," Sykes grunted, wrenching the pistol from her hand.

Caitlin winced at the pressure on her wrist and elbow. She lay still, her mind racing. How had they found her? They couldn't have been following her since the apartment—that was hours ago. They must have known she was coming here, but how? Had Max tipped them off? She didn't want to believe he was capable of that, but hadn't thought he'd turn her away, either. She didn't know what to believe.

Footsteps echoed in the hall as Captain Decker came from the direction of the door. He crouched next to Caitlin and frisked her. When he found nothing but empty pockets, he demanded, "Where is it?"

Caitlin shook her head. "Where's what?" Sykes leaned on her arm a little harder, and Caitlin gasped.

"Don't play games with me, Farland. I know you have the memory card. Tell me where it is."

When she didn't reply fast enough to suit Sykes, he twisted her arm again. He seemed to take great pleasure in it, no doubt enjoying the payback. Even in the dim light, Caitlin could see his swollen nose from where she'd clocked him with the fire extinguisher. "The Captain asked you a question."

"I hid it. At home."

Decker wasn't buying it. "Nice try. We tore the place apart."

"Well, maybe someone stole it," Caitlin said through gritted teeth. "There've been a lot of break-ins in the neighborhood lately." Sykes tried to twist her wrist out of its socket. She cried out, slamming the floor with her free hand.

The lights turned on, startling all of them.

"What's going on here?" Standing near the doorway, his hand still on the light switch, stood the elderly Father Jim Cranston. Dressed in a dark robe and sandals, his white hair was mussed from sleep.

Decker flashed his badge, and said in a firm voice of authority. "Peacekeeper business. Everything's under control. You should go back to your home."

As if to lend credence to his story, Sykes bound Caitlin's hands with zip-ties. The relief of the strain on her arm had her choking back a sob. Sykes then yanked her to her feet.

Once she was up, Father Cranston recognized Caitlin almost immediately. "Caitlin?" he exclaimed, and started walking towards them. His sandals clicked against his feet as he crossed the church.

Decker stepped forward held out a hand "This isn't your concern, Father."

"I know this girl, Officer," the priest insisted, never being one to take no for an answer. "She was one of my wards here. I demand to know what's going on." Caitlin found herself hoping against hope that somehow Father Cranston would help her get out of this mess.

Sykes leaned in to mutter in Caitlin's ear. "Make him go away, or this is going to get messy. Understand?"

Caitlin swallowed hard, suddenly afraid for the old man. After what happened in the square, she knew not even a priest would be safe. "It's all right, Father." She struggled to keep the fear out of her voice. "It's just a misunderstanding."

"What is it you think she's done?" the priest asked, turning to Decker.

Decker frowned, losing his patience. "She's being held under the Internal Security Act on terrorism-related charges. That's all I'm at liberty to say."

Doubt clouded Cranston's face the minute Decker mentioned "terrorism." He had always feared that Caitlin would follow in her father's footsteps. She wanted to shout that it was all a mistake. She didn't want to leave with him thinking the worst of her, but anything she said would be putting him in greater danger. Catching his eye, all she could do was repeat, "It'll be all right, Father."

Decker motioned for Sykes to lead Caitlin out. She limped along awkwardly, his fingers an iron vice digging into her shoulder.

After a moment, Father Cranston called after her, "Don't worry, Caitlin. We'll get you a good lawyer and we'll sort this out. Have faith, child."

Faith was something she was a little short on at the moment, but Caitlin struggled to hold on to it. As soon as they were outside, Sykes let out a quiet chuckle. His cold words sent a chill straight through her.

"You ain't going to need a lawyer where you're going."

[[—✳—]]

Alex heard the gunshot when he was still two blocks from the church, and immediately knew Caitlin was in trouble. He quickened his pace, drawing his own pistol. It was foolish to be going toward the gunfire. Any Peacekeepers in the area would be doing the same thing. But it had been equally foolish for Caitlin to cut through his zip-ties that night in the ambulance, with a squad of soldiers standing just outside. He couldn't turn back now.

He arrived at the church just as the front doors were opening. Ducking back behind the corner, he watched as three figures emerged. The tall, burly one had to be Sykes. He shoved the second person, whose hands were bound. Caitlin limped along, her shoulders hunched. The third figure he could only assume was Captain Decker. Alex leveled his pistol at the trio, but he couldn't get a clear shot at this distance. Cursing silently, Alex lowered his weapon.

He would have to hit them before they made it to Fort McChord. Nobody could mount a rescue operation in the Peacekeeper stronghold. He trailed them from the shadows, far enough behind them that he wouldn't be spotted.

When they reached Fifth Avenue, they turned east. Alex frowned. Fort McChord was in the opposite direction. Where the hell were they going? Caitlin paused, looking between her two captors. She might have asked something, but Alex was too far away to hear it. In the end, Sykes gave her a rough shove, nearly causing her to fall. She caught herself and they headed east, into the heart of the industrial district.

Alex continued to follow them, growing more perplexed by the moment. If he had known where they were heading, he could have tried to get ahead of them to mount an ambush. But now he didn't dare let them out of his sight. All he could do was bide his time and hope for an opportunity.

[[—＊—]]

Jack was in a foul mood by the time they finally made it back to the warehouse. Capturing Caitlin had taken way more effort than it should have. She was a damn paramedic, and the fact that she had gotten away in the first place still gnawed at him. But now they had her, and soon enough she would give up the location of the memory card and anyone else who knew about it.

"What is this place?" Caitlin asked, frowning as they approached the abandoned warehouse. Located in the heart of the industrial district, surrounded by other storage units, it didn't see much traffic even during daylight hours. At night the place was a ghost town.

Sykes smirked. "Just a little home away from home for us. See, the commander doesn't like it when we torture prisoners at the base." Caitlin faltered a step, her pale cheeks growing even whiter.

Lieutenant Hale met them at the door. The young officer looked flustered. "I have the other…"

Jack held up a hand to silence him. "Take her upstairs. Put her in the second room." Sykes led Caitlin away, and Jack turned his attention to Hale.

"Sir, with all due respect, what are we doing here?"

"Getting some answers," Jack replied tersely.

"But—"

"All you need to know is we're dealing with a threat to colonial security. What I need you to do is go through the records. Find me some leverage."

"Sir, this all seems highly irregular," Hale said, shifting uneasily. "Standing orders are to take all prisoners to the Fort."

Jack glared, his patience wearing thin. "You have your orders, Lieutenant. Now park your ass at that computer and get me the information I need. Is that clear?"

Hale gulped and nodded. "Yes, sir."

Jack watched him move away, wondering if it had been a mistake to bring the green lieutenant along. Once again he cursed his lack of manpower.

The upper floor of the factory once housed the management offices. The walls contained some soundproofing, presumably to drown out the noise of the forklifts and machinery on the ground floor. Jack had converted one into an interrogation room. The bland office furniture had been stripped out, replaced with a traditional table and opposing chairs. Caitlin sat in one, her zip-tied hands resting on the table. Sykes stood impassively in the corner.

"No more games, Caitlin," Jack warned. "Where's the memory card? Did you hide it somewhere? Give it to someone?"

Caitlin stared back at him in silent defiance. He suspected she would be a hard one to crack. Her family history gave her years of pent-up resentment toward the Peacekeepers.

Jack perched on the edge of the desk. "We can make this very unpleasant for you. It's Sykes' favorite part of the job, really." He saw her eyes flick to the big sergeant, who offered a mirthless smile in return.

He paused, letting the wheels turn in her head. He could see the fear in her eyes, much as she tried to hide it. "But it doesn't have to be like that. I'm a reasonable man, Caitlin. You give me what I want, and no one has to get hurt. In fact, I'm so reasonable that I'll even offer you something in return."

"There's nothing you can offer me," Caitlin spat back.

Jack smiled. "Oh, I wouldn't be so sure about that." He stood up and began pacing around the table. "Your father's been in prison a long time. I could pull some strings to make things easier for him. Medium security. Regular visiting hours. How long has it been since you've seen him?"

Caitlin's throat moved visibly as she swallowed. "There's no way I could trust you to keep your side of the bargain."

She was right, of course, but the point of the game was to sow doubt. Weaken her defenses. "He's a means to an end, Caitlin. You have something I want. I have something you want. You think I care whether some old man serves the rest of his sentence in general population or not?"

Caitlin hesitated, before finally shaking her head. "I don't believe you."

Jack slammed his hand down on the table, making her flinch. "Believe this: No one holds out forever. You *will* break. You'll tell me what I want to know, and both you and your father will spend the rest of your lives in a maximum security hellhole." He let the words sink in for a moment. "Take the deal, Caitlin. It's your only option."

Caitlin raised her eyes to meet his gaze directly. "Fuck you."

Shaking his head, Jack stepped back. He glanced over at Sykes and gave him a nod. Sykes stepped out of the room.

"I'm sorry you feel that way," Jack said, his voice filled with mock sincerity. "And I'm sure Vince is, too."

CHAPTER 20

ALEX WATCHED THE WAREHOUSE FOR a few minutes, but saw no further signs of activity once Decker and Sykes had taken Caitlin inside. He thought he had seen another soldier in the doorway briefly, but couldn't be sure. He had to figure there were at least three armed men inside. He needed backup.

Taking out his com, Alex dialed Samantha. Her voice answered with a brisk greeting.

"It's me," Alex said, not using names over the open airwaves. "I need you to meet me at the corner of Fifth and Hamilton, soon as you can. Bring some extra firepower."

"What's going on?" Samantha asked in alarm. "Are you okay?"

"I'm fine," Alex assured her. "But a friend's in trouble. I need your help to bail her out."

Samantha didn't hesitate, which Alex was grateful for. "Fifth and Hamilton. I'll be there."

Alex crept cautiously toward the building, doing some recon while he waited for the others. He reached the side of the building and peered through a dirty window. Most of the ground floor was one big open area, and it seemed completely deserted. He couldn't tell what was going on upstairs. For all he knew, there could be an entire squad of soldiers up there. Going in blind was a huge risk, but he didn't see any other choice.

The almost-silent buzz of his com startled him. Beating a hasty retreat back across the street, he answered the call.

"What the hell do you think you're doing?" Ben's angry voice demanded.

"A friend's in trouble. I have to try to help her."

"So you're going off on some kind of half-baked rescue mission? What's gotten into you? Who's this friend?"

Alex sighed in frustration. The longer they waited, the more risk there was of the situation spiraling further out of control. More troops might arrive, Decker might try to move Caitlin, a patrol might come along and spot Alex… there were a million things that could go wrong. He debated how much to say over the phone.

"No one you know. She helped me escape, and she took care of you at the square. The PKs have her now."

"At the Fort? Are you insane?"

"No, at a warehouse in the industrial district. Look, we should cut this short." They didn't like to stay on the air more than a minute or so, for fear that the Peacekeepers might trace the call. "What's your ETA?"

"We're not coming," Ben said firmly. "We've taken enough losses today. I'm not going to risk an extraction."

Alex gaped, disbelief giving way to anger. "She saved our lives! Maybe that doesn't mean much to you, but it does to me. I can't just turn my back on her."

"That's exactly what you're going to do. She's not one of ours. We can't risk it."

Alex hung up and switched off his com. He wasn't going to let Ben talk him out of this. Caitlin had put everything on the line for them, and he owed her the same. Even if it meant he was on his own.

[[—✳—]]

Caitlin gasped in horror as Sykes dragged Vince into the room. "Vince…" Her mind reeled with denial.

The sergeant attached Vince's bound hands to a hook hanging from the ceiling, stringing him up with his arms above his head. Vince said nothing at first, his jaw clenched tightly. She had never seen him truly afraid until now. Finally he met her gaze and said, "Cait, I'm sorry. I…"

Sykes cut off his sentence with a powerful blow to the stomach. "You're not the one we want to hear from."

Caitlin flinched as Vince was struck. "Leave him alone!" She stood up, prepared to charge across the room to do something— anything. Decker shoved her back hard into the chair.

"He's got nothing to do with this!" she cried.

"He does now," Decker replied evenly. "And what happens next is up to you." He left the room for a moment, returning with a small cylinder barely the length of his forearm. Her nervous eyes tracked him moving closer until he was behind her. Decker asked casually, "Ever been hit by a stun stick? We use them for riot control."

"You mean when you're not shooting the crowd?" Caitlin spat back.

She felt an explosion of pain, as if a live wire had touched the back of her shoulder. She screamed, her muscles going rigid. It lasted only a few seconds, but that was enough to leave her weak and dizzy. Her left arm felt like it was asleep, a pins and needles sensation that was slow to fade away.

"I just thought you should have a frame of reference before we got started." Decker tossed the stun stick to Sykes, who offered Caitlin a dark smile before jamming it into Vince's ribs. He left it on far longer than Decker had. Vince's scream cut right through her, a million times worse than any pain from a physical blow.

"Stop it! For God's sake, stop it!"

Mercifully, Sykes stopped. Vince slumped, drained but still not unconscious.

"You're the one doing this to him, Caitlin," Decker whispered in her ear. "You have the power to stop it. Just tell me what I want to know, and this will all go away."

The words were seductive, but Caitlin knew the truth. "If I tell you, you'll kill us."

"You're going to tell me eventually. It's just a matter of how much you and your friend want to suffer in the mean time." The Captain was sickeningly self-confident. And worse—he was probably right.

Decker motioned to Sykes, who resumed shocking Vince. Caitlin closed her eyes, but she couldn't shut out the screaming. She had the almost childish desire to cover her ears with her hands, but the zip-ties prevented that. Tears squeezed through her eyes.

Time blurred. She didn't know how long the screams went on, but finally she couldn't take it any more. Vince was her partner. Her best friend. She couldn't go on letting them torture him because of her.

"That's enough!" she sobbed. "Please stop."

Sykes stopped, but it was Vince who spoke.

Gasping, barely able to stand, his words sounded surprisingly strong. "Don't… tell them…"

That earned him another shock, which went on until Decker gestured to the sergeant to halt.

Vince's words had thrown her for a loop, causing her to doubt. Caitlin shook her head, her voice broken. "I can't let them do this to you, Vince. This isn't even your fight." He had never cared about politics, always trying to stay neutral in a world where Peacekeeper and rebel sympathizers clashed on a daily basis. He didn't belong here, mixed up in this.

"They made it… my fight." Vince replied, with as much defiance as he could muster.

Decker leaned in, blocking her view of Vince. "Your friend is giving you extremely bad advice, Caitlin. I'd expect more from a family man—someone with a lovely wife and kids to go home to." His voice was calm and quiet, but there was no mistaking the sinister undercurrent. He moved away, walking back around behind the table. "Talk to me, before anyone else gets hurt."

Caitlin stared at Vince through tear-filled eyes. He shook his head, just a little, and she understood. He didn't want them to win any more than she did. Lifting her jaw slightly, Caitlin told Decker, "Go to hell."

Decker sighed, looking frustrated. "Then we start again."

Sykes raised the stun stick again, but before Decker gave him the signal to start, the door suddenly opened.

Another Peacekeeper stood there, taking in the scene with a grim expression. "Captain, I have a call for you." He held out a com.

Decker cast a withering look at the other soldier. "It'll have to wait, Lieutenant."

The Lieutenant shook his head. "No, sir, I'm afraid it can't. It's Colonel Isakovich. He'd like to speak with you. Sir." The young officer set his jaw, standing straighter as if bracing himself for impact.

Caitlin looked between the two of them, baffled but feeling the tiniest spark of hope. Maybe the Colonel would put a stop to this insanity.

Decker stalked out of the room, saying nothing. He snatched the com from the Lieutenant as he brushed past him. Sykes and the other officer followed, the door slamming shut behind them. Their departure left Caitlin and Vince alone.

"I'm sorry, Vince," she said tearfully. "I'm so sorry I got you into this."

Sagging against the wall, Vince grimaced. "No. I told them. St. Michaels. I told them where you'd go. They threatened to arrest Adelle, take the kids..."

Caitlin stared at him, a cold shock running through her. "God, Vince..."

"I'm sorry, Cait. I'm sorry," he whispered.

There was no way she could be angry with him. "You had to. Anyone would have done the same."

The fear receded, replaced with a fierce determination. She blinked back the tears. "I'm going to get us out of here."

CHAPTER 21

JACK LEFT THE INTERROGATION ROOM, wondering what the hell Isakovich wanted from him at this hour. He raised the com to his ear. "Decker here."

"You have exactly fifteen minutes to get your ass in my office, Captain."

"Can I ask what this is about, sir?" Jack asked, eyeing Hale. The young lieutenant stood stiffly in the corner, in a perfect parade rest, not letting his eyes fall on anything in particular.

Isakovich snapped back, "You know damn well what this is about."

Jack sent Hale a look that could have cut glass. Sykes looked about ready to tear the lieutenant limb from limb. Forcing himself to take a breath, Jack said into the com, "Sir, I suggest that we meet in an hour. I believe we're on the verge of a major breakthrough in the case, and—"

Isakovich didn't let him finish. "This isn't a discussion, Decker. Fifteen minutes, or I'm sending out a squad of MPs to bring you in. Are we clear?"

"Yes, sir." Jack said, and hung up. "Damn it!" They were so close! He knew Caitlin couldn't hold out much longer. If he stopped now, he would lose precious momentum, but Isakovich wasn't bluffing. Jack stepped up to Hale, getting in the young man's face. "Just who the hell do you think you are?"

Hale gulped, but didn't flinch. "This is wrong and you know it, sir. It was my duty to report it."

"Duty?" Jack scoffed. "What do you know about duty, you spineless little prick? Our duty is to stop these terrorists, whatever it takes."

Hale finally looked at him, his face ablaze with indignant anger. "Those people in there aren't terrorists! You're torturing two innocents!"

"Nobody here is innocent!" Sykes roared, pointing to the room. "That bitch attacked me, and they both let a known killer escape from their ambulance. They're in this up to their goddamn necks."

That caught Hale off-guard, but still he shook his head. "Even if they are, what you're doing is no better than the people you're trying to stop."

Scowling in disgust, Jack snapped. "Spare us your idealistic crap." He looked to Sykes. "I'll go smooth things over with Isakovich, and then we can get back to work."

Sykes nodded, but his reply was interrupted by Hale.

"Request permission to return to the Fort, Captain."

"Denied," Jack snapped. He wanted to talk to Isakovich alone, before Hale could do any further damage. "Wait downstairs. I'll deal with you when I get back." Hale turned and stalked downstairs without a word. Once he was gone, Jack said to Sykes, "Keep the pressure on Farland, but don't do any serious damage."

Sykes nodded, that sadistic smirk back again. "Yes, sir."

Jack cocked his head warily. "I'm serious, Sergeant. They can't tell us what we need to know from a hospital bed. We clear?"

The smirk turned somber. "Crystal."

Jack gave a satisfied nod. Sykes had a temper, and he didn't like the idea of leaving the prisoners alone with him. But a long reprieve would give them time to recover their determination and regain their strength, and that would undo all the progress he had already made. With any luck, by the time he returned Caitlin would be ready to tell him anything he wanted to know.

$$[[-\ast-]]$$

Eyeing the door, expecting the Peacekeepers to return at any moment, Caitlin tugged against her bonds. The zip ties dug painfully into her wrists, but she pulled and twisted against the back struts of the chair. Precious seconds ticked by, marked by her heart pounding in her ears. Finally, the plastic gave way. She was free.

Caitlin rubbed her sore wrists and rushed over to Vince, still hanging from the hook overhead. His chin touched his chest, his eyes closed.

"Vince, wake up," she hissed. "Come on, we're going to get out of here." He didn't respond at first, but she rubbed a knuckle hard across his breastbone until he stirred.

Caitlin dragged her chair over. "Stand on this. Lift your hands off the hook." She steered his feet onto the chair and held him steady while he struggled to straighten up and take the weight off the ropes binding his wrists. As soon as his hands cleared the hook, his knees buckled. His dead weight was too much for Caitlin to stop him from falling, and they both ended up in a heap on the floor. Caitlin winced as her injured ankle cracked against the concrete. Vince's eyes rolled back in his head.

"Vince? Wake up! Come on, wake up, please." She tried the sternal rub again, to no avail. "Damn it!" Now what? She wouldn't get past the Peacekeepers dragging him, and she'd be damned if she was going to leave him behind. Her eyes frantically scanned the room for options, but she could see only one: *Fight*. If she could take one of the soldiers by surprise and get his gun, she might be able to turn the tables on the others. But three soldiers versus one injured medic? She shuddered at the odds.

Caitlin scanned the room, desperate for anything she could use as a weapon. Decker had taken the stun stick with him, and only the table and chairs remained. She hefted her chair experimentally. It wasn't much, but it would have to do. A noise by the door caused her to jump. Heart in her throat, she hobbled over to stand to the side of it, flanking whoever came in.

The door opened, and a smug Sykes strode into the room. He jerked to a stop after just two steps, freezing when he saw Vince on the ground. His hand had just touched the butt of his pistol when Caitlin swung the chair with all her might. It thudded against his back, and Sykes went down in a heap. She hit him again while he was down. The cheap aluminum chair shattered to pieces in her hands, raining down onto Sykes' back. He grunted, stunned.

The commotion caused Vince to stir, rubbing his head with a soft groan.

"Vince! Get up!"

Sykes recovered faster than she expected. Turning and pushing himself off the ground, he launched himself at her midsection. Slipping past her feeble guard, the sergeant wrapped his burly arms around her legs. Next thing she knew, her feet had left the ground and Sykes was slamming her hard into the floor. Her head cracked against the tile hard enough to make her see stars, and the impact drove all the air from her lungs. Caitlin flailed out desperately with one arm, managing to rake her fingernails across Sykes' face. The sergeant barely flinched. He retaliated with a backhanded punch that nearly put the lights out.

Sykes pinned her arms, gripping hard enough to leave a bruise. His leaned down, his hot breath touching her cheek. "You're gonna pay for that."

A shape loomed behind Sykes. Vince had staggered to his feet. Snarling, he looped an arm around the sergeant's meaty neck, pulling him off Caitlin.

Caitlin rolled up onto her hands and knees, gasping for air. The room tilted like a ship on choppy seas.

Vince clung to the sergeant's neck with all he had. Sykes hammered at his arm ineffectually and tried to shift his legs for a hip throw, but nothing broke Vince's grip. The blows became weaker as Vince cut off the oxygen to Sykes' brain. Any second now, the sergeant would be out cold.

Caitlin saw Sykes reaching for his pistol. Time seemed to slow, and a sudden panic seized her when she realized what was about to happen. "No!" Fingers tightening around one of the broken chair legs, Caitlin charged toward the two men.

She wasn't fast enough. The pistol cleared the holster, and Sykes twisted it around behind him, against Vince's side. The booming sound of three gunshots in rapid succession felt like a bucket of ice water dumped over her head.

"Vince!" The strangled cry barely made it past her lips.

Vince staggered backward, looking down in shock at the bloodstain spreading across the lower half of his shirt. He met her gaze for just a moment, and she saw a wide-eyed panic. Then he toppled backwards.

Sykes hunched over, sucking in air like an asthmatic. He saw Caitlin coming and started to swing his gun to cover her. She closed the distance before he could aim, swinging the chair leg at his arm. She heard a satisfying crack, and Sykes howled in pain and dropped the gun. Caitlin threw her entire body behind another wild swing aimed at his face. It broke his nose and sent him reeling, but somehow the big soldier stayed on his feet.

Caitlin's eyes locked on Sykes' pistol, which had skittered under the table a few feet away. She dove for it. Her fingers closed around the handle just as Sykes grabbed her ankle. He pulled her out from under the table, his hand pulled back ready to strike.

A shocked realization filled his eyes when he saw her spin around with the pistol in her hand. He realized he was screwed an instant before she pulled the trigger. The gunshot boomed in the confines of the small room. Sykes jerked back, blood pumping from his neck in a horrifying spray. The strangled gurgling sound he made would haunt her nightmares. Sykes futilely clamped a hand over the wound. He slumped to the side, blood pooling under his head. It only took a few seconds for him to lose enough blood to pass out. A few more and he'd be dead. Caitlin scooted away from him in horror.

My God, what have I done?

As she stared slack-jawed at the dying Sykes, the door to the room burst open. The Peacekeeper lieutenant was there, eyes wide as he took in the bloody carnage of the room.

His pistol snapped up to Caitlin. "Drop the gun."

Caitlin hesitated, fear twisting her insides. Fear of what would happen to Vince if she didn't get him out of here. Fear of what Decker would do when he got back.

"Listen to me," the lieutenant continued, "What Decker's doing is out of line. Put down the weapon and I'll call an ambulance for your friend. Don't make this worse."

Searching his face, Caitlin saw an earnestness tinged with guilt, something she'd never seen from a Peacekeeper before. She believed him. But he was just a lieutenant. Could he really stand up against Decker? What other choice did she have?

A pair of gunshots rang out, and Caitlin jumped in fright. For an instant, she thought the lieutenant had double-crossed her, but then her brain registered that she wasn't hit. The officer, on the other hand, staggered forward and collapsed.

Struggling to process what was happening, Caitlin blinked as a figure appeared in the doorway. Shock and relief flooded through her. "Thank God," she breathed. "Alex..."

CHAPTER 22

ALEX SCANNED THE ROOM FOR threats, but saw only a bloody mess. His eyes widened, then narrowed to furious slits as he realized what had been going on here. "PK bastards," he muttered.

The relief on Caitlin's face was short-lived. She scrambled over to her unconscious partner, ripping open his T-shirt. "Vince, can you hear me?" She kept calling his name, wadding up the shirt and pressing it against his chest to staunch the heavy bleeding. "Vince, please…"

"Caitlin, we have to go." They didn't have much time. He'd heard the gunfire outside, and couldn't be the only one. More soldiers would be on the way. Caitlin didn't respond. Crossing the room, he clasped her arm. Even his light touch caused her to wince and pull away. He didn't want to think about what all the Peacekeepers had done to her. He repeated gently, "We have to go, Caitlin. Now."

"We can't leave him." Caitlin looked up at him, tears streaming down her face. "He's still alive—we have to get him to the hospital."

Alex shook his head. "We'd never make it. We have to leave him."

Caitlin clung to the makeshift bandages, still not moving. "No. I can't."

It wouldn't be much of a rescue if he had to drag her kicking and screaming from the building. Alex tried to think of a compromise. "One of them probably has a com. Call the ambulance." He could see her hesitating. "Caitlin, it's the best we can do. We can't take him with us. He needs more help than we can give. This is his only chance."

Caitlin finally nodded, pulling herself together with effort. "We have to take him outside." When Alex looked confused, she said, "They won't come inside until they're sure the scene is safe. I don't want them to waste any time. Please." Alex nodded, went to Vince's side and started to lever the paramedic into a fireman's carry. As he rose, grunting at Vince's weight, he noticed Caitlin standing over Sykes' body. She was staring at him in horror, afraid to go near him. "Caitlin, we don't have a lot of time. Get the com and let's go."

That seemed to snap Caitlin out of whatever she was thinking, and she crouched down beside him. Her features paled to a sickly color as she rooted through his pockets. Caitlin finally found Sykes' com. After a visible hesitation, she also picked up a pistol from the floor nearby.

Alex started for the door, wishing Vince weren't such a big guy. The weight put a strain on his still-healing shoulder, and he grimaced as he hurried downstairs. Caitlin limped along behind him.

"Where are we?" Caitlin asked. Alex gave her the address, and she dialed a number on Sykes' com. "Yes, I need an ambulance at 618 Hamilton Street." Her voice wavered brokenly. "My friend's not breathing. Please, you have to hurry!" She hung up as they reached the bottom of the stairs, wiping her eyes. The com buzzed quietly, probably the dispatcher trying to call her back, but Caitlin switched it off and tossed it aside.

A hallway at the bottom of the stairs led to the main exit. Without Alex having to prompt her, Caitlin opened the door a crack, peering outside. Alex watched her as she scanned the dark street, noting the intense concentration on her face. "It's clear," she announced.

Once outside, Alex lay Vince down carefully on the sidewalk. Blood drenched the paramedic's shirt, his skin ghastly pale. Alex didn't think he was going to make it, but he didn't have the heart to tell Caitlin that.

She bent down to squeeze Vince's hand, murmuring in his ear. "Hang on, Vince. Help's coming. I'm sorry. I'm so, so very sorry."

The pain in her voice was palpable, and Alex really felt for her. "We have to go. Come on."

This time, she let him take her hand. He helped her up, and they fled off into the night.

[[—＊—]]

Jack's footsteps echoed through the admin building, the only sound in the quiet corridor. He fought hard to restrain his indignant anger at having to come down here to justify his actions. Isakovich was a pencil-pushing lightweight who'd been hiding behind a desk for years. He had no idea how things really worked on Mars, and he didn't want to know. Like most Peacekeepers commanders, he had a history of looking the other way when his men stepped over the line. Only this time, Hale was making him take notice.

The light from Colonel Isakovich's office spilled into the dark hallway. Isakovich sat at his desk, intently studying something on his terminal. He looked up when Jack knocked on the inner office door, and his expression darkened in a severe frown. "You know why you're here, Captain?"

"I assume you got a call from Lieutenant Hale. Whatever he told you, sir, I can assure you there's a reasonable explanation."

"There sure as hell had better be," Isakovich snarled. He slammed a clipboard down on the desk. "Do you know who I just got off the com with?   The Bishop. Why? Because some damn local priest is up in arms about two of his parishioners being arrested. The same two paramedics you harassed the other day. What, Decker, do you think they're setting bombs at night and patching up their victims by day?" Jack opened his mouth to speak, but Isakovich cut him off with a wave of his hand. "And as if all that weren't enough, I've got your Lieutenant calling me up to tell me that you've got these two prisoners tied up in the back room of a warehouse somewhere? Just what in the hell do you think you're doing out there?"

Jack was taken aback. He wasn't surprised that the priest at St. Michael's had made a fuss about Caitlin, but how did the Bishop know about Vince? He never would have imagined that

Adelle Castellano would watch them haul off her husband and then jump right on the com with the family priest.

Conscious of Isakovich staring at him expectantly, Jack cleared his throat. "I did what I felt was necessary to recover that footage, sir. I believe your exact words were to do 'whatever it takes'."

Isakovich slammed a fist against his desk, rattling the pen holder and other knick knacks. His face reddened, a vein pulsing in his forehead. "It's a goddamn figure of speech, Captain! Kidnapping? Torture? What the hell were you thinking?" The Colonel let out a frustrated sigh. "You get results, Decker, and because of that I give you extra latitude. But this time you've gone too far. Hale's report—"

Jack ground his teeth together. "I can deal with Hale." He wasn't going to be outmaneuvered by some pissant Lieutenant.

"And the civilians?"

That was even easier, in Jack's eyes. "As far as anyone else knows, we've just detained Farland and her partner under the Internal Security Act. I've got enough to bury them both. Nobody's going to believe the word of two convicted terrorists."

Isakovich pondered that, and then pointed a finger at Jack. "Fine, but I want those two back here and in a proper cell within the hour. And I don't want to hear another word about you taking prisoners to that warehouse of yours. Understood?"

"Yes, sir." Jack decided not to push his luck for now.

"Clean up this mess, Decker. And for God's sake, be more discreet next time. I've got enough to deal with; I don't need this crap. Dismissed."

Jack saluted and left the office, both irritated and relieved. Farland would probably see the move here as some kind of moral victory, and would be even less inclined to talk. He would have to find some other way to get what he needed from her. He contemplated his options on the short walk back to the warehouse.

As he rounded the corner of Sixth and Hamilton, he saw red strobe lights splashing against the buildings up ahead. Stopping dead in his tracks, he was stunned to realize that the light was coming from an ambulance parked right in front of his warehouse. His first thought was that Sykes had gotten carried away and hurt one of the prisoners. But the Sergeant would have known better than to call an ambulance. What the hell was going on?

Breaking into a run, Jack quickly covered the distance to the scene, his gun at the ready. Two paramedics were loading a stretcher into the back of the ambulance as he approached. Intent on their work, they didn't notice him at first. He held up his badge and demanded, "What happened here?"

Both the medics looked frazzled, but the older one seemed on the verge of losing it. He bent over the patient, working with a palpable desperation. Jack realized that the man in the ambulance was Castellano.

It was the younger of the two who actually responded to Jack's question. His nametag read "Tierney". "No clue. We got a call for a man down and found one of our medics lying on the sidewalk. He's been shot."

Jack cursed under his breath. "Has anyone gone inside?"

"Hell, no. Could be some crazy-ass sniper in there for all we know. Dispatch said the MPs were on the way. Guess you're the first." Tierney closed the back doors on the ambulance and said something about heading over to the Med Center, but Jack wasn't listening. He was already on his way inside.

Jack moved up the stairs, his pistol and flashlight at the ready. Nothing, though, prepared him for what he saw when he opened the door to the upstairs office. There was blood splattered on the table, the chairs and the floor. Both the prisoners were gone, and one of the chairs in pieces. Lieutenant Hale had crumpled a few feet inside the doorway, and Sykes lay across the room, near the table.

Jack walked over to Sykes, staring down impassively at the sergeant's body and the staggering pool of blood surrounding him. Jack thought he should have felt more about the Sergeant's death. Though far from friends, they had worked together for years. Jack had come to depend on him more than anyone. But all he could think of now was how Sykes had failed him. He turned his rage on the nearby chair, kicking it across the room in frustration. "Goddamn it!"

A quiet moan came from behind him, and Jack was surprised to see that Lieutenant Hale was still alive. At the same time, he cursed his luck. Why did it have to be him, and not Sykes? Hale's eyes fluttered open, and his face immediately contorted in a grimace of pain. "He shot me," he croaked, sounding more shocked than anything.

Jack knelt down beside him. "Who did this?" When Hale didn't reply right away, Jack repeated the question, more harshly this time, "What the hell happened, Lieutenant?"

"It was him," Hale replied breathlessly. "The one from the bombing and the riot—'Ty'. Farland called him Alex. She knew him." He pulled open his shirt. A dark hole marked where a bullet had embedded in the young officer's protective vest. Another had struck his collarbone, just above the rim of the vest. Blood stained his undershirt as he fumbled with the straps.

Jack sat in stunned silence, his brain kicked into overdrive by Hale's revelation. They finally had a name for their suspect, and Caitlin had been working with him all along. The escape from the ambulance, her presence at the riot, taking the memory card… all the pieces seemed to fall together.

Hale's asked, "Are the medics on their way?" Jack leveled a cold stare at the young man. "Captain?"

"I ought to let you bleed out right here," Jack snapped. "Your petty crap has jeopardized this entire operation. You split up the team. You let the insurgents get the drop on you. Hell, your little call to the Colonel is probably how they knew how to find this place. The escaped prisoners; Sergeant Sykes' death—this is all on you."

Hale lifted his eyes, blazing with defiance. "I'm not the one who brought them here, Captain. If we were at the fort, none of this would have happened."

The lieutenant had grit, Jack had to give him that. Maybe he wasn't hopeless after all. Jack keyed his radio, "Citadel One to control. Alert the medics outside and the incoming squad that the building is secure." He then said to Hale, "Official word will be that we raided an insurgent safe house." Hale frowned, but Jack held up a finger to stave off his protest. "The Colonel's on board. Don't piss against the wind, Hale."

Jack glanced over to Sykes' body. "Remember who the real enemy is."

CHAPTER 23

ALEX AND CAITLIN HAD MADE it to the tunnels without running into any Peacekeeper patrols. He listened closely for sounds of pursuit, but the tunnels were quiet. It seemed they had made good their escape.

"We're under the residential district now," he whispered. Caitlin looked up instinctively at the rocks overhead. She was clearly in pain, probably exhausted, but she hadn't said a word of complaint the entire time. "There's a safe house. It's not much further."

True to Alex's word, they soon reached the ladder up to Second Avenue. Ten minutes later, they were in the building's lobby, riding the elevator up to their apartment. As the elevator carried them up, Alex took a moment to study Caitlin. A red mark on her cheek had already started to swell up, and her limp had gotten worse the farther they walked. She'd slumped against the wall of the elevator, radiating exhaustion, yet she hadn't said a word of complaint the entire time.

"Thank you," she said, noticing him staring. "I didn't really have a chance to say it before."

"You're welcome. I was glad to return the favor." Her brow creased in puzzlement, and Alex had to clarify. "When you helped me in the ambulance?"

"Oh. Right. God, that seems like forever ago." Shaking her head, she looked up at the ceiling and mumbled, "This morning seems like forever ago."

It had certainly been a hell of a day for all of them. The quiet ding of the elevator saved him from having to respond. He offered a hand to Caitlin, but she waved him off and limped along on her own.

Ben rose from the couch when Alex walked in the door. He looked like he might fall over at any moment, his features pale and gaunt. Samantha was hard work at her laptop, but she looked over long enough to offer a quick, worried smile.

There was no smile from Ben. He scrutinized Caitlin, a severe frown on his face, and then turned his glare on Alex. "I didn't think you'd have the nerve to come back after pulling a stunt like that."

Alex lifted his chin, catching Caitlin's concerned frown out of the corner of his eye. "Sam, why don't you take Caitlin and help her get cleaned up." Samantha nodded and led Caitlin into the back bedroom, leaving Alex and Ben alone.

"I did what I had to," Alex said, meeting Ben's gaze head-on. "They would have killed her."

"This isn't a damn social club," Ben spat back. "We don't run things by committee. You risked our entire operation. You didn't even think about what you might be getting yourself into. Getting *us* into! What if it had been a set up? You just blindly bring her back here—"

"It wasn't a set up!" Alex interjected. "And I didn't blindly do anything. You didn't see what was going on there, Ben." He pointed to the bloodstains on his jacket from carrying Vince. "This is exactly the kind of thing we're fighting to stop."

Ben seethed with quiet fury, barely raising his voice. "No, what we're fighting for is independence for an entire damn *planet*. You have to start looking at the bigger picture." The condescension in his voice only infuriated Alex further. "It's more important than you, or me, or some pretty girl you want to rescue."

"No, it isn't!" Alex countered. "You talk about the war like it's some grand game, but you're playing with people's *lives!* Lives that you seem a little too eager to sacrifice." Alex's mouth twisted in a grim frown, realizing that this went beyond Caitlin's rescue. "How many people were killed today, because of what we did? Our own supporters! Caitlin put her ass on the line for us. She deserved our help."

His words fell on deaf ears. "That wasn't your decision to make. I'm the leader of this cell. I give the orders." Ben lowered his voice, and there was a dangerous edge to it. "If you ever try anything like this again, you're out. Understood?"

Alex clenched his jaw, stung. He never thought he'd see the day when Ben would threaten him like that.

Ben seemed satisfied by his silence, and eased off a little. "You need to learn to accept that sometimes there are sacrifices we have to make. She's an outsider, Alex. She's not one of us."

"She is now," Alex said.

$$[[-\ast-]]$$

Caitlin overheard snatches of the argument through the bedroom door, wondering what she'd gotten in the middle of now. She wanted nothing more than to collapse for a week, but it seemed like she had to keep her guard up even among her potential allies. She realized that Samantha was talking to her, and forced herself to pay attention.

"My stuff's probably too small, but Julio's might fit." There was a sad note in Samantha's voice as she rummaged through the drawers.

The older man didn't strike her as a "Julio". "How many of you are there?" Caitlin wondered.

"Just the three of us now. Julio…" the young woman's voice faltered, and she swallowed before continuing, "He was killed today."

"At the rally?" When Samantha nodded, Caitlin said quietly, "I'm sorry."

Samantha just nodded once more, wiping away tears before they could fall. "Here, try these," she said abruptly, changing the subject. "The bathroom's out in the hall." She handed Caitlin a bundle of clothes and left her alone.

Caitlin felt that she should have said something more, but her own grief was still a hollow ache inside of her. She found the bathroom and turned on the water in the sink. Cool water coursed over her hands as she solemnly scrubbed away Vince's blood. She kept telling herself that she had no choice but to leave him, but nothing helped to ease the gnawing guilt and worry. She'd abandoned him, just as she'd abandoned Tom in the square. Now she didn't even know if he was all right. *He had to be*, Caitlin thought desperately. She couldn't lose him, too.

Caitlin splashed some water on her face, struggling against tears, and looked at herself in the mirror. Seeing the bruises, the haggard exhaustion and sorrow, it was like looking at a stranger. The clothes Samantha gave her didn't fit very well, but she rolled up the sleeves and pants and made do. In the process, she was treated to the sight of a very bruised and swollen ankle. Caitlin moved it experimentally, wincing at the sharp pain, and left the borrowed shoes off until she could tend to it.

Sykes' pistol sat on the shelf where she'd left it. Caitlin picked up the weapon like it was a snake that might bite her. She'd killed a man with that gun. The sheer horror of the thought made it hard for the reality to sink in. She and Vince would likely be dead if she hadn't, but her conscience didn't care. She wanted to throw it away and never see it again, but a horrible dread told her she might need it again. Yesterday she'd never even fired a gun, but now she didn't dare go anywhere without one.

Returning to the bedroom, Caitlin laid her pistol on the nightstand and she sat down one of the twin beds. Her eyes stared blankly at the wall, but her mind was still back in the warehouse. Over and over again, the events played out in her head. She didn't dare close her eyes for fear of what she might see in her dreams.

A short while later there was a quiet knock at the door. Alex stepped inside, a frustrated look on his face.

"Your boss—he didn't want you coming after me, did he?" Caitlin asked.

"It's all right," Alex assured her. "Ben and I don't always see eye to eye."

"Well… thanks for not listening to him."

Alex offered a quick shrug. "He'll get over it. He just doesn't trust strangers."

Caitlin looked up, a worried frown creasing her brow. "Does he want me to leave?" The possibility frightened her. She had nowhere else to go.

"No. You can stay here for a few days at least. After that— we'll work something out." Alex moved closer. "Are you all right? We have a doctor we can call."

"I'm fine," Caitlin said automatically, though she was conscious of just how far that was from the truth. Her body ached from a dozen bruises, but none of them seemed serious. "My ankle got the worst of it, but I don't think it's broken." The mention of a doctor spurred a sudden idea. "Your doctor—can he find out how Vince is? I can't stand not knowing if he's okay." No matter how much she feared the answer, being in the dark was a torture all its own.

Alex nodded. "I'll send him a message." He reached under the second bed and drew out a bag stuffed with medical supplies. Setting it down beside her, he rooted around until he found an athletic bandage. "Here, let me wrap your ankle." He knelt down and began to do so, quickly and confidently. Though he was as gentle as possible, she winced at a sharp twinge.

"There are some pain pills in the side pocket there," Alex told her. "Low dose—takes the edge off but keeps your head clear."

"Thanks," Caitlin murmured. She found the pills, noted the dosage, and downed two of them dry. As she tucked the bottle back into its pocket, she observed, "Not so different from the jump bag we have in the ambulance." Reality hit her like a punch in the stomach, and she whispered, "I won't be able to go back."

Alex pinned the wrap in place and sat back on the other bed, opposite her. He shook his head, a sympathetic look on his face. "No, you won't."

Caitlin looked around the sparse bedroom, struggling to take it all in. Was this her life now? Hiding out in an anonymous apartment, running from the Peacekeepers? She had nothing—no photographs, no mementos. She wouldn't be able to talk to her father again, or to Vince, or anyone else she knew. The loneliness hit her like a wave, so powerful she could barely catch her breath.

"I want my life back." As much as she wanted to put on a brave face, she couldn't stop the tears stinging her eyes.

"Caitlin," Alex's voice was gentle. "The life you knew is over."

Caitlin shook her head, a painful tightness in her throat. "There has to be some way…" But even as she said it, she knew it was impossible. She was in too deep.

Alex didn't say anything at first, letting her come to the inevitable conclusion on her own. When he saw the defeat registering on her face, he asked, "Could you really go back? After what you've seen? What they've done to you, your friend—all those people they murdered at the riot?"

He had a point. Things would never be the same after this. Even if the Peacekeepers weren't after her—how could she possibly pick up the pieces? Tom was gone. After what had happened tonight, Vince and Adelle would never speak to her again. What did she really have to go back to?

Still, a part of her resisted. "I didn't choose this life. I could have. I had plenty of opportunities. My father… he was with the rebels. Max tried to recruit me after Dad went to jail." Caitlin swallowed. "I didn't want it. I didn't want to end up like them."

"You did choose, Caitlin," Alex replied evenly. "You cut off my zip-ties with a dozen Peacekeepers standing less than ten feet away."

Caitlin stared at him. "So you're saying I brought this on myself." The worst part was that she believed it herself.

"I'm saying you chose a side. You did what you knew was right." Alex spoke with the same passion she'd heard in her father's voice a million times. "We need people like you, Caitlin. You've shown your strength, your determination. I saw it the first time I met you. It's in your blood."

"I'm not a killer, Alex."

"You killed Sykes, didn't you?" There was no accusation in his voice; it was a simple statement of fact.

All she could see was Sykes' gurgling form writhing on the ground. She closed her eyes against the terrible image, feeling queasy, but it didn't help. It was still there, burned into her brain. "That was different," she insisted desperately.

"It was self-defense. I understand." Alex's mouth curled downward. "But believe me, Caitlin, that doesn't make it any easier. Despite what the Peacekeepers say, we're not all cold-blooded murderers."

Caitlin frowned as well. "I didn't mean…"

"We're soldiers. Maybe we can't put on uniforms and meet them on the battlefield, but that doesn't change the fact that we're waging a war against an incredibly powerful enemy." He paused. "There's no shame in fighting for your home."

Killing for your home—that's what he really meant. Caitlin swallowed hard, and admitted, "I don't know if I could do that again. Take another life."

"I know," Alex said quietly. "And it doesn't get any easier." He shook his head grimly. "If you don't want to join us, we can help you get away. Set you up on Earth with a new identity. Somewhere out of the Federation's grip."

"Run and hide?" Caitlin scoffed.

"You'd be safe, with some precautions. You could lead a normal life."

Caitlin tried to imagine herself just getting up and going to work every morning; hanging out at the bar with the guys. The images of normalcy seemed so jarring. She shook her head. "I can't. Those bastards killed my husband; they tortured my best friend. I can't just walk away from that. They want to make sure that video never sees the light of day..."

Her voice trembled with a determined fury. "I'm going to shout it from the damn rooftops."

CHAPTER 24

JACK STARED AT THE MAP on his office wall, a half-empty cup of cold coffee in his hand. He had been staring at it for half an hour, but was no farther along than when he'd started. Alex and Caitlin were out there somewhere. He just had to anticipate their next move.

A footfall in the doorway drew his attention as Lieutenant Hale strode in. His right arm was in a sling, and the dark circles under his eyes mirrored Jack's.

Jack frowned. "I thought they discharged you back to the barracks to rest."

"They did. But I'll be more use here." Hale stood stiffly in the doorway, braced for a challenge.

Squinting at the young officer, Jack sipped his disgusting coffee to give himself a minute to think. The events of last night aside, Hale had promise. He was sharp, diligent. If he could be cured of his naive idealism, he could be useful. "Tell me why I shouldn't have the colonel transfer you back to Earth."

"Because you need me." Hale glanced around the empty office for emphasis. "And because I want to catch these people. Edwards, Sykes, the others…they all deserve justice, and we can stop the rebels from hurting someone else. I just want to do it the right way."

Jack put down the mug. "Hale, this is asymmetric warfare. They don't fight fair. They use ambushes, assassinations, intimidation, lies—weaponized fear. Sometimes fighting them means getting down in the mud with them. If you can't live with that, then go home. Or take a posting to the MPs, or admin. Somewhere you don't have to make the tough calls."

"Captain, I'm not an idiot," Hale insisted, adjusting the strap on his sling. "I understand tough calls. But there are some lines we shouldn't cross. Castellano's in critical care because we crossed them, and I don't think he had anything to do with this." Jack started to open his mouth, but Hale headed him off. "And don't give me that 'collateral damage' crap. That's the rebels' justification. We're better than that."

Jack's lips thinned, considering Hale's words. At least the kid had convictions. Time would tell how they'd hold up after more than a few days of seeing the depths the resistance would sink to. And he did have a point about Jack's lack of manpower. "Pull up a chair, Hale." The lieutenant, relaxing, came closer to the wall map. "I've been analyzing the insurgent movements."

Jack pointed to some markers, one by one. "This is Alex's path after the bombing. The shaded zone is where their hacker blacked out the street cams that night. City maintenance reported finding blood on a tunnel ladder here this morning." At the last report, he tapped the map with his pen. "Lab's still running the evidence, but I'd put money on it being our targets. See any pattern?"

Hale stared at map, frowning thoughtfully. "It's all concentrated on these few blocks in the residential district," he said finally, motioning with his good arm. "You think it's their safe house?"

Jack nodded. "I'm thinking it's probably one of these buildings here." He tapped the map again. "The apartments on the fringes are closer to the warehouse district. Easier to get things in and out there. It's mostly working-class people. Less security. Street cams always going down."

"There have to be hundreds of apartments in that area, though," Hale observed dubiously.

"At least a thousand, probably."

"That's like a needle in a haystack." Hale snorted. "What do we do? Set up surveillance and hope for the best?"

Jack shook his head. "The MPs leak like a sieve. And if we put out more patrols, our targets are bound to find out and pick up stakes." *If they haven't already.* Jack shoved that grim thought to the back of his mind. "No, the way we find them is good old-fashioned legwork. So let's get to it."

[[—✳—]]

Caitlin didn't think she'd be able to sleep, but when she finally jolted awake in the safe house bedroom, her watch told her it was almost noon. Samantha's bed was already made and the young woman nowhere in sight. The boys had slept in the living room, and Caitlin could hear soft voices coming through the wall. Caitlin took a minute in the bathroom and then limped out to join them.

Ben was sitting on the couch, and someone with curly black hair knelt on the floor beside him. The new arrival turned to put a stethoscope away in a black satchel, and Caitlin saw his face. She stared for a moment, before realizing aloud, "Doctor Ross?" Alex had told her the rebels had a doctor, but she hadn't expected it to be one of the ER docs.

Noah Ross cast a quick grin over his shoulder. "Miss Farland. Good to see you up and about."

"You two know each other?" Ben asked, his eyes narrowing at Caitlin.

"Just professionally," Noah replied easily. "I know most of the medics, but Farland's one of the best."

Was. Her current situation made her mentally correct him. Caitlin remembered the last time she had seen Noah, frantically juggling multiple serious patients in the ER on the day of the riot. Vince had been there, too, which made her blurt, "Is Vince all right?"

Noah's brow creased. "I got Alex's message, but I don't have any details, sorry. I wasn't on last night, and it would raise red flags if I started asking around randomly or dug into the records. My shift's this afternoon, so I'll check on him then."

Waiting that long for news made Caitlin want to scream, but he was right about the risks. She forced herself to say, "Thanks."

Alex came out of the kitchen, drying his hands on a towel. "The fact that there's nothing on the news is a good sign. They're trying to bury it, which would be harder if he'd died."

Somehow that didn't reassure her. What if their way of burying the truth was to lock Vince away somewhere and throw away the key? What would happen to Adelle and Zac? Guilt smacked her like a two-by-four.

"I'll keep you posted as soon as I have some news," Noah promised gently. "Now, how about you let me take a look at that ankle? Alex said you banged it up pretty good."

Caitlin submitted to Noah's exam. He waved a scanner over her foot, frowning at the swelling, and cleaned up the gash on her arm. An injection of antibiotics was her reward for not getting it tended to right away.

Noah put a fresh dressing on her arm and re-wrapped her ankle. "Doesn't look broken, but this scanner's not sensitive enough to pick up really small fractures. Try to rest it and ice it as much as you can." He rose, packing up his satchel and admonishing Ben, "You need to take it easy, too. Give your lung time to heal. At least you've got a medic here to keep an eye on you." Ben didn't look thrilled.

Noah headed for the door. "Try to be careful. I think you guys have had enough house calls this week."

Alex snickered. "We'll try." He thanked the doctor, who then saw himself out.

Once Noah had gone, Samantha emerged from the kitchen with a plate bearing an omelette. "You missed breakfast, but I whipped this up for you." Caitlin took the plate, murmuring her thanks. As she started eating, she noticed Ben staring at her.

"Alex says you have proof that the Peacekeepers are covering up what happened in the square?" Ben asked.

"I have the footage from the Chronicle camera crew. They were right up front when..." Caitlin's voice faltered. "They saw it all."

"How did you get it?"

"I just took it," Caitlin whispered. She stared at the plate, but her mind was seeing Tom's broken body in the square. "I found Tom and Harry in the square…" She swallowed hard, fighting to get the story out. "I saw their camera, and I knew the Peacekeepers would try to use it somehow. Twist it. I couldn't let them do that."

"Tom." Alex echoed the name. Caitlin looked up and saw a flicker of realization in his face. "The reporter at the square—he was your husband." Caitlin sucked in a breath, forcing herself to nod. Alex murmured, "I'm sorry." Samantha echoed the sentiment.

Ben did not. "What were you planning on doing with it?"

Caitlin shrugged. "I don't know. I didn't really have a plan, I just didn't want them to have it." She set aside her half-eaten omelette, robbed of her appetite. "It seems kind of stupid now. I should have known they'd be transmitting and the Chronicle would have its own copy." If she hadn't grabbed that storage card, none of this would have happened. She wouldn't be on the run, Vince would be all right…

Alex must have guessed what she was thinking. "It's good you did, though. Now we have a better chance of holding them accountable. If we show what the PKs cut out from the Chronicle footage they already released, it's going to make them look like asses."

"Yeah, but how do we get the word out?" Caitlin found herself replaying all the scenarios she'd considered and rejected before she'd approached Rachel.

Ben shook his head. "First things first. We need to get the video. I assume you didn't have it on you when they grabbed you."

"No, I hid it in the ambulance." Seeing their alarm, she said, "Don't worry. It's in a compartment nobody uses. They won't find it."

"I don't know," Alex ventured. "Decker might guess you hid it in the ambulance or the station and tear the place apart. We shouldn't take any chances." Everyone agreed, then Alex paused thoughtfully. "It would be great if we could get something else to support it. Show the extent of the cover-up."

"What about the medical records?" Samantha suggested. "We could prove how many people were really hurt and what happened to them. I could try to get access to the database..."

"The Med Center's not connected to MarsCom," Caitlin pointed out. "The hospital has its own internal network."

Chatter broke out, discussing their options. Noah was the obvious choice, until Caitlin told them that it would leave an electronic paper trail that would surely lead to him being compromised. They continued brainstorming, until suddenly the bolt of an idea made Caitlin sit up straighter.

"What about the ambulance records?" she suggested. When everyone just stared at her questioningly, she explained, "We have our own patient records, separate from the hospital. It won't count the ones who bypassed EMS and walked over, but it'll cover most of the serious cases."

Ben considered for a moment. "Can you get to them from here?"

"No, but I can access them from the station. We have to go back there for the memory card anyway."

More debate ensued. They could get the storage card while the ambulance was out on a call, but the records would require a trip into the station itself. Something the Peacekeepers might anticipate.

Ben made the final decision. "It's worth the risk. Alex, you and Caitlin can head over there tonight and get the video and the records."

Caitlin nodded, but found herself filled with trepidation at the thought of heading back to the fire house, and the life that now felt so far away.

$$[[-*-]]$$

Jack and Hale spent all day digging through records and video footage. Jack had even ventured out to the scene of the tunnel report, hoping that he might gain some insight just by seeing the place. The ladder, marked with bloody handprints, had to have been the work of Alex and Caitlin. But where had they gone afterward?

Hale came into the office with a bag of sandwiches from the mess hall just as Jack finished skimming yet another batch of reports from the housing authority. "Anything?" the young lieutenant asked, hoping Jack had made some breakthrough while he was fetching dinner.

Jack tossed his pen down on the desk in frustration. "No. Still sifting through records from the Bradbury apartments."

After handing Jack a sandwich, Hale sat back down at his terminal. "The facial recognition scans I ran should be about done," Hale said. A few one-handed keystrokes brought them up on the central wall monitor, and faces began flashing across the screen. "These are from street cams on the days of the bombing, the riot, and the escape last night. Coverage inside the zone of interest is spotty, so I also included the streets heading into and out of the zone."

"Good thinking," Jack admitted. He unwrapped his sandwich and began munching as he watched the parade of faces. Halfway through his ham and cheese, he sat up straighter in his chair. "Hang on. Go back one. No, one more."

The screen paused on a man, maybe forty, with curly black hair and a serious expression. He carried a black satchel, and the camera had caught him looking over his shoulder. "I've seen him before." He noticed that the man was wearing scrub pants, and it clicked. "He's one of the docs at the Med Center."

Hale read the timestamp for the picture on the screen. "This was taken an hour after the riot."

"All the docs would've been recalled to the Med Center for the mass casualty event, yet here he is, heading into a shady section across town. And he's got a satchel. Medical kit, maybe?"

"You think he was making a house call?" Hale reasoned.

"Maybe. We know Holstrom was hit in the square. Someone must have taken care of him."

Hale pressed a few more keys, and two other images of the doctor appeared. "He turns up in all three of our time windows."

"Alex was shot after the bombing. Holstrom in the riot. Farland was limping when we picked her up. It tracks." Jack rose and grabbed his pistol, abandoning his sandwich. "Keep digging. Send me whatever you can find on this guy to my com."

"Where are you going?"

"To have a chat with our mysterious doctor," Jack explained on his way out the door.

A short walk took him over to Lafayette Medical Center. Jack had seen the guy in the emergency department, so he started there. He flashed his badge to get the desk clerk's attention, then brought up the man's picture on his com and asked if she knew him.

"Doctor Ross? Yeah, I think he's over in trauma room two."

Jack thanked her, then started in the direction she'd pointed. The doctor from the picture stepped into the corridor right in front of him. He mumbled an 'excuse me', and seemed puzzled when Jack didn't move. Jack held up his badge. "Doctor Ross. I'm Captain Decker, counter-terrorism taskforce. I need you to come with me." From the way all color drained from the doctor's face, Jack knew they had their man.

And he would lead them to the others.

$$[[-\!\ast\!-]]$$

Unlike Farland, Noah Ross proved easy to crack once they had him in an interrogation room in the fort. However squeamish Hale might have been about their methods at the warehouse, he put on a good act with Ross. He convinced the doctor that their flimsy suspicions were actually a mountain of hard evidence. Coupled with threats of prolonged interrogation and jail, Ross crumpled like a wet blanket. In just a few hours, they had the names of Alex's cell, and—more importantly—the location of their safe house.

Now, Jack crouched behind a shrub at the mouth of the alley between two apartment buildings. Around him, the ten men from Captain Cerulli's squad waited impatiently along the wall. Decked out in their assault gear, their rifle barrels glinting in the moonlight, they looked like an impressive strike team. But these were also the same trigger-happy idiots that had opened fire at the riot, and that didn't fill Jack with confidence. He wished he had his own team, but with Sykes dead and Hale on desk duty from his injury, he'd gone from short-handed to no-handed. He had no choice but to rely on the MPs.

"All right, everyone, remember the plan," Cerulli said. He acted as if it were his plan, rather than Jack's, but Jack just frowned and let him have his moment. "Captain Decker and I will take Alpha Team up to breach. Bravo, you've got the lobby and the alley covering the fire escape." The latter had been added at Jack's insistence, remembering how Farland had escaped from him before.

"Weapons free, sir?" asked one of the corporals, wondering if they were authorized to fire without following the usual 'shoot only if they shoot first' rules of engagement.

Jack pre-empted Cerulli's response, "Yes, but remember we need Farland alive." If the storage card wasn't in the apartment, he needed Caitlin to tell him where it was—and who else knew about it. "These are dangerous terrorists, and they'll be heavily armed."

Cerulli nodded, fixing the squad with a grim stare. "These bastards killed our friends. None of them walk away from this."

CHAPTER 25

"SO THIS IS WHAT YOU do all day, huh?" Caitlin asked, a smirk creeping across her face as picked up the cards Alex had dealt. They sat opposite each other at the small kitchen table, killing time until they could venture out to the ambulance station to retrieve the video. Glancing at her watch, she saw it was nearly midnight. They'd be heading out soon. Barring a late-night emergency call, all of the firefighters would be asleep by then. Samantha and Ben were in the living room, the former lounging on the couch with her tablet and the latter refusing to get the rest Noah had ordered.

"Sometimes," Alex admitted, arranging his own hand of cards. He grinned. "Why? Not as glamorous as you'd imagined?"

"I don't know what I imagined." Caitlin's smile faded as she let her eyes drift across the room. "My dad had a job, a life at home… it wasn't like this."

Alex shrugged. "People chip in different ways. Like Noah. His job actually puts him in a better position to help. Not just his medical skills, obviously, but being able to sneak things into and out of the hospital."

"Yeah. I still can't get over him being involved in this. I've seen him at the hospital dozens of times… I had no idea."

"I bet he's thinking the same thing about you," Alex pointed out.

A pensive frown settled on Caitlin's face. She said nothing as she exchanged a few of her cards.

Alex understood; she still didn't consider herself to be "involved"—not like the rest of them. "Look, Caitlin, I know you didn't ask for any of this. Once we figure out what to do with the video, we can still help you start fresh somewhere. I mean, if that's what you want. But I hope you'll stay with us."

Was he being selfish, encouraging her to join this dangerous life? No doubt she'd be safer fleeing to Earth, but Alex had never met anyone quite like her. Tough, smart, passionate. He didn't know many people would risk so much for a total stranger, as she had.

Tilting his head, he wondered, "You never thought about it before? Joining the cause? There's obviously no love lost between you and the PKs, after what happened to your father."

"There isn't, no," Caitlin admitted. She chewed on the question for a minute while arranging her cards, then said, "But when my dad was arrested, I was as mad at him as I was at the Peacekeepers. I'd already lost my mom, and he didn't stop to think about what would happen to me if he got caught. For a while I thought maybe he just didn't give a crap." The remembered pain practically radiated across the table. "I didn't think I could ever forgive him for that. Following in his footsteps wasn't high on my list."

Alex nodded, feeling a pang of sympathy. "Did you two ever work things out?"

"More or less, yeah. They wouldn't let me visit him, but we send messages. He blamed the Federation for the mining accident that killed my mom. He wanted to hurt them; make things better for me. I could understand that. I wanted the Federation gone as much as anyone, I just…" She trailed off uncertainly.

Laying down a pair of jacks, Alex said, "It's hard to cross that line from sympathizing to active rebellion. Putting everything you have on the line. Most people never make that leap."

"It's not just that, though." Caitlin hesitated before venturing, "You remember six years ago—there was an explosion in one of the transit tubes?"

Alex frowned. "I remember. It wasn't us, but I heard about it. They were trying to hit a troop transport, but something went wrong. A dozen civilians killed."

"Fourteen. Our ambulance was first on scene. Pulling people out." Her throat bobbed, eyes haunted. "Then pulling bodies out. One of them was a little boy." Voice hushed, she said, "Getting the truth out about what happened yesterday is one thing, but I don't think I could be a part of anything like that."

Alex put the cards down, the game forgotten. His face turned grim. "I know. That day hit all of us hard. That's not what we're about." He sighed. "But no matter how careful we are, we can't always control what happens. A bad timer, a stray shot, someone in the wrong place at the wrong time… it's a war, and people get hurt."

Lips drawing together, Caitlin said, "That's a poor excuse for killing an eight-year-old boy."

"It's not an excuse," Alex insisted. "There is no excuse for killing an innocent. Just like there's no excuse for the PKs shooting your friend, or ruining your life, or killing all those people in the square."

"That sounds like some 'both sides' justification crap to me."

"Maybe. But you know the difference between us and them?" When Caitlin shrugged, he went on, "When we screw up, we own it. We feel guilty. We care. The PKs would gladly sacrifice anyone and everyone on Mars without batting an eye."

Caitlin didn't argue with him. Instead she asked, "What made you take the leap into helping?"

"I was in grad school, and the advisory committee decided my thesis was too 'controversial'." He made air quotes with his fingers.

"What was it about?"

"Parallels between the exploitation of the Mars colony by the Federation and the American colonies by the British Empire."

Caitlin snickered. "Yeah, I'll bet that went over well with the university admin."

Alex made a face. "Pompous asses." He hitched a shoulder. "I raised a fuss, which got me invited to a MLS meeting. Eventually someone introduced me to Ben. He can be pretty persuasive." He didn't blame Caitlin for arching a skeptical brow. She'd only seen Ben's stern, suspicious side. "Give him a chance. Paranoia is an occupational hazard. He'll warm up once he gets to know you."

"*You* don't even know me," Caitlin pointed out mildly.

"Fair enough. But I figure saving each others' asses goes a long way." He smirked.

A soft ding, not unlike a doorbell, sounded in the living room. Alex had long ago learned to tune out Samantha's early warning alarm; the damn thing got triggered every time one of their neighbors came home. This time, though, was different.

"Oh my God," Samantha cried from the living room. "Peacekeepers in the stairwell."

Alex and Caitlin looked at each other, jolted by adrenaline. Alex was on his feet in an instant, heading for the living room. Caitlin trailed close behind. Samantha had her surveillance camera feed up on the wall-mounted MarsCom unit, giving them all a split-screen view showing a team of Peacekeepers in full tactical gear heading up the stairwell, with more guarding the lobby.

Samantha was already gathering up essentials and stuffing them into her backpack. Alex beelined for the coffee table and hauled out a duffel bag of weapons.

"How did they find us?" Samantha asked.

Ben's eyes narrowed suspiciously at Caitlin, but Alex headed him off before he could comment. "Doesn't matter. We've got to move." Even if he hadn't seen what the Peacekeepers had done at the warehouse, the wide-eyed look of panic on Caitlin's face when she heard the warning told him she had no part in this.

Alex started handing out submachine guns from the bag. Ignoring Ben's frown, he held one out to Caitlin. She took a half-step back, uncertain. Alex didn't blame her for the reluctance. It was one thing to defend herself in the heat of the moment; actively taking up arms against the Federation was another level. He handed the weapon to Samantha instead.

"I'll get the back door open," Samantha offered, heading for the back bedroom.

"Cait, go give her a hand," Alex said. He checked his weapon and slipped it over his shoulder.

Caitlin's brows knitted in alarm when he took a pair of grenades out of the pack. "What are you going to do?"

"Slow them down a bit. Go on through. We'll be right behind you." With that assurance, Caitlin took off after Samantha. Alex frowned at Ben. "You should go with them. You're in no condition to fight." The older man could barely stand.

"I'll set the door charge," Ben acted as if Alex hadn't said anything, his jaw set in a determined line. "Let's give those bastards a surprise."

[[—✳—]]

Jack's team moved up the west stairwell. He heard the sharp clang of something metal hitting the stairs above them. It bounced, hitting several more times before finally coming to rest on the landing. Even in the dim light of the stairwell, Jack recognized the object immediately.

"Grenade!" he shouted, diving to the side. He hit the stairs with a jarring thud, banging both shins on a sliding skid down to next landing. Behind him, the grenade exploded with a series of deafening booms. The stairwell lit up brighter than daylight.

It was just a flash-bang. Jack got to his feet, nursing bruised legs and bruised pride. His ears were ringing. Around him, his team also picked themselves off the ground, disoriented. The trooper who'd been closest to the grenade lay on the top step, cradling his head.

A second grenade went off just after the first. This one emitted a shower of sparks and then started gushing a thick, white smoke. It quickly filled the stairwell, stinging Jack's eyes.

"They've made us," Cerulli announced needlessly. "Keep moving! We need to secure that hallway."

Jack grabbed the soldier nearest him, giving him a light shove upstairs. "Go! Go! Go!"

[[—∗—]]

Caitlin followed Samantha into the back bedroom, convinced she was about to do another leap off a fire escape. Her ankle twinged just thinking about it. She certainly hadn't seen a real back door, but then Samantha had surprised her by opening the closet. Pushing aside some coats, the young woman pulled up a rug to reveal a ragged hole cut into the floor. Samantha crouched and reached into it.

"Where's that go?" Caitlin wondered.

"Empty apartment downstairs," Samantha replied absently, grunting with the effort of fiddling with something Caitlin couldn't see. "Just need to get the ceiling tile out of the… there!"

They both jumped as a series of bangs reverberated through the walls.

"Flashbangs," Samantha explained, lips thinning. "We don't have long." She shoved her backpack through the hole in the floor and dropped down.

Caitlin made sure her pistol was secure in her zippered jacket pocket before following. The landing sent a jolt of pain up her ankle, and she just stood still for a moment, wincing. The apartment below must have had a different layout, for they came down in a bedroom. From the knick-knacks and photos on the dresser, and the mussed bedsheets, it was clear someone lived here.

"I thought you said it was empty?" Caitlin whispered.

"It *was*."

The bedroom door opened, and Samantha's weapon jerked up as a frowning man in a robe walked in. He took two steps before he saw them and froze, his eyes going wide. "Who are you? What do you want?" His eyes drifted past them to the hole in the ceiling.

"We're not going to hurt you," Caitlin assured him. She pointed to the living room couch. "Just go sit down."

The man acted like he was going to comply, Caitlin and Samantha following him into the other room. Suddenly he bolted for the front door.

"Stop!" Samantha trained her weapon on the man.

"Don't shoot him!" Caitlin shouted. Ignoring the pain in her ankle, she ran to intercept him at the door. He had just started to open it when she slammed into him, using their combined body weight to pin the door closed. The impact smacked his face against the door jamb.

Samantha came up behind them, jamming the barrel of her submachine gun against his temple. "Sit your ass down." The stern order seemed incongruous coming from the mousey young woman's mouth, but there was no mistaking the menace in the words. Holding up his hands in surrender, the man complied. As he sat shakily on the couch, Caitlin saw blood trickling from his nose.

She winced, guilt washing over her. How many other innocent people would get hurt by all of this? Chewing her lip, Caitlin stared up at the ceiling.

Come on, Alex. Where are you?

[[—✳—]]

After lobbing his grenades down the stairs, Alex raced back to the apartment. Ben closed the door behind him, then clipped a few wires into place to act as a tripwire for the block of plastic explosive taped to the back of the door.

"That should buy us a minute," Alex said. Grabbing his "bug-out" backpack, ready for just such an emergency evacuation, he headed for the back bedroom.

"Help me move this in front of the bedroom door." Ben was already pushing the sofa over.

Alex hesitated, confused, then lent his weight to the end of the furniture. His eyes flicked to the screen, which showed the Peacekeepers beginning to recover. "This isn't going to slow them down."

"It's not for them," Ben declared flatly. "It's for me."

"What?" Alex just stared in confusion.

Ben dropped the duffel of weapons on the floor behind the couch, ready to use it as cover. "I'll keep them busy for as long as I can."

Confusion turned to dread as Alex realized Ben's plan. "Come on, Ben, that's crazy—"

Ben cut him off. "I'm only going to slow you down. This will give you time to get out."

"Fuck that," Alex snapped. "I'll carry you out of here if I have to."

"We don't have time to debate this, Alex." Ben pointed to the screen, where the soldiers were beginning to advance up the hallway. "You're in charge now. Get the girls and get out of here." He paused a moment before giving Alex's arm a somber clap. "You were right to go after Farland. About what we should be fighting for. Now go. Get the hell out of here and go see this through."

Alex looked between Ben and the screen, mind spinning desperately for some other way out. He would have traded places with Ben in an instant if he could, but Ben couldn't make it out on his own. His throat tightened painfully. "Ben, I…" He couldn't find the words to thank the old man for all had done, and what he was now doing.

But Ben seemed to read his expression well enough. His own face softened, and he just nodded. "Go," he urged again.

This time, Alex listened. He ducked through the bedroom door just as the Peacekeepers prepared to breach.

[[—※—]]

Jack brought up the rear of Cerulli's squad as they exited the stairwell, the dazed soldier just ahead of him. Two troopers readied themselves on either side of the door, then looked to their Captain. Cerulli gave the hand signal to breach, and the lead soldier hammered the door in with a hand-held battering ram.

An explosion ripped into the hallway, sending the door—and the lead soldier—flying into the opposite wall. The man crumpled to the ground, singed and shredded, and didn't get back up. Plaster and splintered wood rained down on the other soldiers. The shattered doorway smoldered.

Jack half-ducked, his ears ringing. He cursed under his breath.

Cerulli staggered backward in a daze, pressing a hand to a cut above his eyebrow. When the other captain said nothing, Jack shouted, "Move in! Get your asses moving!"

The authority in his voice spurred the other soldiers into action. The one closest to the door moved through it in a standard room-clearing drill. A burst of gunfire cut him down before he'd made it five feet.

Jack's pulse quickened. He had expected the rebels to be making for the fire escape. Why would they stand and fight? They had to know they didn't have a chance.

He had them now.

[[—*—]]

Caitlin breathed a sigh of relief when Alex rushed into the living room of the downstairs apartment. "We've gotta go," he announced curtly, stopping short when he saw the man on the couch holding a bloody dish towel to his nose. Cocking an eyebrow at Samantha, he left the obvious question unasked.

The hacker shrugged. "Apparently they rented the apartment. It's handled." She peered behind him. "Where's Ben?" Alex's silence sparked a growing sense of dread, and Samantha's voice pitched up in concern. "Alex? Where is he?"

"He's not coming."

Caitlin sucked in a gasp. She had worried how the injured Ben would make it out with them, but she had never thought that he wouldn't.

Samantha shook her head, taking a few more seconds to process. "What? Wait. No. He can't— " She started back towards the hole connecting the apartments. "We have to go back for him."

Alex caught her arm, stopping her. The loud whomp of the door charge going off above them rattled the ceiling light, causing bits of dust and plaster to rain down. They all jerked their heads up at the sound. The guy on the couch shrank back against the cushions in a panic, looking like he might throw up.

"They're going to kill him!" Samantha cried desperately.

"And if we go back, they'll kill us too!" Alex snapped. "I want to charge back in there as much as you do, Sam, but it's his choice. He's buying us time. Let's not piss it away."

Samantha jerked her arm free, and for a moment it looked like she was going to try to push past him. Then her expression shifted. Resignation sparked a grief that she struggled to tamp down. A burst of gunfire above them made her wince. "Fine. Let's go."

Caitlin opened the door, but looked back at the guy on the couch. "I'm sorry about all this." He just stared at her, the disgust on his bloody face making her want to crawl into a hole. She hastily ducked through the door.

Alex and Samantha hid their weapons as they followed her out into the hallway. Smoke from Alex's grenade had begun to drift in from the stairwell, but wasn't enough to trip the smoke detector. Most of the neighbors kept their heads down and their doors locked, but a few dared to open their doors to investigate.

They passed an elderly woman pulling her housecoat hastily around her. "What's going on?" Seeing the smoke, she sniffed the air. "Is something burning?"

Though it made her nervous to have all these people so close to a firefight, Caitlin shuddered at the idea of sending a panicked exodus headlong into jumpy soldiers. "Peacekeeper exercises upstairs, ma'am." She raised her voice to address them all. "Everyone back inside for your own safety." Caitlin didn't look like much of an authority figure in her baggy, borrowed clothes, but her commanding firefighter voice sent most scurrying back inside.

The sound of gunfire upstairs followed them on their way down the hall. The muscles on Alex's jaw stood out in sharp relief with the strain of leaving their comrade behind. Samantha looked close to tears. They rounded a corner and neared the end of the T-shaped hallway. At the end of it was a window leading out to a fire escape, similar to the one Caitlin had used from her own apartment.

"They might be watching the alley," Sam pointed out.

"I know," Alex admitted, "But it's on the opposite side of the building, so hopefully they won't have as many guards. If we're lucky, they won't have a full perimeter. We'll have to move fast. Once we hit the fire escape, we'll be pretty exposed."

"What about the freight elevator?" Caitlin suggested, gesturing to a nearby alcove containing the elevator and a few vending machines. "It lets out right by the back door. We take patients out that way sometimes."

"The elevators are recalled." Alex had noticed that when he went out with the grenades before.

"Not if you have a firefighter code."

Alex weighed the risks. "Worth a try," he decided. A quick glance at Samantha got him a nod of agreement.

They moved into the alcove. Caitlin thumbed a code into the beige keypad, marked 'Fire Department Use', embedded into the elevator's control panel. The red lock light on the panel turned green an instant before a powerful explosion shook the building.

[[—❋—]]

Two soldiers leaned around the door jamb, trading fire with those within the apartment. Jack moved up, past the useless

Cerulli. He readied a flashbang grenade in one hand, his pistol in the other. "Flashbang up," Jack alerted the squad over the radio. The guy by the door gave Jack a little nod, then laid down some covering fire while Jack tossed the grenade into the apartment.

As soon as it went off, the squad crashed into the room in a well-oiled formation. Each man cleared a sector and set up interlocking fields of fire. Jack followed them in, swiftly realizing there was only a single gunman defending—the old guy from the square, Ben Holstrom.

Holstrom took down a second soldier and winged a third before Jack finally silenced him with two bullets to the chest. As the rebel toppled, the soldiers continued their sweep.

"Main room clear!" someone reported in Jack's earpiece. Soon others confirmed the bathroom and kitchen were clear as well. Jack fell in behind the pair of soldiers who moved into the apartment's single bedroom, feeling a rush of anticipation.

But there was no one.

"Bedroom clear!" reported the corporal on Jack's left.

Damn it. Where were they? Their thermal sweep had shown four people in the apartment before the raid. They couldn't have vanished.

Jack keyed his radio. "Bravo Team, Charlie Team, report. Any movement?" They both responded negative. Jack frowned. "Charlie, you sure? Nothing on the fire escape?" The soldiers confirmed, and Jack frowned.

Cerulli's voice filtered back to him from the living room. "Where are the others, old man? We know they were here." There was a soft 'oof' as one of the troopers kicked the prisoner in the side. "Give me something, and maybe we can get our medic in here."

Holstrom let out a bitter chuckle, his labored breathing making it more of a rasp. "Long gone," he hissed. "Good luck finding them from hell."

Cerulli snorted. "What's—" He stopped talking abruptly, and Jack turned in time to see the shock register on Cerulli's face.

"IED!" Cerulli yelled.

Jack had a split second to dive into the bathroom before Holstrom's improvised explosion ripped through the living room.

CHAPTER 26

THE PEACEKEEPERS WERE TOO BUSY dealing with the aftermath of the explosion to pay attention to the freight elevator or back alley, allowing Alex, Caitlin, and Samantha to escape. On the way out, Alex had allowed himself one last look back at the blown-out windows and damaged bricks on the fourth floor that marked Ben's final sacrifice. He had always said he'd never let them take him alive.

An uncomfortable silence lingered as the trio made their way into the tunnels and then distanced themselves from the apartment. They saw no signs of pursuit; Ben had done his job well. A hollow ache gnawed at Alex. No matter how logical Ben's delaying tactic had been, it still felt like he'd abandoned his mentor; his friend.

Alex paused beneath one of the access ladders, a dim light filtering down from the streetlights above. The streets at this hour were almost deserted. "We can rest here a minute while we figure out what to do."

Samantha slid off her backpack and sank to the ground. Silent tears streamed down her cheeks. Alex sat beside her, draping an arm around her shoulder.

Gingerly sitting down on Samantha's other side, Caitlin stretched out the leg with the injured ankle. "I'm sorry about Ben," she murmured, watching the other two with a quiet sympathy.

Alex nodded. "He always told me he wanted to go down fighting," he said, grief making his voice strained. "Take as many of the bastards as he could with him."

"'A life in jail is no life at all.'" Samantha quoted with a tearful sniffle. "That's what he used to say to me." After a pause, she asked plaintively, "How could this happen, Alex? How did they find us?" Alex had no answer for her.

It was Caitlin who spoke up, her voice weighed down by guilt. "Ben thought it was my fault." Alex started to shake his head, but Caitlin cut off his protest, "He did. I saw the way he looked at me when Sam saw the Peacekeepers coming. All of this is because of me. Vince, Ben, God knows how many people were hurt back there…" She trailed off, pinching the bridge of her nose. "I never should've taken that damn vid."

Samantha shifted towards the other woman, pulling free from Alex's arm. "This isn't on you, Caitlin."

"Sam's right," Alex said. "There are a hundred ways the Peacekeepers could've found us. That's the risk we all take for doing this. Ben knew that. It's the PKs who killed him; hurt your friend; killed all those people in the square. That's why we're all here. That's why we have to stop them."

Alex looked between them. "The last thing Ben said was how important that vid was. He wanted us to finish this. Show the world what the PKs really did. So let's go do it."

[[—✶—]]

"I'm standing outside the Bradbury Apartment complex, where a shootout and explosion just a few hours ago has left at least six dead. Early reports indicate that a Peacekeeper squad struck an insurgent cell. The insurgents fought back, armed with grenades and automatic weapons. Peacekeepers secured the building, killing at least one insurgent and capturing a stockpile of weapons and explosives. Several residents suffered minor injuries when the terrorists detonated an IED, and the building owner estimated that repairs for the resulting damage could exceed thirty thousand credits. As you can see here behind me..."

Colonel Isakovich switched off the MarsCom, cutting the reporter off in mid-sentence. He fixed Jack with a hard stare. "You had a full squad. Ten soldiers against three insurgents and a civilian. What the hell happened, Captain?"

Standing opposite Isakovich's desk, Jack tugged at the bandage on his forearm. The pipes in the wall of the bathroom had protected him against the worst of the blast, leaving him with only a few scratches and one ruptured eardrum. Captain Cerulli and a few of his men hadn't been so lucky, leaving Jack to answer for the debacle alone. "They knew we were coming, sir. They hit us in the stairwell before we even made it to their floor."

"How? You think there's a leak in the MPs?"

Jack shrugged, wincing as the motion tugged on a shrapnel wound in the back of his shoulder. "It's possible, but if they had advanced warning, I think they would have been gone before we got there. More likely the MPs botched the entry and tipped them off inadvertently. We'll never know."

Isakovich leaned back in his chair, letting out an expansive sigh. "What a goddamn mess. Where's that leave your investigation? Please tell me you at least found something in that apartment."

"We're still going through it," Jack said, an indirect admission that they hadn't found anything yet. "It looks like they had an escape hatch in the closet and went out through the floor below. Lieutenant Hale is trying to pick up any traces of their movements on the city cameras."

"What about that doctor who was working with them?"

Jack frowned. "He claims he only knew about the one safe house. We'll keep leaning on him to be sure he's not holding out. We have the account they used to communicate, so we'll be ready if they try to contact him again."

"And in the mean time, you've got nothing," the colonel concluded with a stern frown.

Jack bristled, drawing himself up straighter. "Sir, our intel led us to them once. We took out one of their team—probably the leader, judging by his age and experience. Captured a lot of their gear. Their safe house. They're reeling. They'll make a mistake. And when they do, we'll find them. I just need a squad of MPs on standby for when we do."

"You'll have it. But Captain, let's be clear—you're already on thin ice. No more screw-ups. Are we clear?"

Jack let the threat sail over him. He wasn't going to fail again. "Crystal, sir."

"Good. Now get out there and find those bastards!"

[[—∗—]]

Up until a few days ago, Caitlin had spent much of her life at the Waycross Fire and Rescue station: four 12-hour shifts every week since the day she graduated from the fire academy. Since Tom had moved out, it felt more like her home than her empty apartment. As she keyed in her access code to the lock panel on the front door—the only door she could get into without her keys—it didn't feel much like a homecoming. She, Alex, and Samantha had spent the better part of an hour watching the station from afar, looking for signs that the Peacekeepers had anticipated them coming here. They saw nothing, but worry kept Caitlin on edge as she pulled open the door. Samantha was right behind her. Alex remained across the street to cover their escape if needed.

An oppressive silence hung over the station, broken only by the drone of Chief Daniels' snoring in the upstairs bunk room. It was past two in the morning, and even the night-owls like Zhang would have gone to sleep by now. Caitlin and Samantha slipped into the garage, walking alongside the ladder truck and crossing behind the two ambulances.

Down the main hallway, they found an open doorway. "We're in the office," Caitlin whispered, just loud enough for the microphone on her collar to pick up the words. She didn't turn on the main light, but the monitor cast enough light for her to see the keyboard as she switched on the computer and sat down at the desk.

"Still no sign of activity out here," Alex's voice reported in her ear.

Caitlin had never been much of a typist, but this time her fingers flew over the keyboard, logging into the system and bringing up the ambulance call records. She searched for all patients treated on the day of the rally. She pointed to the screen. "There. That's what we need." This violated just about every law related to patient privacy, but Caitlin didn't hesitate, or even feel guilty about it. Maybe this was what it was like to be a criminal—to fall down that slippery slope where you convinced yourself that the ends justified the means.

Samantha took over the seat in front of the monitor, popping in a storage card. "Okay. I got it from here. Go get the vid."

Leaving Samantha to copy the records, Caitlin headed back to the garage. She had just put her hand on the ambulance door when a melodic alert tone sounded over the base radio. Caitlin froze as the dispatcher's voice followed the alert. "Medic Five-One: Code 2 dispatch at 200 Duncan Avenue for a 76-year-old male complaining of chest pain." The alarm klaxon blared loud enough to wake the dead.

"What the hell is that?" Alex's voice came over her earpiece. He could probably hear the klaxon from outside, and see the upstairs bunk room lights turning on automatically in response to the alarm.

Caitlin mumbled, "They just dispatched the ambulance to a call."

"Get out of there," Alex said.

"I've got the records," Samantha responded. "I'll meet you by the back door."

"Stand by. I don't have the video yet." Caitlin jerked the door open and climbed up into the back. The ambulance just dispatched was the same one she and Vince had been driving the day of the riot; it was where she had hidden the memory card. If the crew took it out on a call, heaven only knew when she'd get another chance to get it back. If she hurried, she ought to be able to grab the memory card and get out before the crew made it downstairs.

Pulling the main jump bag out of its compartment, she unzipped the pouch where the med scanner should have been.

It was empty.

"Shit!" Caitlin hissed.

"Cait, I see people moving upstairs." Urgency had crept into Alex's voice. "Get the hell out. Now."

Caitlin took a breath. They couldn't work without a scanner; it had to be here someplace. Conscious of the seconds ticking by, Caitlin searched the jump bag's other pouches. She shoved the bag back into the compartment and slammed the door in frustration. As she turned around to look in one of the other compartments, she spotted the scanner on the long bench seat. Wanting to throttle whoever had forgotten to put it away, Caitlin grabbed the scanner unzipped the side pouch. There, just where she had left it, was the memory card from Harry's camera.

Caitlin breathed a sigh of relief. Tucking the card into her jacket pocket, she rushed out the side door—and ran right into Andy Park.

The older man let out a little cry of surprise. "Caitlin?" He took a few steps backwards, fear flashing in his eyes. "What are you doing here?"

"Doesn't matter," Caitlin said with a quick shake of her head, relieved to see Park. Of all the people in the station, Caitlin got along with him better than anyone except Vince. He wouldn't turn her in. She wanted to just turn and make a run for it, but she couldn't leave without finding out one thing. "Andy—how's Vince?" she asked, her voice catching a little. "Is he all right?"

Before Park could answer, his partner came around the front of the truck. "Come on, old man, what's the…" Chris Tierney's voice trailed off when he spotted Caitlin. "I'll be damned…" he breathed. He just stared in shock for a moment, but then his hand went to his radio speaker. "Medic Five-One to dispatch…"

Caitlin felt a cold wave of dread, knowing that he was calling the Peacekeepers. Without thinking, she drew the pistol from her jacket pocket and leveled it at Tierney. It stopped him cold, his jaw dropping open. Caitlin stared at the weapon in her hand, unable to believe what she had done. But she was committed now.

"Go ahead, Medic Five-One," the dispatcher replied.

"Tell them to disregard," Caitlin ordered. Her hand trembled, and she hoped that Tierney couldn't see it. "Do it, Chris. I don't want to shoot you."

"Like you shot Vince?" Tierney spat back.

Caitlin blinked, dumbfounded by the accusation. "What?"

"Spare us the innocent routine. They found your prints on the gun. Why'd you do it, Cait? Why Vince? He was your friend!"

Caitlin shook her head, stunned that anyone—even Tierney—would consider her capable of such a thing. "They're lying!" she protested. She knew it was impossible for them to have found the gun, because she was holding it. Pointing that out wasn't likely to help her case with Tierney. "I would never hurt Vince. How could you even think that?" She glanced to Park, but saw only fear and suspicion in his eyes. Her face crumpled, as she realized that neither of them believed her.

"Medic Five-One? Medic Five-One are you en route?" The dispatcher's persistent queries were getting more agitated, as they tried to figure out the status of Park and Tierney's ambulance. Caitlin knew that if they didn't reply soon, the dispatcher would assume something was wrong.

She swallowed past the painful lump in her throat. "Answer him," she told Park. "Tell him you're on the way."

Park nodded, his hand going slowly to his microphone. He never took his eyes off Caitlin, but activated the mic and spoke into it. "Dispatch this is Medic Five-One…" he paused, taking a breath, and then said, "We need Peacekeeper assistance at our station, Code 3."

Caitlin flinched as if he had struck her. She stared at him, shaking her head in pained disbelief. How could everyone turn against her so easily? Park braced himself, seemingly waiting for her to shoot him, but Caitlin didn't move.

"Just tell me, please—is he alive?" she pleaded.

It was Tierney who replied, "He's in the ICU. Still touch and go, but they think he'll pull through." He added bitterly, "No thanks to you."

Caitlin closed her eyes, letting out a breath in relief. She wanted to shout at them that she didn't do it, but she knew the words would fall on deaf ears. Vince was alive. Let them think whatever they wanted. It didn't matter anymore. This part of her life was over. Keeping her gun trained on them as she backed away, Caitlin reached the main door and dashed out of the station.

CHAPTER 27

THE SAFE HOUSE WAS A dingy one-room apartment above a clothing boutique that had gone out of business years ago. Ben had some kind of arrangement with the owner, who had returned to Earth. There was a sofa with a pull-out bed, a small table, and a dilapidated loveseat tucked into the corner. Alex had led them all here after another hasty retreat into the tunnels.

"You sure this place is safe?" Samantha wondered as she dumped her backpack on the couch.

"Safe as we're going to get." Alex replied, lowering the blinds over the dusty windows. "Ben said the owner was an old friend who let him stay here sometimes, so there shouldn't be any paperwork or anything tying him to the place. He and I are the only two who knew about it." Alex frowned, the loss of his friend casting a pall on his features.

Caitlin sank down onto the loveseat. Taking the storage card from her pocket, she sat there staring at it with a distant expression on her face. She hadn't said much since the fire station. Whatever happened there had left her shaken and subdued, and Alex was worried about her.

"Sam, can I borrow your tablet?" Caitlin asked abruptly. Samantha brought the device over, and Caitlin popped the storage card into the slot on the side.

"Are you sure you want to watch that?" Alex asked, his brow creasing.

The dread in her eyes said no, but she swallowed hard and whispered, "I have to. I owe him that much."

Alex squeezed her shoulder. "Okay. We'll be here if you need us."

There wasn't much privacy in the tiny apartment, but Alex and Samantha afforded her what space they could. Alex busied himself pulling out the sofa mattress and setting up the bed. Samantha disappeared into the bathroom for a few minutes to change, then came over to help him.

The silence was broken by a soft weeping. Caitlin sat hunched with the tablet still in her lap, her face buried in her hands. Alex and Samantha exchanged concerned glances. After the briefest hesitation, Samantha abandoned the pillowcase she'd been fussing with and joined Caitlin on the couch. Quiet words were said, and then Samantha opened her arms and engulfed the other woman in a hug. They cried together, each mourning the man they had lost that day.

Thinking of Julio, Ben, and all the others who had been murdered by the Peacekeepers, Alex mourned as well in his own quiet way. He glanced over at the tablet and its impactful recording. Now they had the means to make the Peacekeepers pay for all of it.

[[—✳—]]

When the tears ran dry and Samantha and Alex had their chance to watch the recording, it was after three AM and everyone was dead on their feet. Alex had initially insisted on being chivalrous and taking the loveseat, but after seeing him trying to get comfortable with his long legs draped over the edge, Caitlin offered to switch places with him. She didn't think she'd be able to sleep anyway. But then Samantha, being the shortest of the group, insisted that she was the most logical choice. "Don't worry, he's a gentleman," the young hacker had assured Caitlin with a smirk. "Besides, he knows we'll both shoot his balls off if he tries anything."

Despite the scratchiness behind her eyelids, sleep eluded Caitlin. Seeing Tom on the video had torn open the scab of grief. Tom's cameraman Harry had been the first to fall, sparing Caitlin from having to see Tom shot in real-time. But seeing the fear on Tom's face, and his anguished cry of his friend's name had proved a torture all its own. She tossed and turned for an interminable period of time before finally sitting up with a sigh.

"Can't sleep?" Alex's soft whisper made her jump. "Sorry. Me either." Caitlin wiped at her eyes, saying nothing. Alex sat up and reached over to squeeze her shoulder. "Anything I can do?"

Caitlin started to shake her head, but something in his earnest expression gave her pause. "Could you…" Words failed. Tentatively, giving him ample chance to move away, she scooted along his arm until she was nestled into the crook of his shoulder. Alex stiffened briefly in surprise, but then relaxed and curled his arm around her back. He added his other arm, wrapping her in a protective embrace. "Thank you," she murmured.

"Sure," Alex said easily. "You know, if you want to talk or anything…I'm sure that was really hard to watch. Hell, it was hard for me to watch."

"I thought I was ready for it. I'd seen what happened to them. But it was so much worse." Her throat tightened painfully, tears pricking at her eyes. "I know your friend was killed there too. I'm sorry."

Alex thanked her, and they both fell quiet. Caitlin rested her head against his chest, listening to the steady rise and fall of his breathing. She hoped she wasn't giving him the wrong idea. Romance was really the farthest thing from her mind. Yet she had to admit some part of her enjoyed having those strong arms wrapped around her. It had been a long time since she'd felt such tenderness. She shut down that train of thought, feeling disloyal.

"Can I ask you something?" Caitlin ventured. "Do you ever see your family?"

"Not for a long time." Hearing the sadness in Alex's voice, Caitlin regretted asking. He went on, though, "It was around Christmas, about five years ago. Not long after I joined the rebels. I'd just finished explosives training with some guerrillas in South America. I stopped by my parents' place in Florida on the way back. It was hard. Knowing I might not see them again. Not being able to tell them anything about what I was involved in." He blew out a soft breath. "Even if I could have, I don't think they would've understood."

Caitlin bobbed her head. "That sounds rough." She sighed. "I haven't seen my father in almost fifteen years. Just messages. I kept hoping that someday he'd be transferred to lesser security so I could visit him, but now…" She trailed off. "I'll never see him again."

"You can't let yourself think that way, Cait. You have to believe that we can win. That someday Mars will be free and you'll be able to go back to your life, and see your family again. It's the only thing that keeps us all going. You can't give up hope."

Tilting her head up, she studied his face. "Do you really believe that?" She wanted to, but right now it felt like an impossibly distant goal.

Alex quirked a sad smile. "Some days more than others," he admitted. "But I try to remind myself of it whenever we hit a rough patch." He held her gaze, his expression intense. "Just remember…you're not alone. We're in this together."

For the first time, Caitlin felt like she was a real part of their team. And perhaps, with Alex, a part of something more.

[[—☀—]]

Samantha was already up and making breakfast when Alex awoke. Caitlin slept on, still tucked in against his side, her arm draped across his chest. Loathe to wake her after the restless night she'd had, and feeling more comfortable in that embrace than he probably should, Alex lingered for a few more minutes before gently extricating himself. She was still asleep when he emerged from the bathroom a few minutes later and joined Samantha in the kitchen.

Flipping some just-add-water pancakes at the stove, Samatha looked pointedly at the sleeping Caitlin, then gave Alex an amused side-eye. "I'm not going to have to shoot you, am I?"

Alex leaned against the counter, ripping open a bag of breakfast pastries. He rolled his eyes. "Nothing happened. She was just upset."

Samantha gave a soft mmm hmm, then slanted him a smirk. "You like her, though." Alex shifted, a half-hearted protest forming on his lips. "Don't bother trying to deny it. I know you too well."

Scowling, Alex said, "Come on, Sam. She just lost her husband. I'm not that much of an asshole."

"She told me they'd been separated for awhile." Samantha shrugged, the smirk fading. "Got to take your chances while you have them, right?"

Alex knew she was thinking about Julio, and gave her shoulder a little squeeze. He didn't know what to feel about the rest of it, but there wasn't time to dwell on it. Caitlin had stirred, padding her way over to join them.

"Morning," she mumbled sleepily, offering Alex an awkward smile. He wondered if she was embarrassed about the night before, and wished he could tell her that she needn't be. But then Samantha was pointing her to a plate of pancakes and Caitlin was distracted thanking her and pitching in to get everything to the table.

As they gathered around the table to eat and plan, Alex flipped through the morning headlines on Samantha's tablet. The incident at their apartment building last night was at the top of all the local news sites. Seeing Ben's mugshot was like a kick in the gut, but Alex forced himself to read the rest of the article. He felt a grim sense of satisfaction that Ben had taken out almost an entire squad single-handedly. But then, near the end, another set of photos made him frown.

"What is it?" Samantha asked.

He flipped the tablet around so they could both see, and pressed the play button. *"Peacekeeper commander Colonel Andrei Isakovich has issued warrants for three suspects wanted in conjunction with the attack. Two are believed to be from the group responsible for the bombing at Fort McChord early Friday morning."* It showed the same sketch they'd been using for Alex since the bombing, and another rough artist's sketch of Samantha—probably from the neighbor. *"The third is Caitlin Farland, a paramedic with Waycross Fire and Rescue."* The report went on, but it was clear Caitlin was no longer listening. She just stared at the monitor, a dumbstruck look on her face.

Alex remembered the first time he had seen himself on the news, after a raid on the Fort McChord vehicle depot a few years ago. They didn't have his name, or even a decent picture of him—just a few grainy surveillance photos of him and Julio, wearing masks. It had nonetheless been a sobering experience, to realize he was officially a wanted fugitive. He could only imagine how it must be for Caitlin, to have her name and face up there for the whole world to see.

"I'm sorry," he said lamely. It didn't really fit, but he couldn't think of anything better to offer. There were no ready platitudes for a situation like this.

Frowning in concern, Samantha changed the subject. "So we've got the video and the records. How are we going to get anyone's attention? Anywhere we upload it, the censors are going to have a field day."

Alex set down the tablet. "I have an idea. Something that will make a splash too big for them to ignore." He looked at Caitlin.

"But to do it, we're going to need to get into the Chronicle, and I think Tom might have had something to help."

$$[[-*-]]$$

Caitlin stared up at the dome, watching the clouds drift across the pale pink sky. The streets bustled with activity—people on their way to work, or to get in some early morning Christmas shopping at the marketplace. The scenes of normalcy were jarring compared to the tatters of her own life. Caitlin felt her heart skip a beat every time a person passed by, afraid that someone would recognize her or Alex and call the Peacekeepers. Thankfully, their hat-and-glasses disguises seemed to be working; no one paid them any attention. Samantha had gone off separately to get some other supplies for Alex's plan.

Shiro Gardens Hotel was a posh-sounding place that didn't live up to its name. The only gardens in sight were the hydroponic ones at nearby Shiro Solarium. The rear entrances were locked to guest keys, but they lurked around until a pair of tourists returned from an early morning jog, then slipped in before the door closed behind them. Taking the elevator up to the seventh floor, Caitlin led the way to room 703.

"This should be it," Caitlin said, standing outside the door of the hotel room. She had never been here before, but Tom had given her the address in case she needed it.

"Do you have the key?" Alex asked. When she shook her head, he took a quick look up and down the hallway to make sure nobody was around, then slammed his shoulder against the door. On the second hit, the locking mechanism gave way with a quiet crack, and the door swung open. Caitlin hesitated just a moment before venturing inside. Alex followed quietly behind her. If he wondered why her husband was living in a hotel, he didn't ask.

Caitlin looked around, feeling a hollow ache at the impersonal cleanliness of the room. Apart from Tom's laptop computer, sitting out on the desk, everything was put away in drawers or cabinets. Neat and tidy, just as Tom liked it. A single photograph on the nightstand drew her attention immediately. It was the same photo Caitlin had on her mantle—she and Tom smiling happily on the couch last Christmas. She ran her finger along the edge of the frame.

"You want to grab the laptop?" Alex asked gently.

Caitlin snapped out of her thoughts, reminded they were there for a reason. "Yeah, okay." Under the desk was a carrying case. She slid the computer inside and slung it over her shoulder.

They kept searching, until Alex said, "Found it." On the top of the dresser, a little worse for the wear from the last time he'd accidentally let it go through the wash, was Tom's press badge. Alex held it up for her to see, then pocketed it. He watched her for a moment, concern furrowing his brow. "You need some time, or…"

Caitlin lingered for a minute, running a hand over the clothes in the closet, then reluctantly closed the closet door. Crossing to the nightstand, she picked up the photograph and tucked it into the carrying case beside the laptop. "I have what I need." Taking one final look around the room, she followed Alex out and closed the door behind them.

[[—✳—]]

Jack rubbed his eyes tiredly, switching off the MarsCom screen. He'd been pouring over old records for hours and found nothing. He and Hale had grilled Dr. Noah Ross, but the good doctor had already told them all he knew. Caitlin's Uncle Max claimed he hadn't seen her in years. Jack suspected he might be holding out, but it was a flimsy instinct, not worth stirring up the Syndicate over. Ben Holstrom had been an equally dead end —any known associates were either dead, in prison, or had vanished into obscurity. Jack still hadn't turned up any details on the real identities of the other two. First names alone weren't much to go on, and he was beginning to think that someone had deliberately erased them from any public databases—probably the same person who was always screwing with the street cams around them. They were ghosts.

He was running short on leads, but there had to be something here; Jack couldn't accept that the trail had gone so cold so quickly. The colonel doubled security at the spaceport, but so far all they had accomplished was scaring the tourists. Jack couldn't ignore the possibility that his quarry had skipped town before the Peacekeepers tightened security at the starport, or taken a rover around the canyon. He had squandered so many chances to get them; he was beginning to wonder if he would get another one.

"Captain, I think you'd better take a look at this." The excited words came from Lieutenant Hale, working at his desk with his arm in a sling. He held out a piece of paper.

Jack studied the printout. "A hotel break-in? What the hell does that have to do with anything?"

Hale said, a hint of a smile on his face, "Look at the name, sir."

"Tom MacIntyre," Jack read the name of the room's occupant, wondering why that sounded familiar. Then it clicked. "Farland's husband. I'll be damned."

"The maid found the door broken open when she went to do her cleaning this morning. She said nothing looked disturbed, and the only things that seemed missing were MacIntyre's laptop, and—get this—a photograph of him and his wife."

Jack cursed himself for not having checked out the husband sooner. Sykes' initial investigation showed that MacIntyre had been killed in the riot, so Jack didn't look into it any further. "Get over to the Chronicle and track down MacIntyre's network information. See what their IT guys can do and contact Net Security. If they connect that laptop to the MarsCom net, I want a trace put on it immediately."

Hale nodded and moved off, leaving Jack to stare intently at the printed report.

"What the hell were you doing there, Caitlin?" Jack murmured under his breath. At the same time, he felt a wave of exhilaration. He was back on their trail.

CHAPTER 28

CAITLIN GAZED UP AT THE glassy exterior of the Carter Building, unable to see anything behind its mirrored windows. The tallest structure in Waycross, it towered over the rest of the downtown office buildings. Small groups of men and women in suits emerged from the lobby, heading out early for lunch, and Caitlin felt a pang of nervousness every time someone looked her way.

It must have showed on her face, for she heard Alex's voice beside her, "Relax. I doubt even your friends would recognize you." They had gotten a table at a cafe where they could watch the building's entrance.

"He's right," Samantha's voice echoed in her earpiece, the young hacker positioned across the street. "I barely recognized you."

Caitlin wanted to believe them, but that did little to calm her nerves. Despite the wig and sunglasses Samantha had purchased for her, she still felt terribly exposed.

Alex's disguise would definitely hold up to casual scrutiny. A short black wig covered his close-cropped hair, and he had glued on enough fake whiskers to turn his goatee into a full beard. In glasses and a shirt-and-tie, he looked more like an accountant than a rebel soldier.

She tried to push her worries to the back of her mind, and took a sip of the lukewarm coffee she'd been nursing. "I haven't seen anything unusual," she said. No Peacekeepers, no extra security—nothing to indicate that the Peacekeepers had anticipated their next move.

"Me either. It looks clear."

"Are you sure we're not rushing things?" Caitlin wondered aloud. It had been only a few hours since retrieving the laptop and making the final preparations.

"We've got a solid plan." Alex tore his eyes off the building, and looked at her intently. "But it's not too late to back out."

Caitlin set down the cup. "No," she said resolutely. "Let's do it." He just nodded, his feelings buried behind a stoic mask. She wondered if he was as nervous as she was.

"First sign of trouble, we bail. You have the tunnel route memorized?" When Caitlin nodded, Alex stooped down to grab his briefcase, which had been sitting on the ground between them. "All right. Give me five minutes, and then head in." He hesitated a moment, then finally bent over and planted a quick kiss on Caitlin's cheek. "Good luck."

Without waiting for a reply, Alex quickly turned and started heading for the entrance.

By the time Caitlin recovered from her surprise enough to say something, he was already halfway across the street. "Be careful, Alex."

$$[[-*-]]$$

Alex strode through the Carter Building lobby with a purposeful gait. All the pre-mission jitters were gone, replaced with the quiet calm he always felt once things were in motion. Even so, he stopped short when he spotted a lone Peacekeeper standing by the security desk, talking to the guard there. He recognized the officer, who had one arm in a sling.

Striding over to the public water fountain, he bent over and pretended to take a drink. "We may have a problem," he said, the words picked up by the microphone clipped to his collar. "One of Decker's guys is in the lobby. The one I shot at the warehouse."

"Did he see you?" came back Caitlin's started voice.

The security guard motioned for the Peacekeeper to head into the Chronicle offices. Alex straightened, stepping away from the fountain and taking a moment to straighten his tie. He casually slipped a hand into the pocket of his sports jacket to check his pistol, and scanned the rest of the lobby. No one seemed out of place, as if they might be undercover PKs on a stake-out. "No. It looks like he's alone, but he went into the Chronicle."

"So what do we do?"

"Stick to the plan. Head around back and wait for my signal."

The offices of the Martian Chronicle occupied most of the first two floors. Alex walked through the lobby, sneaking a glance at the lobby security guard. The guard seemed more interested in his cellcom than in the people passing through, and Alex spied a puzzle game on the screen as he passed.

Heading through the frosted glass door of the Chronicle's main entrance, Alex flashed a quick, confident smile to the middle-aged receptionist, remembering what Ben had told him was the key to infiltration: *If you look like you belong, and act like you belong, nobody's going to question you.* He swiped his stolen press badge—doctored to show a fake name and Alex's face instead of Tom's —across the lock panel. The door opened obediently, and the receptionist answered an incoming call without looking suspicious.

The Chronicle's bottom floor had a wide-open foyer filled with clusters of seats, short tables, and fake greenery. In the middle of it all, a shiny metallic staircase led upstairs. Surrounding the central lobby were rows of cubicles, with an outer ring of offices and conference rooms along the walls. Upstairs, a mezzanine-type balcony ringed the foyer, giving it an airy height.

Alex passed a handful of Chronicle employees going about their daily business, but none of them paid him any mind as he headed for the rear of the building. Tucked away in the corner, a rear exit led outside. It had an obvious sensor and a sign warning, "Emergency exit only. Alarm will sound." But Alex had come prepared. Thirty seconds later, he had disabled the sensor and fooled the system into thinking the door remained closed. Then he wedged the door open.

"Back door's open," he said over the radio.

"On the way," Caitlin and Samantha each acknowledged, but Alex didn't wait for them. He had his own job to do. He headed back to the central area and climbed the stairs. Film editing suites, the broadcast studio and the media workspaces were all upstairs. Alex waited until the hallway was clear, and then ducked into one of the storage closets. Cramped and filled with old computer equipment and spare vid cameras, the cluttered closet suited Alex's purposes. He set his briefcase on the floor and opened it. Inside, carefully nestled in foam cut-outs, were several blocks of plastic explosives—all that remained of Julio's emergency stash.

It took him about fifteen minutes to get everything ready, and then he checked the wireless detonator control. The status light blinked a reassuring green, so he switched the safety back on and tucked the control away in his jacket pocket. Now, all he had to do was wait for Caitlin's signal.

[[—✳—]]

Nobody noticed Caitlin and Samantha sneaking in the back door. Heading down the row of cubicles, they found Tom's easily enough. Unlike the hotel room, every little detail marked this place as his. From the silly toys on top of the monitor, to the photos on the desk, to the "Martian Firefighters" charity calendar on the wall—the memories took her breath away.

"I've got this," Samantha said, touching Caitlin's arm briefly and then slipping into the office chair. She set Tom's laptop on the desk and turned it on. "We're connected."

Caitlin watched over her shoulder as her fingers flew. The blue and red background of the Martian Chronicle filled the screen, and Samantha opened the messaging app. She loaded the message that they had prepared. It was simple, appealing to a journalist's inherent curiosity.

The Chronicle will be breaking this story within the hour.

The recipients included editors of all the major news networks on Earth, and the branches of the Martian Chronicle in the other cities on Mars. They could have sent the message from anywhere, but felt it would have more credibility if it came from the Chronicle's network directly. Throw in the intrigue of the email coming from a dead reporter, and they figured somebody somewhere would pick it up.

Samantha attached a copy of their evidence to the message—the contents of the memory card, the patient records from the ambulance station, and eye-witness statements she had found on underground message boards. It was all there, if anybody would dare to believe it. She clicked the 'send' button, and they both held their breath as the progress bar filled up.

It had just past fifty percent when Caitlin heard the familiar voice of Rachel Griffiths in the doorway. "Just what the hell do you think you're doing?"

[[—✳—]]

Jack stood in the living room of insurgent's apartment, staring at the wreckage of the room. Apart from the bodies being removed and police tape strung up across the door, nothing had been disturbed since the failed assault. A forensics team had been over the apartment with a fine-toothed comb yesterday, but they hadn't found anything useful. He had come back to the apartment in the hopes that inspiration would strike, because otherwise he was running out of ideas.

Jack's com buzzed for attention. He answered it with a curt, "Yes?"

"Captain Decker, this is Specialist Jameson with Net Security," said a young woman. "We have a trace on that laptop you put a flag on. It just logged into the network."

Jack felt his heart racing, elated at the sudden change in their luck. "Where?" he demanded.

"Carter Building… ground floor…"

Jack finished the sentence for her, his elation turning to dread. "The Chronicle. Damn it!" He had sent Hale there to take a look, but apparently they'd slipped through somehow. He radioed the squads that the colonel had placed on standby. "This is Citadel One to all units. Suspects located at the Carter Building, in the Martian Chronicle offices. Converge on the building."

Jack didn't even bother waiting for a reply. He set off toward the city center at a run.

CHAPTER 29

CAITLIN'S DISGUISE MUST HAVE PASSED muster, because it took Rachel several seconds before she squinted and realized, "Caitlin. What are you doing here?"

"Something you should have done a few days ago," Caitlin replied.

Rachel's eyes narrowed. "You've got no business screwing around on our network." She pulled out her cellcom. "I'm calling Security."

Caitlin snatched the com out of her hand. "I don't think so." Rachel looked more annoyed than afraid, but then Caitlin pulled the gun halfway out of her pocket, just enough to show Rachel it was there.

All the color drained from Rachel's face. "What do you want?" she breathed.

Samantha closed the laptop and slipped it back into her case. She keyed her collar microphone. "It's done."

Caitlin felt a rush of satisfaction, but they weren't finished yet. Sending the message was the easy part. Even if some of the news networks followed up, the Peacekeepers could just deny everything—claim that the rebels had fabricated the "evidence". It might get a little attention, but not the kind they were looking for. They needed something bigger.

"We're going to take a nice quiet walk up to the control room," Caitlin told Rachel, keeping her voice low. "Don't make a fuss." She slid the pistol back into her jacket pocket. As soon as Rachel started moving, Caitlin touched her radio microphone and said, "We're on our way up."

Alex was waiting for them at the top of the stairs.

Rachel stared at him, gasping in recognition. "My God, you're —"

Alex touched a finger to his lips to silence her, and she clamped her mouth shut. Rachel looked between them in wide-eyed disbelief. "Let's go," Alex said.

They followed the railing that ringed the upper level, forming a sort of balcony around the lobby below. Arriving at the main studio, a red light blinked above the doors to indicate that filming was in progress. A big bay window let them see inside to the control room, with the actual set through another set of doors beyond. They went inside. A lone technician studiously watched a bank of monitors, occasionally pressing a button on the complicated control panel. It took him a moment to even register their presence.

"Have a seat." Caitlin motioned Rachel toward one of the chairs.

The tech pulled his headset off of his ear. "Rachel? What's going on?"

As she sat down, Rachel folded her arms across her chest. "This is insane."

Samantha approached the technician, flashing her submachine gun. "We're making a small addition to your programming schedule. Move aside."

Paling, the technician scooted his chair away from the control panel. Samantha pulled over a stool and took his place, sliding a storage card into the reader slot. Caitlin knew it held a teleprompter script and video for them to air.

Rachel's gaze drifted between the three rebels. "Do you really think you can get away with this? You start broadcasting some nonsense, and the Peacekeepers will be here in minutes. Do you really want to end up in jail?"

"Jail?" Caitlin snapped back. "They tried to kill me to keep this quiet." The tech blinked in shock, but Rachel shook her head, nonplussed. Caitlin went on, "They'd rather kill more people than admit what they did." Her eyes blazed with rage, thinking of Vince. "And you're the one that sent them after me."

"Oh, stop acting like everything is black and white," Rachel countered. "They've got the security of the entire colony to think about. They're trying to protect us. If word about this got out, the rebels would have jump all over it. There would be more attacks, riots, maybe even a war! Is that what you want?"

Caitlin slammed her fist down on the desk in frustration. "Look around you, Rachel! The war's already started! It's about time we did something to end it."

She caught Samantha's eye, and the other woman nodded and went to work. Caitlin started pacing back and forth, unable to contain her nervous energy.

Finally Samantha looked up at the monitor showing a live view of the studio. "Here we go…"

The anchorman looked puzzled as the teleprompter changed, but he quickly recovered. Caitlin felt her heart racing as he started reading the words they had written.

"And now, we bring you this late-breaking news, a Martian Chronicle exclusive…"

[[— ✳ —]]

It took Jack three tries before he was finally able to get through to Hale on his cellcom. "Hale! They're at the Chronicle. Find them. I'll be there in five minutes."

Hanging up, he continued his sprint across downtown. After an eternity, he reached the building and dashed inside. The centerpiece of the Carter Building's lobby was a large flat-panel monitor tuned to the Chronicle's live feed. Jack's expression darkened when he saw several people gathering in front of it, pointing and gasping. Something had caught their attention, and that couldn't be a good sign. Jack's worst fears were confirmed when the upper right corner of the screen displayed a graphic saying "Massacre in Waycross."

Jack swore under his breath. Hurrying up to the desk of the bewildered security guard, he flashed his badge and pointed to the monitor. "Can we cut the power?"

"To the monitor?"

"No, to the Chronicle. The whole building if we have to. We need to stop that feed."

The guard shook his head. "There's circuit breakers in the basement, but it wouldn't do you any good. The Chronicle's got its own emergency backup generator."

Swearing again, Jack took out his com and dialed back the specialist from Net Security. "Jameson, this is Captain Decker. The Chronicle is doing a live broadcast. I need you to shut it down now."

"Sir, I don't have the authority—"

"I'm giving you the authority, damn it," Jack snapped. "Get it done, or find someone who can. Otherwise I'm going to come down there and you're going to feel the boot of my authority up your ass." He hung up and snapped to the guard, "Turn that damn screen off, and clear out this lobby." As the startled guard scrambled into action, Jack got on the radio again. "Citadel-One here. What's the status on the backup team?"

"Should be there any minute," the controller replied.

On cue, a squad of a half-dozen sweaty soldiers double-timed it into the building. Jack flashed the pictures of their targets and started dishing out orders for some of the men to seal the exits. Then he pointed to two privates. "You two, with me." He dashed toward the Chronicle offices.

[[—✻—]]

Alex felt a wave of relief wash over him as the broadcast began. He clapped Samantha on the shoulder, then caught Caitlin's eye from across the room and offered her a triumphant smile. She returned it with a shell-shocked grin of her own. They'd done it! Now all they had to do was get out of here in one piece. Alex had estimated that they had about ten minutes, give or take, before the Peacekeepers got a squad over from the Fort. And the clock had already started ticking.

"I'll check to make sure our exit's clear. Two minutes, then we're out of here," Alex said. The others nodded.

He'd barely made it ten steps down the hallway before he spotted the Peacekeeper officer from the lobby coming toward him.

"Hands up!" the soldier shouted, raising a pistol with his good arm. The other was still in a sling from their last encounter.

Alex pulled his pistol from his pocket, but the young lieutenant had the drop on him. Gunshots rang out in the hallway, and Alex shouted in pain as he dove for cover.

[[—⁎—]]

Caitlin flinched when she heard the gunshots. She immediately keyed her radio. "Alex? Are you all right?" There was no answer, and Caitlin felt a pang of fear deep in her stomach. Exchanging a frightened glance with Samantha, she drew her pistol and chambered a round.

"Watch them," Samantha said, readying her own weapon. "Make sure they don't stop the broadcast. I'll go help Alex." She rushed out.

Caitlin nodded. The pistol felt heavy in her hand, and the thought of using it again made her mouth go dry. In her mind's eye, she could still see Sykes, the blood gushing from his neck. She tried to push those thoughts aside. More gunfire echoed in the hallway outside, and Caitlin edged tentatively in that direction.

Had she been paying more attention to Rachel and the technician, she might have seen their pointed looks and hand gestures. But the first indication they were plotting something came when the tech launched himself out of his chair and crashed into her. He grabbed her arm, trying to wrestle the gun away. A moment later, Rachel joined the fray wielding a big metal microphone stand. She brought it crashing down on Caitlin's back, driving her to the ground.

CHAPTER 30

ALEX THREW HIMSELF SIDEWAYS, KNOCKING open a door that led to some kind of computer room. A pair of startled workers screamed and took cover behind the desks as more gunshots splintered the doorframe. Alex crouched breathlessly in the doorway, clutching his right arm. The bullet had struck just below his elbow, tearing through his forearm. He could still move it, so he didn't think it was broken. Gritting his teeth, he tried to ignore the pain.

He'd dropped his pistol out in the hall when he'd been shot. Defenseless, he touched the button on his microphone. "Cait, Sam, we've got trouble out here. Need backup." There was no response—not even static. "Sam? Caitlin? Do you read?" Again, nothing. Alex instinctively reached inside his jacket pocket to check his radio. His fingers touched a sharp, jagged edge that wasn't there before, and when he pulled out the radio he saw that it had taken a hit from a stray bullet. "Damn it!"

The gunfire from the hallway had slacked off. Alex could imagine the Peacekeeper officer moving to a better position to cover the doorway, waiting for backup. He had that luxury. The longer they waited, the more soldiers would arrive. Alex and his friends had to get out soon or they'd be trapped in the building.

A burst of submachine gun fire came from up the hall, near the studio. Alex sucked in a breath. More Peacekeepers?

Then he heard Samantha's call, "Alex! Hallway's clear! Where are you?"

Alex rushed out of the computer room, scooping up his dropped pistol. "Sam, thank God. Where's Caitlin?"

Samantha pointed back the way she'd come. "Back in the control room. Are you okay?" Her eyes widened in concern at Alex's bloody arm.

"Just a scratch. We need to get—" Alex stopped abruptly. Across the balcony that ringed the lower foyer, the elevator had just opened. Three more Peacekeepers strode out, one of them Captain Decker.

Alex and Decker locked eyes, sharing a moment of shocked recognition. Ducking behind the balcony railing, Alex squeezed off a few shots that sent the soldiers scurrying for cover. Samantha added her fire to the mix, chewing up the railing on the opposite side.

"We're can't get pinned down here," Alex said breathlessly. "Get Cait and head down that back staircase. I'll meet you by Tom's cube. If I'm not there in five minutes, head to the rendezvous point in the tunnels. Don't wait for me."

"What are you going to do?" Samantha asked.

"Create a diversion." Alex pulled the detonator control from his inside pocket, and Samantha's eyes widened in realization. "Go. I'll cover you." Alex popped up, firing across at the Peacekeepers as the young woman scurried back to the control room. One of the soldiers went down, but then their return fire had him ducking again.

There was only one thing left to do. Alex pressed the trigger on the detonator.

$$[[-*-]]$$

Caitlin's knees buckled as Rachel hammered her with the microphone stand. Grunting in pain, she somehow clung to the gun as the technician tried to wrest it from her grip. Two against one, Caitlin fought with a fierce desperation. She held her own, but took a beating in the process.

At one point, she twisted the pistol free. The tech froze, the same sinking realization his face she had seen on Sykes'. The difference was, this guy wasn't a Peacekeeper. He was just a regular guy caught up in a situation he didn't fully understand. Caitlin let her arm go slack; she wouldn't shoot him.

Rachel came at her again, smacking her upper arm with the makeshift metal club. Pain jolted down to her fingers, and the gun clattered to the ground. The reporter raised the club to strike once more, but Caitlin tackled her. They both went crashing into the workstation, sending papers and electronics flying. The two women wrestled for position, grunting and twisting at limbs.

"Kevin! Damn it, help me! Get the gun!" Rachel cried.

Kevin the tech didn't move. His eyes were locked on the studio monitor, where Tom and Harry's footage from the

Commons was playing for the whole world to see. It made him reevaluate which side he wanted to be on.

Rachel wasn't much of a fighter, mostly slaps and nails. When she grabbed a handful of hair, Caitlin countered with a brutal hook that snapped Rachel's head back.

"You bitch," Caitlin snarled, seeing red. This was the woman who had tried to steal Tom; had sold her out to the Peacekeepers. Bloody knuckles kept pummeling that perfect face, thinking only of everything Rachel had taken from her.

"Stop, please!" Rachel whimpered. Shrinking back, she held up a hand to ward off the next blow.

Caitlin stopped, breathless. Rachel's terror, the pain radiating through her fist, the clatter of gunfire from the hallway, the panicked pitch in the anchors voices on the monitor as they reacted to the gunshots—it all washed over her in a disorienting wave, bringing her back to herself. What was she going to do, beat Rachel to death with her bare hands? That wasn't her. Releasing the reporter's crumpled violet dress shirt, Caitlin stepped back.

The door opened, and Samantha rushed back in. "Get down!" the other woman cried, diving behind the workstation just as a booming explosion rocked the building and turned the big window into a hail of shrapnel.

[[—✳—]]

Jack was reloading his pistol when the thunderous explosion ripped through the hallway. Hot air scorched his face as the blast knocked him to the ground, and he covered his head to shield himself from the shower of shattered building materials raining down on him. He could feel a thin line of blood trickling from his right ear; his already-abused eardrum further damaged by the shockwave. All he could do for several seconds was lay there, stunned.

When he regained his bearings, he saw that the blast had been close—too close. The room just behind him had been all but destroyed. Apparently there had been something flammable in there, because Jack already could see orange flames dancing through the black smoke that drifted from the ruined storeroom. The building's sprinkler system kicked in, dousing the hallway in a fine mist. The fire alarm buzzed annoyingly, dimmed somewhat by the ringing in his ears.

Through the sprinklers, Jack saw a tall figure moving down the hallway. Alex.

The trooper on Jack's left had been knocked flat also, but staggered to his feet when he saw the approaching gunman. He raised his weapon just in time to be shot twice in the chest.

Jack began frantically sweeping aside the debris, searching for the pistol he had dropped. His fingers touched something cool and metallic, but it was just a broken strut, perhaps from a shelving unit. He cursed inwardly.

He thought Alex would come for him next, but two of the troopers Jack sent to the lobby had been drawn by the explosion. They rushed over, shouting at Alex to drop the gun. He responded by opening fire. One soldier went down immediately; the other started trading shots with Alex.

Jack still couldn't find his gun in the rubble, but when Alex stopped to reload he saw his opening. Pushing up off the floor, he charged at Alex like a football player. The rebel saw him coming. Slamming the fresh magazine in place, he managed to get a shot off. Jack felt the bullet crease the top of his shoulder, but barely noticed it before he careened into Alex.

The momentum carried them both backwards, up and over the railing surrounding the central staircase. There was a heart-stopping moment of free-fall, and then they both began an uncontrolled tumble down the stairs.

CHAPTER 31

CAITLIN FELT THE HOT RUSH of air from the explosion, and covered her head as glass flew through the room. Rachel screamed and cowered under the workstation. In an instant it was over. Caitlin cautiously got to her feet as the fire alarm started blaring. Her face and arm had gotten a few nicks, but nothing serious.

The technician, Kevin, hadn't been so lucky. He lay sprawled on the floor, hands hovering over a big chunk of glass embedded in his chest. He groaned in pain, and looked like he was going to pull it out.

"No! Don't touch it!" Caitlin urged, crouching beside him. "It could be tamping down on a blood vessel." She swung her head back and forth, looking for a first aid kit or anything that might help him. She saw nothing.

She was dimly aware of the studio monitor still showing the Chronicle's live feed. One of the anchors was speaking at the camera, moving down a smoke-filled stairwell.

"We're still not sure the extent of damage from the explosion. Initial reports indicate that it was isolated to one wing of the Chronicle offices. What we do know is that we're being told to evacuate the building. You can probably hear the fire alarm going off in the background, but – more than fire – there's the concern of a second explosion. Ladies and gentlemen, we're going to continue our broadcast for as long as we can, as we move to the relative safety of the street outside…"

If even a fraction of the news agencies on Earth had been tuned in for the broadcast, there was no way the Peacekeepers would be able to cover this up. Her satisfaction was tempered by Kevin's bloody wound. God only knew how many others had been injured by the blast. It wasn't supposed to happen like this. The bomb was Alex's last resort.

Samantha scooped up Caitlin's pistol, shaking off the glass before handing it back to her. "Alex's radio is down. He's drawing them off, but he'll meet us by Tom's cubicle." She saw Caitlin hesitating. "We have to go. PKs are closing in."

"Yeah. Shit." Leaving Kevin, injured in a burning building, went against every instinct she had. Being a firefighter and paramedic had been her job—her identity—for all of her adult life. "We can't just leave him. Rachel, get over here." The reporter hesitated, staring at Caitlin like a frightened animal. "Now!"

Caitlin helped Kevin to his feet, taking care not to jostle the shard of glass in his chest. "You need to get him outside to the medics. Make sure nothing touches that shard." She draped

Kevin's arm around Rachel's shoulder, but the woman just stood there with a dumbstruck look on her face. "Go. Now. Do something useful for once."

Rachel took a step toward the door, Kevin leaning heavily against her. She paused to glare at Caitlin, her eye already swelling. "You're nothing but a goddamn coward. Tom would be ashamed of you."

The words landed harder than Rachel's punches, but Caitlin didn't respond. Samantha tugged on her arm. "Come on. Let's go."

Caitlin allowed her friend to guide her out into the corridor. There the sprinklers assaulted them, and smoke filled the air. She squinted through the haze, searching for Alex. A commotion on the lower level caught her attention and she spotted him near the bottom of the stairs, engaged in a brutal melee with Captain Decker.

"There's Alex!" she cried, pointing. From her vantage point, she could see another soldier closing in.

Samantha saw it too. She leaned over the balcony, her submachine gun rattling off a short burst. The trooper ducked for cover. Caitlin left him to Samantha; she was already running for the main staircase. Towards Alex and Decker.

[[—✳—]]

Alex landed with a crash at the bottom of the stairs, feeling like he'd just rolled down ten floors and hit every step along the way. Shaking his head to clear it, Alex picked himself up and took stock. Between the gunshots, the explosion, and now the fire—a mad panic had emptied the lower floor of the Chronicle.

The other soldier was around somewhere, but for the moment Jack and Alex were alone.

Jack was a little slower to get up, blood flowing from a deep gash on his forehead. Alex landed a solid kick to the captain's midsection. It knocked Jack over onto his back, leaving him sputtering for air. Grabbing Jack by the shirt, Alex shoved him up against a nearby cubicle partition. The flimsy plastic gave way, sending them both tumbling backwards.

When they regained their footing, they circled each other, trading blows. Alex landed a few good punches, but they barely fazed Jack at all. Blood trickled down the Peacekeeper's face, but he just wouldn't quit. More gunfire rang out, not far off, and he knew that Samantha and Caitlin must still be fighting.

Finally Alex landed a punch that sent Jack reeling. The officer fell, hitting the carpeted floor with a thud. As he started to get up, his eyes narrowed in a dark, dangerous expression. Following his stare, Alex spotted his pistol peeking out from behind a potted plant near the base of the stairs.

They both lunged for the weapon simultaneously. Jack got a hand on it first, but Alex landed on top of him and grabbed his wrist with both hands. Grunting and snarling, they wrestled for control of the weapon. Alex tried to get enough leverage for a hold, hoping to break Jack's arm, but Jack landed a viscous right cross. Alex saw stars for a moment, and a moment was all Jack needed.

Alex felt the tearing pain in his side even before his mind registered the gunshot. He pressed a hand against his abdomen, gasping, and fell sideways onto the carpet. The bullet had robbed him of air, and now each breath brought fresh agony. Jack planted a foot against his shoulder, forcing him to roll over onto his back. Alex could only look up, helplessly, as the captain loomed over him.

"Just do it," Alex said, raising his chin defiantly. Whatever fear he felt, he'd be damned if he was going to let Jack see it.

Jack sneered, wiping away some of the blood on his chin. "I'll never understand you people. What is it you think you've accomplished today? All you've done is prolong the inevitable. Earth has more resources and manpower than you could ever dream of. You can't win."

Sometimes even Alex wondered why they were fighting what felt like a hopeless war. But now he understood with absolute clarity. "We've got nothing to lose."

Smirking, Jack raised his pistol a little. "Just one thing."

Alex flinched as a series of gunshots rang out, but they weren't aimed at him. His eyes widened as the bullets struck Jack's arm and chest, knocking him sideways. The final bullet tore through Jack's head with a spray of blood, and the captain collapsed like a rag doll. Relief slowly took the place of shock as Alex's gaze shift toward the staircase to his left. Standing there, halfway up the stairs, was Caitlin.

Caitlin lowered her pistol, a dazed look on her face. She stared at Jack's body for a long moment before she was finally able to tear her eyes away and focus on Alex. Paling, she rushed down the stairs to his side. "God, you're hit." Ripping off a strip of his shirt, she pressed that into the wound. Alex bit back a cry of pain.

Samantha came rushing down the staircase a few moments later, pausing to gawk at Jack and snag the pistol before joining Caitlin at Alex's side. "I got the other one," she told them, "But more are on the way."

Tying the makeshift bandage in place with his belt, Caitlin asked Alex, "Can you walk?"

"Maybe." Alex groaned as Caitlin helped him get to his feet, leaning heavily against her. How the hell were they supposed to escape when he could barely stand? "You guys should go," he said through gritted teeth. They had left Ben behind; he deserved no better.

"We're not leaving you here," Caitlin snapped. He opened his mouth to protest further, but Caitlin cut him off with a sharp, "No. We're not discussing this."

Samantha tucked his pistol back into its holster, then slipped under his other arm. "Don't look at me. She's right."

Alex knew he was outnumbered. They moved along at an awkward shuffling pace that was far too slow, making their way toward the windows at the end of the cubicle row. Every step was an effort, and Alex was grateful for the moment's respite when the women lowered him into an empty office chair. He struggled to catch his breath, hand pressed against his belly to staunch the bleeding.

Using a fire extinguisher from a nearby wall, Caitlin began pounding against the thick glass of the office window. At first the extinguisher bounced harmlessly off the pane. "Come on, damn it!" Alex was about to suggest that she just shoot it when a large section collapsed and shattered. It took only a moment for Caitlin to clear the rest of the glass out of the way.

"This is stupid," Alex grumbled through gritted teeth. "There's no sense in all of us getting caught."

Samantha slipped his arm around her shoulder again to help him up. "You wouldn't leave us, so shut up and move your ass."

Climbing out the window was the most agonizing experience of Alex's life, but he managed. He had to sag against the wall on the other side, increasingly dizzy.

The blare of fire engine sirens in the distance greeted them as they emerged onto a side street Although there were a few people in sight, everyone was too distracted by the approaching fire trucks to notice their unorthodox exit from the building.

"We should split up," Samantha suggested, eyeing the street.

"What?" Alex and Caitlin said in unison.

"I still have my tablet; I can wreck some havoc with their signals. Send them on a wild goose chase in the other direction."

"No." Alex shook his head. "It's too dangerous."

"Dangerous is thinking that we can outrun the PKs with you in this condition. We need to be smart. Take this." Samantha pressed Alex's pistol into his free hand. "I'll meet you guys back at the safe house."

"Sam…"

She ignored his protest, and leaned her head against his shoulder in a quick half-hug. "I'll be fine. It's you guys I'm worried about. Be careful."

"You too," Caitlin whispered, giving Samantha a hug as well. The young hacker flashed a worried smile before dashing off, disappearing around the corner. Caitlin settled Alex's arm around her shoulder, and they set off again.

Caitlin dragged Alex around the corner into an alley near the cafe they'd been sitting at earlier. "Hang in there, Alex," she urged, not doing a very good job of hiding the worry in her voice. "Not far now."

No sooner had she said the words, Alex heard an authoritative shout behind them. "Halt!" His blood run cold. They just couldn't catch a break. "Hands up! Turn around!"

Alex slanted Caitlin a look, and saw the dread written on her face. He glanced downward where his hand, covered in blood, had clenched around the handle of his pistol. Caitlin nodded almost imperceptibly. He kept the gun concealed behind the flap of his jacket.

Raising her free hand, Caitlin turned them both around. A pair of Peacekeepers advanced from the mouth of the alley. "Oh, thank God," Caitlin said, puzzling the two young privates. "My friend's hurt—can you help us?"

"Get your hands up! Both of you!" The panicked private in the lead made a motion with his rifle. But his brow furled in confusion, and Alex hoped that it was enough to make him hesitate. With his head spinning, it was still too far for a sure shot, and they wouldn't get a second chance. He waited until they were closer.

Caitlin pumped her hand toward him, palm out. "Okay, okay, take it easy. I'll have to set him down. He can't stand on his own." She lowered Alex to the ground, moving very deliberately so as not to spook the soldiers. Alex did a convincing job of lying there limply. It didn't take much effort.

The soldiers were very close now. "Check him out," the lead soldier said, motioning toward Alex. The second Peacekeeper was just starting to crouch down when Alex drew his pistol. Jerking backward, the soldier tried to bring his rifle to bear, but Alex fired three quick shots into the Peacekeeper's chest and face. The other soldier swung to cover his partner, but Caitlin drew her own pistol in a flash and shot him point blank in the side of the head.

[[—∗—]]

Caitlin stared at the soldier's body as it fell, her horrified face splattered with blood. Her own blood rushed in her ears, and she had to lean a hand against the alley wall to steady herself.

What did I just do?

"Cait. Cait, we have to go."

Alex's words snapped her out of her shocked daze. She safetied the pistol and shoved it back into her pocket with a shaky hand, then draped Alex's arm across her shoulders. He let out a heart-rending moan as she pulled him to his feet, then they shuffled the rest of the way to the tunnel entrance.

"I don't think I can climb down," Alex admitted, grimacing.

"I'll help you," Caitlin said, lowering him down next to the edge of the grate. She went down the first few rungs first, then motioned to him. "Just scoot forward and put your legs over."

Alex canted his head, giving her a skeptical frown. "You sure?"

Caitlin's mouth twisted wryly. "I've taken guys bigger than you down a ladder. Trust me."

Alex followed her instructions, and she used the techniques she'd learned at the fire academy to brace his weight against the ladder and guide him down. When they reached the bottom, she supported him in a light embrace, studying his face. The pain, sweat, and pallor there sparked a gnawing worry in her stomach.

"Come on, lean on me," she told him, slipping under his arm once more.

They shuffled off into the darkness. Alex had made Caitlin memorize the tunnel route, but all the twists and turns had her second-guessing herself. At least Samantha's distraction must be working, for they heard no signs of pursuit. They made it a few blocks before Alex finally collapsed. She managed to slow his fall, but they both landed in an inelegant heap.

"I can't…" Alex breathed, panting as if he'd run a marathon. Sweat drenched his face, visible in the light filtering down from a small grate above. "Can't go any farther."

Caitlin helped him lean against the rough-hewn rock wall and checked his wound. Blood had soaked through the makeshift dressing and his clothes. His abdomen was completely rigid, a dire sign, and even light pressure from her probing fingers elicited a strangled cry of pain.

Despite the the dim light, Alex could see the expression on her face. "I'm not going to make it," he concluded with a resigned grimace, saving her from having to say it.

Caitlin swallowed, her throat painfully tight. "I think it ruptured your spleen. You're in shock. Bleeding internally. If we get you to the hospital right now, you might have a chance." She couldn't force confidence into her words, having experience enough to know how slim of a chance it would be.

"A chance at what?" Alex whispered. "A life in prison? You know how that ends."

She knew. She'd seen the hopelessness in her father's eyes every time he sent her a message. But she didn't want to accept it. Desperate, impossible scenarios started running through her mind. Maybe Dr. Ross could stabilize him, and then they could sneak him into surgery. Could she even get him back to the safe house? If she called the medics, he'd be arrested, but could they get him out after he was treated?

Alex interrupted her thoughts, bringing her back to reality. "Cait, those guards back there—I know you're already beating yourself up about that." Caitlin flinched. She'd been trying not to think about it, but he was right. "You did what you had to."

"Did I?" Caitlin challenged, guilt smothering her. What Sykes and Decker had done made their deaths easier to bear, but that guard in the alley was different. "He was just a kid, doing his job…"

"You said it yourself—there's a war on. He picked his side. He was a soldier. And now so are you. A good one." Alex's voice grew weaker, blood loss taking its inevitable toll. "Sorry I won't be there to fight with you." He reached up a bloody hand to cup her cheek. "I wish things had worked out differently for us."

His tender gaze made it clear he wasn't just talking about the rebellion any more. She leaned into his hand, the words causing a conflicted swirl of emotions. The grief of losing Tom was still raw, but she couldn't deny the strength of the bond between her and Alex. In time, who knew where it might have led. Now, he too was being snatched away from her. Tears blurring her vision, she whispered, "So do I."

Alex's hand shifted to the back of her head, and she let him gently pull her closer until their lips met. It was slow and soft, a kiss goodbye as much as anything else. Afterward, he leaned back and smiled sadly. "I've wanted to do that since I met you."

Caitlin didn't know what to say. Her feelings were more complicated, but she wanted him to know that she did care; that he meant something to her. "I'll never forget everything you've done for me, Alex," she said. "You saved my life. You *changed* my life." And though she had once told him she wanted her old life back, she now realized that wasn't true. "What we did today —we made a difference."

A corner of Alex's mouth curled upward in a moment of proud reflection. "Yeah. We did." He let out a slow breath, his gaze becoming unfocused. "Think I just…" He trailed off, eyes closing, and then slumped forward.

"Alex?" Caitlin's voice broke, the tears spilling over and leaving tracks down her soot and blood-stained cheeks. She checked for a pulse to be sure, but it just confirmed what she already knew.

He was gone.

She scooted over and pulled him close, holding him as she wept. In the dark, lonely quiet of the tunnel, she could hear sirens in the distance. Echoes of another life.

CHAPTER 32

The voice from the MarsCom faded into indistinct noise as Caitlin passed the monitor on her way through the bar to the booth in back. Self-consciously, she dipped her head and tucked an errant strand of her newly cut and dyed (brown, at Samantha's recommendation) hair behind her ear. She still hadn't gotten used to seeing her face plastered all over the news; likely she never would. The Peacekeepers were combing the city for her and Samantha. Even with a disguise, every trip out of their new apartment became a nerve-wracking experience, but they couldn't stay glued to the MarsCom feed forever.

After ordering a drink and waiting a few minutes, Caitlin murmured for her microphone, "Any sign of him?"

"Not yet," came Samantha's response in her ear. She was positioned in another cafe down the street, watching the outside via security cameras.

Caitlin waited. She was beginning to think that the meeting would be a bust when Samantha said, "I've got him. He's on his way in now. Bodyguard's stationed outside but I don't see anyone else following."

A few minutes passed, then her uncle, Max Farland, sat down at her table. "Thanks for coming, Max." She wasn't sure he would, after his last speech saying he couldn't stick his neck out. "You sure you weren't followed?"

Max smirked. "Girl, I was doing tradecraft while your parents were still dating. Still, it's risky, meeting like this. You and your friend are radioactive." He scrutinized her face, turning more serious. No amount of makeup could completely hide all the bruises, scratches, and dark circles she'd accumulated over the past few days. "You all right?"

It was strange, she thought, that she didn't even know how to respond to that simple question. "I'm alive. They killed Alex."

"I saw on the news. I'm sorry. He was a good man. That was a hell of a thing you guys did, though. The Earther press is all over the story. Even the Federation censors couldn't keep it down. Your old man would be proud."

A sad smile touched Caitlin's lips briefly. "I've been thinking a lot about him. All those years you and he spent fighting the Peacekeepers, I never really understood. But now…" Shaking her head, she let her voice trail off.

"Look, Cait, you should lie low for a while," Max said, watching her in concern. "Let all this blow over. I can get you off-world? Australia's independent—no extradition treaty with the Feds."

"Is that where you went?" She had always wondered, when he disappeared after her father was arrested.

Quirking a smile, Max nodded. "Always reminded me of home."

For a brief instant, she pictured it. Relaxing at the bar after work with her friends; taking a holiday at the beach; not having to constantly look over her shoulder, or carry a gun everywhere she went. It was hard to imagine going back to a life like that after everything she had seen. Everything she had done.

She shook her head. "Thanks, Max, but that's not why I'm here." She paused, taking a breath, and then said, "I need you to put me in touch with the rebels. Sam and I need to link up with another cell."

A disapproving frown twisted Max's mouth. "Now's not the time to go looking for trouble. You need to think about your future. You'd be safe on Earth."

"They've taken my family from me. Everyone I care about. I can't just run and hide."

Max's frown deepened. "If it's revenge you're after, you're kidding yourself. It's not worth it. Believe me."

Caitlin couldn't deny the rage that burned inside her. There was an edge to her voice as she replied, "If you had any idea what those bastards had done, you wouldn't say that." Shaking her head, she continued, "But this isn't about revenge. This is my home. I'm not going to let them run me out of it."

The old man sighed. "All right. I'll help you if you're sure that's what you really want. I owe you that much. But Cait, listen to me. There's no future in this life. Odds are you end up like your dad, or your friend. Why throw your life away?"

Maybe Max was right, but all Caitlin could think about was what the Peacekeepers had taken from her—her father, Tom, Vince, Alex, her career—and what they would take from others if given the chance. All she had left was the hope that someday the Peacekeepers would be gone, and that all of this wouldn't have been for nothing. It wasn't much, but it was enough to keep her going.

Caitlin offered Max a bittersweet smile. "I've got nothing to lose."

About the Author

Linda Naughton has been writing stories for as long as she can remember. She is the author of several novels, children's books, and the blog Self-Rescuing Princesses. A proud geek and gamer girl, she enjoys sci-fi, disaster movies, and role-playing games. She is a software engineer, paramedic, and mother of two.

Visit her website: www.lindanaughton.com to learn more, or join the newsletter for blog posts and updates on future books: www.lindanaughton.com/newsletter.html

Your Review Matters

If you enjoyed this book, please take a moment to provide a review at the point of purchase. Your reviews are extremely helpful for independent authors.